PROTECTING MEDUSA

ELIZABETH ANDREWS

Protecting Medusa
The Medusa's Daughters Trilogy, Book 2

Being the Medusa puts a real crimp in a woman's social life. Lucky for Philomena Gregory, she gave up on men long before Athena's curse landed on her head--she learned as a child men don't stay, a lesson reinforced when she was a lovesick teenager. The hot naked man in her bathroom won't change her mind.

Ryder Ware has waited six years to meet Mena in person. She's managed to avoid him every time he's visited his son, her nephew. Flirting on the phone and via email is no substitute when a man is so intrigued. But now that Athena's Harvesters have found her, Mena has no choice but to let him keep her safe--and close, *very* close.

Philomena may have to accept his protection, but, even with chemistry hotter than Hades, she won't change her mind about a relationship, even after a little sex. Or even a lot of sex. Good thing Ryder's a patient man. After waiting years, what's a few more weeks to convince the woman of his dreams he wants forever?

Forced to flee to ensure their family's safety, Mena and Ryder *mostly* stay ahead of the Harvesters on her trail. The longer they're together, the harder it is to keep believing all men are cut from the same cloth. Ryder may be bossy, but he proves he'll be there when she needs him, even though she'd never have asked for his help. It will take a long time to break down her walls, but with the deadly Harvesters turning up everywhere they go, they may not have long enough.

Mena must decide if she can trust herself as much as she trusts Ryder. Otherwise, Athena's curse on her family will mean her end, instead of her happily ever after.

Protecting Medusa
Copyright © 2021 by Elizabeth Andrews
Ebook ISBN: 9781734668940
Paperback ISBN: 9781734668957
Cover by Aleisha Knight Evans

First Electronic publication: August 2021
First Paperback publication: August 2021

This book goes again to my husband and my two sons, as well as my father who is no longer with us. It's for everyone who protects their family from harm, in big ways and in all the small ones, too, from making sure they have a safe place to live, to ensuring they stay dry in the rain. Family is important, and those who keep theirs protected have a difficult job. Thank you all.

THE LEGEND

Millennia ago, a beautiful young Gorgon made a fatal mistake, one her descendants still pay for today. She so angered Athena that the Goddess cursed Medusa, changing her lovely hair to snakes and causing her gaze to turn any living thing to stone. As if that wasn't bad enough, Perseus then set out to kill the unfortunate Medusa.

Perseus didn't know she'd already found a way to protect her descendants from some of the Goddess's curse: she created an amulet which would transfer from one future Medusa to the next, either when she fell in love or died. This cup prevents the curse from wreaking constant havoc on the women's lives, instead limiting it to once each month for the current Medusa. And you thought you had PMS from hell.

Along with the Goddess's curse, Perseus's descendants have also followed the Medusas through the centuries, trying to take the amulet as they hunt, or harvest, the Medusas. Over time, details about the amulet and how the curse passes from one Medusa to another have been lost or forgotten.

These Harvesters have so far failed to find the amulet, called Medusa's Goblet, and, for several generations, have also failed to kill the reigning Medusas. But they persist and are closer now to achieving at least one of those tasks: finding the current Medusa.

A few years ago, one of their own fell in love with the Medusa he was destined to kill. Now his family is more determined to kill her successor, and they won't let anyone stand in their way this time.

CHAPTER ONE

R yder Ware stood at the window, watching the man stride along the road in the dark. The other man couldn't see him, but Ryder remained frozen anyway, barely breathing. After tracking this guy for weeks, his patience had finally paid off. The man was a Harvester, and his quarry was one Philomena Gregory, the current Medusa.

Ryder wouldn't allow the man to have her.

He watched as the Harvester walked toward him, not even bothering to skulk in the early dark of winter as he made his way toward Philomena's mother's house. The stranger must've believed no one was home, despite the faint light shining from between the living room curtains.

He knew exactly where the guy was heading. He'd have gone to the same spot if he were a Harvester. And Ryder would beat him there. Catch him off guard.

Ryder headed upstairs. He stripped and turned on the water in the bathtub, aiming the shower head straight down to minimize how wet he'd get, and waited at the back of the tub, curtain shut, pulse only beating slightly faster than normal. He could ignore the fruity-smelling shower gel and shampoo that he'd bet belonged to Philomena for a few minutes.

The guy thought he'd be getting one of the women by surprise, but he'd find out in a hurry he was dealing with someone *much* more dangerous.

~

PHILOMENA PARKED BESIDE HER MOTHER'S HOUSE. She'd arrived first, and she needed to get dinner on in a hurry. Once Jason got home, she'd be too distracted to focus on cooking.

She went in the back door, balancing a grocery bag while she reset the alarm, then hit the light switch with her elbow as she continued into the kitchen.

She took her mother's cast iron skillet from its hook over the counter and put it on the stove, turning the heat to high and dropping in some ground beef before she shed her coat. As she put away the rest of the groceries, the meat began to sizzle.

She rolled up her sleeves and dug a spatula out of the utensil drawer, but froze when she heard a creak from upstairs. She waited, then shook her head. It was a hundred year-old farmhouse.

She stirred the beef in the pan, adding chopped onions she'd picked up at the store--not out of laziness but because she knew she needed to move quickly after three days away and with an excitable six-year-old on his way home. She could take time tomorrow to do her own prep work for dinner.

The sound came again from upstairs. She set the spatula on the spoon rest and turned the flame under her pan down to low, then tugged up the hem of her long skirt to pull her dagger from its leather sheath on her thigh.

A loud thud reached her ears, and her heart beat faster.

Dear Gods, someone really was in the house.

She crept up the back steps, keeping to the edges where she knew her weight wouldn't make the stairs creak, the smooth handle of her long knife comforting in her sweat-damp hand.

More thumping, accompanied by running water.

She frowned when she got to the top of the steps, wincing as something hit the porcelain bathtub, followed by muffled cursing.

She stuck her head around the corner, but the partially-closed bathroom door at the other end of the hall blocked her view. All she could see were shadows.

Two people? In her mother's bathroom? She wished she'd grabbed the phone on her way up so she could call the police. No, she should've called before coming upstairs. Too late now.

More thumping and a crash.

Her jaw clenched, and she stepped into the hallway, her pulse pounding in her ears.

"I've called the police," she lied, moving slowly along the hall. Frigid air drifted toward her. Either the bathroom window was open, or something was seriously wrong with the furnace. She frowned, holding tighter to her knife.

A dark blur went out the window, and her eyes widened. It was quite a drop to the ground, even with all the snow mounded below from the big storms so far this winter.

When a large, naked man with a gun went to look out the window, she froze in the middle of the hall, her dagger shoulder high.

Naked.

She swallowed, and then he turned around. Her lungs stopped working.

"Hello, Philomena. Have I ever told you how much I love a woman who can handle a blade?" He caught the edge of the door and pulled it wide open.

She'd know that voice anywhere, and that face, even if she'd only seen him in photos. Ryder Ware, Jason's father.

And wow, *was she seeing him in person.*

He smiled, a cocky grin that revealed dimples in both cheeks, his eyes dark like melted chocolate. Lower, wide shoulders, muscled chest with a veil of dark blond hair, darker yet where it narrowed over his muscle-rippled belly, leading to his groin.

Where he was visibly aroused and getting more so by the second.

She forced her gaze back to his face and found his expression had shifted to something dangerous. Predatory. She forced her lungs to take in some air. "Ryder. What are you doing here?" *Besides standing naked in my mother's bathroom.* She inhaled slowly again, attempting to make her heartbeat slow down, but it just kept galloping along under her ribs. She hoped her sweater was heavy enough to hide the way her nipples had started to tighten. Leftover hormones, she told herself. Or the cold from the open window. Nothing to do with the nude man in front of her.

"Saving your life." He winked at her, completely unself-conscious about his nakedness. Or his arousal.

She refused to look. Not that she had to. She had very good peripheral vision, and *wow!* "What are you talking about?"

"Harvester." He clicked something on his gun and laid it on the counter beside the sink.

She went cold, colder than even the open window

warranted. "What...I...how..." She didn't want to think about all the implications in that one word, her eyes closing for a second before she met his gaze.

"I need to go after him." He grabbed a pair of jeans from the rumpled heap of clothing on the floor, then paused, a wicked grin slanting over his face. "Are you done staring?"

Philomena realized she *was* staring, and scalding heat rushed to her face as she dragged her gaze up to his.

"We can continue this later, Mena." He crossed the small room in one step and pressed a hard kiss onto her mouth, startling her. "Keep the alarm on." Then he grabbed his gun, went to the open window, and ducked outside.

She rushed across the room in time to see Ryder roll to his bare feet in the snow, running across the yard behind the other man's footprints as he shrugged the snow from his naked back.

When goosebumps lifted along her arms after several minutes of staring into the darkness, she realized she was freezing. And the shower still ran. Giving herself a shake, she lowered the window and flipped the lock, then frowned, wondering how someone had reached it to unlatch it. Pondering that, she turned off the water.

After six years of successfully avoiding Ryder in person, it seemed she'd finally have to deal with him.

She shivered, and this time, it wasn't from the cold, but from the mingled fear and adrenaline racing through her veins. Sheathing her dagger, she smoothed her skirt back down and returned to the kitchen, pushing thoughts of the bossy, sexy father of her nephew out of her head.

The beef was browning, and she dragged the spatula through it to loosen it from the bottom of the pan, before she dropped in chopped peppers and tomato sauce.

She hadn't seen Jason or her mother in three long days, and she hadn't imagined their reunion might occur like this.

She rubbed one hand over her forehead, trying to banish the mental image of Ryder, naked and aroused.

By what? she suddenly wondered. *The thrill of the fight?*

She supposed it was likely. She knew he was something of an adrenaline junkie. After all, his stint in the military had been rounded out by some secret missions he still couldn't talk about, and she'd heard several stories from Jason about his dad jumping out of airplanes. Ryder had followed that up with some other secret intelligence agency job for a few years.

The only other possibility was that the arousal was because of her.

She laughed. Yeah, right. She knew she was reasonably attractive, but men didn't fall to their knees at their first sight of her. Not even men who had flirted via email and over the phone as frequently as they were in contact. Actually, *never*, even when she'd dated with actual hope of finding 'The One'. Or, um, leap to attention that way. Certainly not men who knew the sort of monster she truly was.

She swallowed hard, but her mind didn't want to cooperate with her, making her senses all go haywire and sending heat into her belly. *And he had kissed her.*

A tap at the back door made her jump and drop the spatula into the meat and sauce.

Ryder stood outside, gun still in his hand, his face somber, though something sparked in his eyes when she got to the door and turned off the alarm. "Gone, but I know where to find him later," he said shortly as he came inside.

She stepped away, desperate for something to distract her from his naked chest. The spatula. She fished it out of the bubbling pan and rinsed it at the sink. "You should have let us know you were coming." It came out sharper than she intended.

He laughed as he leaned over the stove to inhale. "So you could keep avoiding me, Mena?"

She didn't look at him right away, but her pulse tripled its pace. Of course he knew she'd been avoiding him all these years. The man wasn't an idiot. "In case we had other plans," she said instead, remaining at the sink instead of returning to the stove to stir their meal.

"As it happens, I spoke to Aggie this morning." He grinned. "She knew I was coming."

Philomena bit her lip and looked away for a second.

"What's wrong, Mena?" He moved nearer. "Are you angry I didn't give you another chance to hide, or are you still turned on?"

Her eyes widened and her mouth dropped open. "I was not."

He touched her chin. "Liar." His gaze flicked to the front of her sweater. "You are."

She blushed furiously, aware of the way her nipples had tightened under her sweater again. Dammit. "Cold."

He slid his thumb along her lower lip, his smile fading. "You don't need to be embarrassed about it, Mena. The feelings are reciprocated," he said softly. "You know that."

She jerked away when he leaned nearer. Her heart raced crazily, and her legs felt like rubber. "I'm not interested in a relationship with you, other than as you are Jason's father and I am his aunt." He didn't need to know she'd admired the photos Jason had of him, or that just the sound of his voice when he flirted on the phone caused her to shiver on occasion.

He lifted one eyebrow. "Desi's been telling stories? After all this time?"

She moved around him to stir the sloppy joes. "Desi's got nothing to do with it. Though, now that you mention it, her taste in men is known not to be very good, and my type is completely different from hers."

For a second, he remained silent, but then Ryder laughed behind her. She ground her teeth together.

"I've seen your type, Mena, and your taste in men isn't so hot. I think it's time you tried a different flavor." His hands settled on her shoulders, making her tense even more.

"You should get dressed. Mom and Jason will be here any minute," she said, hearing the quaver in her voice. "And put your gun away."

His breath warmed the top of her head, and she held her own, waiting. But he simply gave her shoulders a gentle squeeze and moved away.

Leaving her to wonder how he'd seen any of her dates.

Better than imagining him going upstairs to finish dressing.

She frowned into the skillet, stirring more vigorously than she needed to. Had he really been spying on her? For how long? She didn't even remember the last date she'd had.

When her mother's car pulled into the driveway beside hers, she inhaled deeply, forcing some of the tension from her shoulders and neck. After three days of forced solitude, she wanted to see her family. Very much.

Jason burst through the back door. "Aunt Phila!"

She smiled and held out her arms, bracing when he flung himself at her. "Hi, baby." She scooped him up, even though he really was getting too big for that. She kissed one of his cheeks, then his mouth, then his other cheek, while he giggled. It was their ritual for whenever she'd been away. A kiss for each day they'd been apart.

He wrapped his arms around her neck, tight. "I missed you."

"You know I missed you, too." She caught sight of her mother coming in and gave her a strained smile. Her mother lifted one eyebrow, and Philomena shook her head. "How was school today, buddy?" She set him on his feet and unzipped his coat.

He shrugged out of his superhero backpack and his coat, bouncing the whole time. "You know the hamster in our room? Harvey? He got out of his cage during recess today, so we had to crawl around looking for him till Nita found him hiding under the bookcase in the back corner. Oh, and we got a new girl in our class today. Her name is Rose, and she has red hair and a million billion freckles on her face. And Eddie brought a picture of his new German Shepherd puppy with him. Eddie's gonna train him to be a guard dog an' keep bad guys away. He said I should come see him this weekend. Can I go?"

Philomena relaxed a bit more, listening to him while she heated some frozen vegetables and set the table.

When Jason came up for air, he frowned at the table. "Hey, how comes there's four plates, Aunt Phila?"

Her spine stiffened, and she took a quick breath as she turned from the stove.

"Because I came to visit, little guy," Ryder said from the foot of the stairs.

"Daddy!" Jason shrieked and met his father halfway across the room.

Ryder's grin was as big as Jason's, and he swung his son around in a big hug while Jason clung tightly to him.

Philomena watched as they greeted one another, doing

silly guy stuff--funny handshakes and high-fives, and hugging again--and her heart squeezed in her chest, painfully. She'd never seen such naked delight on her nephew's face. Or imagined it in his father's.

"What's got you so uptight?" her mother asked quietly.

"You should have told me he was coming." She kept her voice low, too, and shot a sharp glance at her mom.

Agatha Gregory smiled instead of looking abashed. "You needed to come anyway, and I couldn't tell him 'no'." She shrugged with one shoulder. "You'll have to deal."

Philomena opened her mouth to tell her mother what she thought of her suggestion, but Ryder crossed the floor to them, Jason at his side. "Supper's ready," she said instead.

"Let me help." Ryder winked at her.

"I've got it." She moved around Ryder to the stove, shutting the burner off and scooping the beef mixture into a bowl. When she turned around, he blocked her way, a dangerous glint in his brown eyes. "I'm fine, Ryder," she said stiffly.

"Yes, you are," he breathed, leaning closer and cupping the bowl, his hands directly over hers, sending bolts of heat shooting along her arms. "But I'm going to help whether you like it or not."

"Here. Take it." She slid her fingers free and let him have the bowl. Somehow, though, she didn't think he just meant supper preparation, and that made her nervous.

She sat across the table from her mother, as always, with Jason between them on her right, which meant Ryder sat to her left. Even though there was more than a foot of space between then, his nearness made her stomach do back flips. She answered Jason's questions automatically, though tonight, unlike every other month when she'd been gone for three days, most of his attention was on his dad. She ate little, tension stealing her appetite.

Between the Harvester and Ryder's unexpected appearance, she thought she might prefer another three days of suffering through Athena's infernal curse.

It wouldn't have been so bad, really, except he kept touching her.

First, while she passed the buttered peas, he made certain to slide his fingers over hers when she handed him the bowl. Then he nudged her foot with his under the table while he talked to Aggie. Tiny, innocent things, really, except for their encounter earlier in the bathroom. That was far from innocent.

By the time Jason shouted it was time for his favorite show, she wanted to jump from her chair and run out into the snow just to get away.

Ryder caught her wrist when she started to push her chair back. "I want to talk to you and Aggie," he said quietly when his son had left the room.

Her mother linked her hands and rested her chin on them, concern lining her brow. "What's wrong, Ryder?"

"I've been following a Harvester."

Philomena tugged her hand free and clasped her fingers in her lap, looking at her half-empty plate. Her stomach squeezed, and she was grateful she'd hardly eaten.

"Met him here earlier, right, Mena?"

Her mother's gasp made her shoot a glare at him.

"I think you should take Jason to Mena's tonight, Aggie. Just in case."

"I think you're right," her mother said after a moment. "How did he find us?"

One of his big shoulders lifted. "I wish I could say for sure, Aggie, but I imagine they're just tracing families like when Kallan was still hunting. But this guy seems to know, or at least to believe, that Mena's the Medusa. He's been in town for two days, checking out the lay of the land, driving by the house." His dark gaze slid to Philomena's face. "I'm going after him again."

She swallowed, feeling a little guilty for wishing he'd leave, and averted her gaze.

"Will you go right away, Aggie?"

"Well, yes. But what about the two of you?" Her mother got to her feet, her frown deepening as she looked from one of them to the other.

"We'll be fine here for tonight," he said. He rose and caught one of Aggie's hands. "I've got a buddy coming tomorrow to upgrade your alarm system, though. Everything needs to be sensored, not just the first floor. This guy came in upstairs."

Her mother shut her eyes, no doubt imagining what would have happened if she and Jason had been home, or if the Harvester had come in the middle of the night. "Whatever you think is best, Ryder." She squeezed his hand. "Let me get some things together."

That left Philomena alone with him, and the tension ratcheted a few degrees higher.

"You don't think he'll come back, do you? Tonight, I mean?" She remained seated, not wanting to bump into him while she cleared away the remains of their meal, keeping her gaze on the table. Flitting from her plate to the leftover peas and sloppy joes. The open bag of rolls. Jason's empty plate.

"I don't know. He seems to believe this is your primary residence, which means your mother and Jason need to be out for now. But I winged him earlier, so he'll have to patch himself up first." He inhaled deeply. "We'll be fine until my buddy gets here."

She arched one eyebrow. "'We'?"

His lips curved into a cocky smile that made goosebumps lift on her arms. "Yeah. I think I can protect you."

"Who'll protect me from you?" It was out before she could stop it, and she colored again.

"If you need protection from me, I'm sure you'll do fine. You wear your knife all the time, right?"

"Not to bed." *Dammit, what is* wrong *with my mouth?* More heat crawled up her throat to her face.

"Well, that's reassuring," he drawled, his eyes darkening. "Why don't you let me help you clean up?"

"Why don't you go sit with Jason?" she countered, pushing to her feet. Standing made her feel slightly better, though he still towered over her by a good six inches. "I'm sure he'll be happy to catch you up on his show." She carried her plate to the sink and scraped the remains of her meal into the disposal, turning it on and drowning out any response he might have made.

When she turned around, she saw his back as he went into the living room, where Jason greeted him enthusiastically. The back looked as good as the front, she admitted, faded jeans clinging to a tight ass, strong thighs and calves.

"Gods," she muttered, shutting her eyes. Her hormones ought to have settled since her three days of exile were over till next month.

She very deliberately didn't think about him while she put away the leftovers and started the dishwasher. Or about the intent look in his eyes earlier, right before he kissed her. Instead, she focused on the website she was creating for a new client. She'd nearly finished tweaking the design, and in another day or two, it would go live, and a nice fat check would deposit into her bank account.

"Philomena."

She glanced over her shoulder at the strained sound of her mother's voice. "Are you okay, Mom?"

Aggie nodded. "I'm worried about you."

"I'll be fine. You know I'm armed," she joked, patting her thigh.

Her mother didn't smile back. "If he's tracked you here, it's only a matter of time before he finds your house, too."

She couldn't disagree. She'd thought it herself while poking at her dinner–what if he'd arrived at her house in the past three days while she was alone and bed-ridden? "Looks like I need to add to the protection here," she said instead of responding to her mother's last comment. "Aside from Ryder boosting the alarm system, that is. Do you mind?"

Her mother shook her head. "Of course not. We have to make sure Jason is safe. I should have thought of refreshing the wards sooner."

Ryder came into the kitchen, Jason clinging to his back like a little monkey and giggling all the while. "I told Jason he's going to stay at your place tonight, Mena."

She frowned. "It's Philomena," she said, realizing he'd been calling her Mena since his arrival. He did the same thing when they spoke on the phone, too, no matter how many times she'd corrected him over the years.

The grin returned in a flash, and heat curled into her belly once more.

So much for not thinking about *that*.

He squatted so Jason could climb off. "Okay, sport, time to get your coat on." Still, his gaze stayed on Philomena's face.

She shifted her weight from one foot to the other,

feeling the heat sink lower, spread. It was a *very* good thing he hadn't arrived right before her period last week, when her hormones were amped up about ten thousand percent, thanks to Athena's curse if she was reacting to him like this now. Even her panties were damp. If he'd been here last week, she might've done something regrettable.

She swallowed and forced her gaze away from him as he rose to his full height again. "Can I help, Jason?"

"Nah, I got it." His fingers fumbled a bit on the zipper, but then he slid it to his chin.

She smiled and knelt in front of him. "I'll see you tomorrow, okay, buddy?"

He nodded and flung his arms around her neck. "I hope you have the best dreams."

She shut her eyes. She loved their bedtime ritual, established when he was barely speaking yet as a baby. "I hope you have even better dreams."

"No, you have the bestest." He hugged her tighter.

"Sleep great, baby." She kissed him, a big, smacking kiss and released him, getting to her feet. "And *you* have the bestest, bestest dreams ever."

He laughed and took Aggie's hand at the door.

Philomena kept the smile on her face while she watched them go, though worry niggled into her chest. They needed to be safe.

The heavy weight of Ryder's arm settled on her shoulder. "They'll be fine for tonight," he murmured near her ear while outside a car started.

She nodded, biting her lower lip. They had to be. If anything happened to them, it was on her head.

"And I have to go." He stepped away and took his coat from the hook behind the door.

She grabbed the nearest jacket, which was too light for

the brisk winter night, but she pulled it on anyway, then walked outside with him, noting her mother's headlights leading away from the house. "You're going to be careful, aren't you?"

"I'm always careful." He shot her a bad boy grin that had her heart racing as they made their way along the sidewalk to the front of the house, where she saw his truck parked out front now beside the mailbox.

"Nothing can happen to you, Ryder. You have Jason to worry about."

He kept walking.

"Are you listening to me?" She glared up at him when he came to a stop beside the truck.

He put his arm around her shoulders. "Are you more worried about Jason? Or me?"

She blinked. "I'm worried about what will happen to Jason if something happens to you." He smelled really good. Her pounding heart sped up still more. He stood too close. She needed a distraction. "You know Desi is a lousy parent. Might as well not even be a parent."

"What if something did happen to me? Would you miss me?" He bent nearer, his mouth almost grazing her temple.

She tried to concentrate on his words, but the awareness rushing through her made it difficult. And dammit, she couldn't even blame it on pre-curse hormones.

"Would you be upset if I were hurt?" His open mouth slid down her cheek, hot, damp. *Tempting.*

Desire raced along her veins. Under her sweater, her nipples tightened in anticipation.

"Mena?" He licked the corner of her mouth.

She gasped, and he swooped in, covering her open mouth with his, and pressed her against the side of the truck, his warmth compensating for the cold metal at her back.

He was aroused again. The heavy erection nudging her belly made her panties wetter.

Shocked by her reaction, she couldn't resist anyway, lifting into his kiss.

"Wrap your legs around me, Mena," he whispered against her lips.

She forced her eyes open, trying hard to distract herself from the temptation of Ryder.

"I bet you're wet for me. Is your pussy slick enough for me to slide deep yet?" One of his hard hands cupped her bottom, pulling her tighter to him.

She didn't want to be so aroused by his explicit words. Or by the scent and feel of him all around her, but clearly, her brain had ceded control to her hormones.

"Maybe not yet." His other hand slipped under her sweater, and his thumb stroked around the tip of her breast, once, twice, three times before he rubbed it over her aching nipple. "You smell delicious." He nipped at her lower lip. "I bet you taste even better. If I put my mouth on you, it wouldn't take long before you were wet enough for me." He pinched her nipple, lightly, making her hips jolt toward his.

"Yeah," he continued, sliding his mouth along her jaw, "lick your clit, make you moan, make you scream." His fingers dug into her ass, lifting her nearer. "Wrap your legs around me, Mena." He nipped at her earlobe.

Her body obeyed the command in his voice this time, raising one leg, then the other to wrap around his waist. That let him slide his hand from her ass to the hem of her skirt, pushing it out of his way, up her thigh. She shivered, grabbing his shoulders.

When his fingers skimmed the wet crotch of her

panties, he hummed his approval. "So wet for me, baby." He slipped one finger underneath, along slick folds until he reached her clit, startling a cry out of her.

"It's going to be so good," he whispered against her ear as he plunged two fingers into her quivering sheath. "Deep and slow. It'll be like nothing else for either of us." His fingers stroked over a sensitive spot deep inside, and her body contracted, hard, around his fingers.

She opened her eyes. She should put a stop to this. But...*oh, Gods.* His thumb pressed on her clit, sending fire racing into her belly.

"Later, I'm going to fuck you from behind, and it's going to be even more incredible. Deeper, harder. But right now, I have to be inside you."

She realized he'd freed his erection, his skin searing hot and silky between her thighs. Oh, he felt good.

"Mena." He caught her gaze. "Tell me now."

It took her a moment to comprehend that he was giving her a chance to opt out. Instead of doing the smart thing, though, as she always did, she slid her hands up into his silky hair, guiding his mouth back to hers.

He groaned and eased inside her, slowly filling her, stretching her. It seemed forever before his hips were finally snugged tight against hers.

She couldn't catch her breath, and he shared his with her, his weight pinning her to the truck when she would have rocked her hips.

"Nn-nn," he breathed against her mouth. "Don't move yet, baby."

Gods, she needed to move. Her inner muscles clenched on him, tight.

He groaned, and inside her, his cock jerked.

This time, she tightened those muscles intentionally.

His low chuckle vibrated from her lips, into her belly and aching breasts. "Impatient, are we?" His hips rolled in a slow circle against hers.

"Please." It had been *so* long.

He licked her lower lip, sucked on it lightly. "You're going go have to develop some patience, smart girl." As he withdrew, slowly.

Her whimpered protest cut off when he slammed deep again. Over and over and over, until her body exploded into a million pieces.

He swallowed her hoarse scream in his rough kiss while his release jetted into her.

Her legs shook around his waist, as did her fingers at his nape. If he hadn't been holding her between his hard body and the truck, she'd be a steaming puddle on the snowy ground.

He kissed her more gently now, one hand still beneath her, the other sliding through her hair, fingers grazing her scalp, her nape, her throat, warm, feeling much too good.

Dear Gods, what had she just done?

"Is that amazing brain of yours starting to reform?" he whispered along her lips.

She blushed, grateful for the darkness. How could he know?

"It's okay, Mena. But it's definitely only the beginning." He inhaled deeply. "I'm going to hate this part," he muttered, then eased his hips away from hers, just as slowly as he'd joined their bodies earlier.

She bit her lip to keep in her whimper at the loss of him inside her. Clearly, it had been far too long since she'd indulged in the real thing.

He lowered her to her feet, steadying her when she wobbled a little. He tipped her chin up and planted another brain-melting kiss on her. When he lifted his head, it took her a few seconds to re-focus her gaze on his grinning face.

He adjusted his clothing, smoothed her skirt down, tugged her jacket closed.

Some part of her loved the protective, possessive gesture, and that scared her. A lot.

He studied her for a moment, his smile softening. "I need to go find this guy, but I'll be back later," he said at last, sliding his thumb along her lower lip.

She ignored the tingling his touch left behind and tried to turn her mush-brain into a functioning organ once more. "You don't expect me to be waiting up, do you?"

His low laugh sent a ripple of heat into her middle. "I can find my way."

Her eyes widened. "Find your way where?"

"Back to you." He bent to kiss her once more, hard and fast.

She shook her head. "Not a good idea."

He kissed her again, his mouth slanting over hers so his tongue could delve deep, stroking, sending fresh heat spiraling into her chest, her belly.

Obviously, she was weaker than she'd ever realized.

"You're mine now, witch," he breathed against her mouth. "And I'll see you later." He straightened, still too close.

She slid along the side of the truck carefully, away from him, before she stepped onto the sidewalk to face him. "The guest room is downstairs, Ryder. Your things will be waiting there." She wished her voice wasn't so unsteady.

He just grinned at her, the cocky grin that both aggravated and excited her.

Before the heat in her belly could fully combust all over, she turned and hurried back to the house. Even after she'd gone inside and re-armed the alarm, long after the rumble of the truck's engine faded away, she leaned against the door, legs shaking and heart racing.

The man was dangerous. Maybe just as dangerous to her as the Harvesters, though in a far different way.

She finally pushed away from the door, her legs wobbly as she made her way to the closet in the first floor bathroom.

When Jason was younger, they'd put dowels on every window in the house so they couldn't be raised far enough for anyone to get in or out of them. Clearly, the upstairs windows were a weak spot in the house's defense, so child-proofing would help, at least until Ryder's friend came to expand the alarm system. She gathered the dowels from the back corner of the closet and started on the window right there in the bathroom.

She concentrated for a few minutes on physically securing the house, wedging the dowels into every window on the first and second floors. When she'd finished her task, she sat in the center of the living room floor, concentrating on slowing her breathing. Imagined herself reaching deep into the ground to draw up the Earth's protective energy, which she envisioned wrapping securely around the house, keeping out anyone who wished her family ill. She used only what she needed, then grounded the rest back into the Earth and thanked the Gods.

By the time she finished, she felt a bit calmer. All the curtains were drawn tight, and she resisted the urge to peek out the front window. If the Harvester had returned, he didn't need to know exactly where she was.

Philomena moved to the couch, trying to decide what would work best to relax her. It had been an extremely tense evening.

Not to mention hot.

She covered her face with one hand and shut her eyes, taking a deep breath.

Having sex with her sister's long-ago ex was far from the smartest thing she'd ever done. Outside in the snow, when the Harvester knew where to find her, for crying out loud. At least the nearest neighbors lived about a mile away. She put her other hand over her face, too, laughing softly. Desi had always been the dumb one about men, not Philomena.

Apparently, Ryder Ware brought it out in women.

She sat up straight. She didn't have time to worry about him or her own shocking lack of restraint.

She turned off the lights in the living room, then went to the kitchen where she'd left her purse and tote bag, digging her laptop out. She left only the work light over the sink on, so Ryder could find his way into the house. Carrying her computer upstairs, she went to the room she'd used as a teenager, the room she still used often--when she wasn't suffering through her period and PMS from Hades. Or, rather, from Athena.

She sat cross-legged on the bed and booted up, then realized she hadn't brought her water with her. Sighing, she left the laptop on the bed and returned to the kitchen, grabbing her water bottle from the counter. She took a sip as she climbed the stairs, thinking about the Harvester.

She hadn't seen his face, so she wouldn't recognize him. She couldn't sense them--not like answering the phone when one of her cousins was calling and knowing which one before they spoke, her very own personal caller i.d. And apparently, the protective warding she'd done previously around her mother's property wasn't strong enough, or he couldn't have climbed in the bathroom window. Or maybe it had just been too long since she'd refreshed it. She made a mental note to refresh the protection around her own little house as well.

She sighed and stretched across the bed, tapping keys with one hand. Her email screen came up, and she scrolled through the list. A few new business queries. She smiled when she got to the end of the list and clicked on the mail from her cousin Electra.

"Hey, Philomena, it's been far too long since you've come visiting, though I imagine you have a lot going on there. How is Jason doing? Getting huge, right?

"I wanted to let you know I heard from Desdemona last week."

Philomena's smile faded.

"She mentioned maybe getting back to visit with you and Jason, and I thought you should have a heads-up, because I know she's not good about advance warning people. Of course, she may never show at all, but I wanted you to know. Just in case.

"She said she'd talked to Jason's dad a while ago, that he has some new secret gig, and he opened a security firm. I suppose you already know about it, since you and Aunt Aggie talk to him more frequently than Desi does."

Not if she *could help it.*

"Anyhow, just wanted to give you that warning. And to check in. Maybe one of these days when you haven't got visiting pets, you can take a drive up to see us. Love, E."

'Visiting pets'. That was Electra's tactful way of saying 'sporting deadly snakes on your head'.

Her pulse thudded in her ears. Ryder's new secret gig. Until tonight, she would have assumed he'd taken on another job for the government. Now she wondered if it was Harvester hunting.

She tapped a couple more keys on the laptop and closed the email program, her mind spinning.

Ryder shouldn't even know what a Harvester was. Most normal human men didn't. But he happened to have gotten tangled up with a family dealing with curses meted out millennia ago by ancient Greek deities.

Today was one of those days when she wished *she'd* never heard of Harvesters either.

Her stomach lurched at the thought of the man in her mother's house, bent on murdering her. That would be a horrible thing for her mother and Jason to come home to. Not to mention for *her*.

She inhaled slowly and pushed herself upright once more. She'd never sleep at this rate. She pulled her laptop onto her knees and opened the file for the website she'd been designing before her period hit. She worked on tweaking it until she couldn't see straight, finally shutting it down around eleven-thirty. She stripped and climbed into bed, huddling into a ball under the covers and hoping she actually slept.

She pulled the sheets and blankets tight around her. She wished the Harvester had been killed instead of just winged.

But she didn't want to think about the man who'd wounded him. Nope.

She certainly wasn't going to think about what had occurred between them earlier in the dark winter night. *Absolutely not.*

CHAPTER TWO

Ryder gave up his hunt before twelve. He'd found the bloody trail his quarry left hours earlier, but it had vanished along the main street in town. Obviously he'd gotten into his rental car and driven off to patch up his bullet wound. He wouldn't go to a hospital, since gunshot wounds required police notification. Plus Ryder knew from his discussions with Kallan that Harvesters had abnormally quick healing abilities. By morning, the wound would be mostly healed, as long as it wasn't mortal, and there hadn't been enough blood to indicate that.

He'd found himself a dark corner table at the bar the Harvester had been visiting the past few nights. Ryder waited there a while, sipping soda and eating pretzel sticks in case the other man came for his customary beer, while he tried not to think about Mena. When the Harvester hadn't arrived by ten after eleven, Ryder had to admit defeat, at least for tonight.

His blood warmed at the thought of the woman waiting for him.

Or more likely, *not* waiting for him. He grinned as he steered his truck out of the snow-packed parking lot.

She'd been shocked earlier, but also aroused when they were in the bathroom after the Harvester's escape. Her green eyes had darkened to an incredible shade of emerald when she'd realized he was turned on. Her nipples had tightened under her sweater, and he'd be willing to bet her panties were wet. They sure had been later, outside.

His body tightened just remembering how responsive she'd been, the way her mouth softened beneath his. He hadn't intended to take her up against his truck in the cold of the winter night. Just to tease her a little.

But when she'd wrapped those long legs around him, all his good intentions had evaporated.

He swallowed hard. All these years of her avoiding meeting him in person, and now this... He'd imagined what it would be like to have Mena in his arms and in his bed, had planned for the eventuality, but he hadn't thought it would be quite so instant.

And now that he'd had her, he wanted more.

Her dig about his long-ago non-relationship with her sister made him smile. Desi had been nothing more than a fling while he'd been home on leave for a couple weeks, and he'd been the same for her while she was on spring break. Neither had intended it to be a forever thing. He'd never had any intention of forever, with anyone. He hadn't believed in it.

He smiled again, thinking of Philomena's very first phone call to him after Desi had left Jason with her and Aggie just weeks after the baby's birth.

She'd demanded he take responsibility for this child he hadn't even known existed--while he stood in a tent in Afghanistan, covered in several days' worth of sand and dust, stunned. He'd been careful while he was with Desi, as he was careful any of the rare times he indulged in a fling. Clearly, this was a cosmic slap alongside the head to change his methodical, blinkered way of thinking. Just a month after he'd re-upped for another three years with Uncle Sam. The universe had a twisted sense of humor.

When he'd finally rotated back to the States twelve months later, he traveled straight to Pennsylvania, to his son. Aggie and Mena had sent him pictures and updates regularly, so he'd had time to wrap his head around the fact that he was a father, to watch his son's progress from birth. He still wasn't prepared. But when he'd seen the baby tottering around the living room of the old farmhouse, he'd fallen instantly in love. His son had been wary of the big stranger for only a few minutes, until Ryder offered his hands to help Jason stagger-step across the floor, and the delighted smile on the baby's face had wrapped itself around Ryder's heart.

It had taken a lot longer to warm up to Mena, mostly because she managed to be away every single time he arrived. Aggie had made her excuses--work, last minute client appointment, things like that--for a long time, but Ryder realized quickly she didn't want to meet him. He just didn't know why. Perhaps lingering disapproval over his fling with her sister. Perhaps because she'd been saddled with someone else's child.

They'd spoken on the phone regularly, and he'd been polite at first. Her own tone was more reserved, eventually defrosting to something like civil.

He decided, however, after talking with her and with Aggie, it had nothing to do with raising Jason. She obviously loved his son and took exceptional care of him.

He'd found himself teasing her after a while, via email

and on the phone, hoping she'd warm up to him. After all, she was important to his son. More important even than Jason's actual mother. Still, he only ever got a cool, polite tone from her.

Eventually, Aggie had confided in him about the family's curse.

He hadn't believed her, of course. Who could believe a claim so crazy? A curse carrying through centuries, turning one unlucky woman in the family each generation into a snake-haired creature for three days every month, that had another family still hunting them several thousand years later? It was too ridiculous. Until he'd met Mena's cousin Andrea and her husband Kallan Tassos. A Harvester.

In his travels around the world, Ryder had heard a lot of tall tales and folk stories, but this one, it seemed, incredibly, was true.

He wanted to talk to Mena about it, but as usual, she was nowhere to be found during his visit. Instead, he spoke to Andrea and Kallan for several days, learning everything he could about the curse and the Harvesters.

It made him realize some things about Mena.

Like...she wasn't always away simply because of him. Aggie confirmed that later when he'd asked.

Like...she was determined to protect her family. Which meant going away every month to keep them safe from herself.

Like...she would be especially reserved with her emotions. After all, who could one trust with a secret of that magnitude? Family, yes. Anyone else, probably not.

The next week, he gave his notice to the small intelligence agency where he'd been working since leaving the military. He'd taken on some high-paying freelance gigs after that, but he spent a lot more time trying to keep an eye on his little family to make sure they were safe.

He parked the truck in the driveway beside her car. The back porch light shone, and inside the door, he saw the alarm blinking, "armed". Smiling, he let himself in with the key Aggie gave him several years ago, then reset the alarm. In the kitchen, a low light shone over the sink.

Even though she'd pushed him away earlier, she'd still made sure he could find his way into the house.

He stuck his head into the guest room behind the living room and found his duffel bag in the middle of the bed, just as Mena had told him it would be. He imagined her planting it and thinking 'so there'.

He grinned, moving out of the room and heading for the small bathroom off the kitchen to brush his teeth.

But he didn't plan on sleeping in the guest room. Not now. He would have any other time, would have even tonight, except for what occurred earlier.

When he stepped out of the bathroom, he made his way up the stairs, only a small train engine night light in the second floor hall showing the way. The door to Mena's room was shut tight, which made him stifle a chuckle, right before he opened it and stepped inside. The night light let him see far enough to gauge the distance to the bed, several steps away, and, as his eyes adjusted, to make out the lump on the opposite side that was Mena.

He braced himself on the footboard to untie his boots, toeing them off with only muffled thuds on the wood floor. He stripped and fumbled for the edge of the blankets. Quilt, comforter, cotton blanket--no, there were two--then the flannel sheet. Grinning in the dark, he slid in.

Mena murmured something in her sleep, curling into a tighter ball when he reached out and found her bare back.

He rolled closer and wrapped her in his arms. She was warm. Soft, skin like satin.

Unsurprisingly, his body responded to the feel of hers, but he ignored the stirring arousal. He had excellent self-control, and she'd need her rest for what was coming.

Whether she liked it or not--and he'd stake his life she wouldn't like it--Mena Gregory was going to let him protect her from the men hunting her.

She shifted in his hold, her breast grazing his forearm.

He clenched his jaw as his dick jerked against her soft ass. *Sleep.* They both needed to sleep, because tomorrow would be a long day.

He took a slow breath, inhaling the sweet scent of her. A little flowery, faintly spicy. It made his blood thicken in his veins. Made his body harden still further.

Ryder shut his eyes tighter and concentrated on counting his heartbeats. The distraction always worked.

It wasn't working now.

Especially when she stretched one of her legs out, the sole of her foot sliding down from his knee to his shin.

He swallowed back a groan, his pulse thrumming too quickly. "Mena, baby," he whispered. He didn't want to release her, though.

She made a sleepy sound and shifted so one of her curls brushed his mouth.

He'd imagined this a thousand times, and now he was finally here, she was sleeping.

He grinned in the dark, burying his face in the loose mass of her hair. It tickled his skin, sliding, smelling of the same sweet scent on her skin.

Her breathing faltered. "Ryder?"

"Right here," he rumbled, feeling goosebumps lift on her skin. "Go to sleep."

She didn't move for a moment, then took a deep breath and her breast brushed his arm again.

His cock throbbed painfully.

"You're warm," she whispered, shifting closer to him.

He couldn't stop the moan this time.

She dragged her fingers along his arm, lazily.

"So are you." He nipped at her earlobe, hearing her breathing hitch. And slid his palm up from her ribs to catch her breast.

The taut peak burned his fingers. A surprised sound escaped her when he tugged gently.

"I won't lie and say I don't want you, Mena," he whispered, too aware of how rough his voice was, how thick with desire, "but you should get some sleep. We have a lot to do tomorrow."

She slid her foot back up his leg, which pressed her ass harder into his erection. She shifted her leg forward, and he moved his hips so his cock could slide into the tight, damp space between her thighs.

"Oh, Mena," he breathed. Now that he'd had her once, he wanted more, even if he knew it wasn't a good idea to press so soon.

She inhaled unsteadily, and he felt her body's reaction, the wetness bathing the top of his erection.

So much for self-control. "Roll over, baby," he ground out, pinching her nipple until she arched into his hand.

It took her a moment to obey his order, moving away from him. He rolled with her, pressing both his knees between hers, widening her stance.

"Jesus," he muttered, his cock sliding into her sheath, just the tip.

She sucked in a quick breath.

"Just like I told you earlier, Mena." He dragged his open

mouth along the bared nape of her neck. "Harder and deeper." He eased farther into her heat.

She rocked back to meet him, and his cock went hilt-deep. Her gasp mingled with his groan.

"Easy." He stilled her with one hand on her hip.

Their ragged breathing filled the dark space around them, making him hyper-aware of how alone they were here.

He slid his hand around from her hip to find her clit, the tiny bit of flesh distended already with her desire. "Oh, isn't that nice?" He plucked it much as he had her nipple, and her sheath tightened around him.

Her head dropped, and she quivered.

"It's all right, Mena." He bit her shoulder as he withdrew his cock from her, out, nearly out. "I'll take good care of you." Slowly, slowly, he pushed deep again, feeling her body tremble around his.

Over and over, he repeated the strokes, the thrusts. She came after only a few minutes, her cry muffled in the pillow. Sweat dripped from his forehead onto her back, slick with her own perspiration.

"Not done yet," he ground out, nipping at her nape this time while he strummed her clit.

She huffed a laugh, shoulders shaking with her release and the laughter. "I noticed."

He grinned into her skin. "Really?" He rolled his hips in a tiny circle, stroking over a spot deep inside her that made her laughter turn to a moan.

"Yeah, it's kind of hard to ignore *that*." She clenched her inner muscles around him, stealing his breath for a moment.

"Witch." He caught her hips and jerked them toward himself, wedging his cock even deeper inside her.

A shocked cry echoed around the room, and her body tensed beneath his.

"Not yet." He held still, though his own body screamed for release.

"Please."

He dragged his open mouth to the spot where her neck met her shoulder, teeth scraping gently and making her shudder. "You have to learn some patience." And he needed to exercise his own. Or dig a deeper well.

She whimpered when he pinched her clit again, her hips jerking toward his touch.

"You like that?" He licked the spot he'd just nibbled, tasting salt and Mena.

She whimpered a reply, her inner muscles clinging when he eased his hips away.

"You'll like this even better," he promised, releasing her shoulder to catch both her hips in his hands.

The movement lifted her higher, and she braced her weight on her elbows, her head lowering.

Ryder stroked slowly back inside her heat, his breath hissing out at the feel of her around him. Over and over, he slid out, then in, out, in, gradually increasing his pace until she screamed when the second orgasm broke, her body bowing beneath his.

His own release strained for freedom. He'd never be able to stop it now. One more deep stroke, and it exploded, rushing from somewhere deep inside.

He collapsed onto his elbows, trying not to crush her with his heavier weight, his lungs barely able to get him enough oxygen to remain conscious. In his chest, his heart felt like it might pound itself to pieces.

Underneath him, Mena's heart beat crazily, too, and he smiled into the tangle of her hair over her shoulder.

Eventually, he could think enough to realize he was probably smothering her in the pillow, and he rolled to his side, keeping her tight in his arms.

Their rough breathing still echoed around the room. He felt too hot for all the blankets, but he left them where they were, too exhausted to push them off.

"Sleep, Mena," he whispered, kissing the top of her ear.

She hummed a breathless reply, one hand sliding along his forearm until she reached his wrist. Then her fingers stopped moving.

Ryder smiled in the dark.

He hadn't imagined winning her would be very easy. Perhaps with such explosive chemistry between them, courting his Medusa would be easier than he'd expected.

HE SHOULD HAVE KNOWN BETTER.

When he woke in the morning, he stretched, then put one hand out to find her.

Gone. Sighing, he opened his eyes and looked around the room. Mena was gone. Of course.

He sat up, and the blankets fell to his lap. Listening hard, he heard faint sounds from the kitchen, and he relaxed.

He threw back the mound of blankets and grabbed his jeans, stepping into them before he gathered the rest of his clothing and padded down the steps, the wood cold beneath his bare feet.

In the kitchen, Mena bent at the waist, peering into the refrigerator. She'd obviously showered, her inky hair still wet against her sweater, her wool skirt and boots hiding her long legs. She shot him a wary glance as she straightened and closed the fridge.

"Good morning." He dragged one hand over his head, aware he was rumpled from sleep.

Her gaze slid from his hair to his bare chest to the unbuttoned waist of his jeans, and pink tinted her cheeks before she dragged her gaze back to his face. "I was going to make breakfast. Would you like something?"

Yeah, you, back in bed, naked. "What were you going to have?" he asked instead. He had plenty of time, and Aggie would be here soon with Jason.

"Eggs and toast. I think Mom has some bacon or sausage in the freezer, if you'd like." She bit her lower lip, her green eyes wide and dark. His attention went to the tiny round mole at the right corner of her mouth. He wanted to lick it.

He set his things down at the bottom of the stairs and took a step toward her.

She flinched as if she'd retreat, then held her ground, eyes filled with caution and only the barest shadow of desire.

He smiled, more to himself than at her. "Good morning, Mena." One more step brought him within arm's reach, but he waited.

The pink in her cheeks deepened. "Good morning," she whispered.

He touched her chin. "Are you all right?"

She blinked as her entire face reddened. "Yes." She looked away.

"Good." He tipped her chin up and kissed her, hard.

For a second, she stood there, frozen, and he thought she might pull away, but then her lips parted, and he relaxed, sliding his tongue along her lower lip, dipping into the warmth of her mouth. She'd brushed her teeth, tasted of mint. He changed the angle of the kiss, one of his hands catching her nape to slide his fingers into her damp hair.

She set her hands on his shoulders, and a soft sigh met his tongue.

He gentled the kiss, then lifted his head just slightly.

Her eyes were shut and her mouth swollen. She was gorgeous.

He kissed her again, lightly. And again.

When he straightened this time, her fingers dug into his shoulders, and she swayed just a little. He steadied her, watching her eyes flutter open. Desire and wariness mingled there in opposite proportions now.

"Eggs and toast are fine."

She blinked up at him, a tiny frown marring her forehead for a few seconds.

"I'll just grab a shower, and then we have work to do." He didn't want to, but he released her.

"What kind of work?" She dropped her hands to her sides.

"My buddy is on his way to boost the alarm system. I want him to do your place, too. Then you and I need to go away."

"What?" Annoyance chased the desire right out of her eyes. "I can't go away. I have work to do. And I was just gone for three days."

"At your place. Not quite the same, and not far enough to get this Harvester away from our family."

She clearly wanted to argue with him, sparks snapping in her eyes, but she pressed her lips together instead.

"We can talk about it over breakfast." He picked up his things and went into the guest room. He shut the door, then grinned when something soft hit the door almost at the height of his head. Good thing she'd waited till the door shut and used something light. Her aim was pretty good.

THE MAN HAD SOME NERVE.

Philomena glared into the skillet and dragged the spatula through the eggs vigorously. Too vigorously, as the spatula scraped the side of the pan. Letting out a shaky breath, she tried to push Ryder out of her head for a few minutes.

She'd called her mother when she came downstairs, and Aggie assured her they were fine. Jason was watching his favorite Saturday morning cartoon in his pajamas before breakfast. Philomena felt a bit better knowing he was safe and happy.

Her gaze slid to the window over the sink. She could see the woods that lay between her mother's house and her own. Only a couple miles of distance. Not far enough.

She stirred the eggs at a more normal pace now. Sure, she'd known when the curse fell on her eight years ago that the Harvesters were a serious threat. But somehow, she'd hoped after all this time they wouldn't find her.

She shivered, thinking how lucky they were Ryder had been waiting for the Harvester yesterday. Otherwise, her mother and Jason might have arrived to find her dead in the kitchen. She touched the top of her dagger handle through her skirt. She knew how to wield it, but who knew how the Harvester was armed.

She'd have to ask Ryder.

Her pulse quickened. *Back to him.*

He was showering. She knew because she heard the water running, and it didn't take much effort to imagine him standing beneath the streaming water. After all, she'd gotten a terrific view of his naked body last evening.

Heat pulsed in her middle at the memory, then more when she thought of later.

She shook her head. No, *that* was a mistake. Both times. She turned the burner off and covered the pan, then pushed the bread down into the toaster.

The water shut off in the next room, and she swallowed, trying not to let her brain go there again. She busied herself with getting plates and silverware out, then took butter and jelly from the fridge. While thinking of website coding, she poured orange juice into two glasses.

When he emerged from the guest room, his hair was towel-dried, though still damp, making the blond look darker. He wore a soft black t-shirt over faded jeans. She jerked her gaze to his face in time to see that grin disappear.

She narrowed her eyes, but kept her mouth shut and dished up breakfast.

He waited until she had eggs in her mouth before he spoke. "What work do you have going right now?"

She forced down the eggs and chased them with a quick swallow of juice. "I'm nearly done with a big site, then I have a few smaller ones waiting. Regular maintenance on others."

"You can work on them away from home, right?"

She glared at him. "I'm not leaving."

He raised one dark blond eyebrow. "I don't remember asking you."

She set her fork down. "Just because I made a mistake and slept with you does not give you permission to make my decisions. Also, you are no longer in the military, and not my commanding officer. And, FYI, I will not be sleeping with you again."

He laughed. "Not much sleeping going on, the way I remember it."

Heat scorched her face, and Philomena growled, curling her fingers into fists on the table. "I am not looking for a relationship, and even if I were, you wouldn't be at the top of my wish list." *Good Gods, no.*

Ryder took a drink, though she couldn't understand how, with that miserable grin still spread over his face. "You, Mena, are afraid to be in a relationship with a man stronger than you are."

She blinked at him, her heart pounding faster. "What?" How could a man she'd managed to avoid for so long know so much about the way her brain worked?

"I've seen your 'dates'. Bunch of pansies, without a spine in the whole lot. You pick men who won't argue when you decide you're done with them." He lifted his fork. "It's a tactic I'm immune to." He scooped up more eggs.

Her mouth was dry, but she refused to lift her glass and let him know he'd hit the mark with his assessment of her. "How long have you been spying on me?" she asked instead.

He shook his head, swallowing his eggs. "Just trying to make sure you were safe. Can't have you bringing danger home to Jason."

That was low, and she shot him a fierce glare. "I have never dated anyone who was a danger to Jason," she ground out.

"I know." His grin remained smug, and she wanted to smack it off his face. "You've never dated anyone who was a threat to your remaining single either."

She shoved away from the table, her chair screeching with the sudden movement. "My dating is none of your business." She jolted to her feet and spun away.

"You haven't dated anyone who would present any sort

of challenge to you," he continued from behind her when she walked the few steps to the sink. "Is it because you're really that afraid, or because you were just waiting for the right man to come along?"

She shook her head, anger and fear clogging her throat, and gripped the edge of the sink so hard her knuckles turned white. There was no 'right man' for her. Not for the Medusa.

Behind her, his chair scraped over the floor. "I'm not a spineless wonder like any of those guys," he said, his booted footsteps drawing nearer. "And I've been waiting a very long time, so I'm not going away quietly."

Philomena shut her eyes.

His big hands settled on her shoulders. "But I promise I'll never hurt you, Mena," he whispered, too close to her ear.

She jabbed her elbow into his ribs, hard, surprising him into releasing her. She slid away along the counter. "But I might hurt you." She patted the hilt of her dagger through her skirt as she faced him. "You know I'm armed, right?"

He rubbed his side where she'd elbowed him, still grinning. "Bring it, baby."

Her jaw dropped, and he laughed. Suddenly, his smile vanished.

"Get down."

"What?" She frowned.

He pushed her to a crouch, then moved through the doorway of the guest room, grabbing his gun from the open bag on the bed.

Her heart jumped into her throat at the sight of it.

"We have company," he breathed, peering through the narrow space she'd made when she parted the living room curtains earlier to let some morning light in.

She fumbled her skirt out of her way and unsheathed her dagger, wrapping her fingers tight around the hilt. It felt good against her palm, but her hand shook. Two days in a row was a little much.

"Hang onto that." He stepped to the alarm panel and shut the system off, then eased out the back door, his posture cautious.

Philomena shut her eyes. *Oh Gods, don't let the Harvester hurt him.* She'd never forgive herself if something happened to him because of her. Jason would be heartbroken. She opened her eyes and took a quick breath. She couldn't be sitting here in the middle of the floor if Ryder didn't walk back in. She crawled behind the door, where she could see through the crack between door and frame.

And waited.

It seemed an eternity before she heard steady footsteps crunching in the snow leading to the door, and she tensed even more, pain sliding up the back of her neck to squeeze her skull. Her breath escaped in a rush when she saw Ryder step inside, and she lowered her dagger to her side, eyes closing for a second. *Thank you, Gods.*

He shut the door and knelt in front of her. "It's all right." He touched her cheek with cold fingers, and she shut her eyes again.

"Gone?" She opened her eyes and found his expression somber, his brown eyes hard.

"Dead."

She gasped, the room tilting sharply to one side.

"Either him or you, and I'd prefer him." He helped her to her feet. "I've got to get rid of the body." He cupped her elbows in his hands while he studied her expression. He guided her back to her seat and pushed her into it, then took the dagger from her nerveless fingers. "Drink some of that orange juice, baby. You look mighty pale."

While she wrapped both hands around her glass, he tugged her skirt up far enough to reveal the soft leather sheath strapped to her thigh.

"Nice," he murmured, then put her blade into it and snapped it shut. His fingers, hard, a little rough, lingered along her skin, distracting her from her chaotic thoughts for a couple of seconds. He inhaled shakily, then pulled her skirt into place, rising again. "I'll be back as soon as I can. Do *not* go anywhere without me, Mena." He bent to kiss the top of her head, then strode out to his truck after resetting the alarm.

She rose, still shocked, then stood there at the door, staring out into the snowy back yard as the sound of his truck faded away.

He'd killed someone to protect her.

The thought chilled her. Not necessarily the idea he'd killed someone. She imagined he'd killed before, during his time in the military and working for the intelligence agency. But to keep her safe... Someone who would have killed her given the opportunity. *That* was the chilling part.

The Harvesters had really found her.

She shivered, wrapping her arms around her waist, and turned away from the door. Her mother and Jason were in danger with her here. Far more than she'd ever let herself imagine.

Fear tightened her chest. She needed to go somewhere else. Somewhere the Harvesters wouldn't kill her family to get to her. *Away.*

She scraped her breakfast into the trash, hands shaking so much she dropped her fork in, too. Her breath came too fast, making her dizzy. She retrieved the fork, carrying it and her plate to the sink and turning on the water, too hot, but she put her hands under it anyway, wincing before adjusting the temperature.

Where would she go?

Oh, Gods, *how* would she go? How could she not see Jason again? She bit her lip against the sting of tears in her eyes. She'd had him since Desi gave birth to him six years ago.

The phone rang, startling her, and she sniffed, grabbing a dish towel on her way to pick it up. "Hello?"

"Good, you're still there." Ryder.

She sniffled. "I have to go."

"Not without me." His tone went hard. "That's why I told you not to go anywhere without me. I knew you would get there."

Philomena wiped the towel over her cheek. "It's not safe for them if I'm here."

"I know, baby," he said, more gently. "But wait for me. We'll do this together. I can keep you safe."

She dropped into the chair he'd abandoned, staring at his half-eaten breakfast. "I can't stay."

"Mena."

She stuck his fork into the small mound of eggs on the plate, her mind spinning in too many directions. Her heart pounded loud enough to drown out most of those thoughts, even if she could capture one.

"*Mena.*"

His sharp tone snagged her attention. "What, Ryder?"

"Stay with me here." He took a deep breath and released it. "I'll be back at the house in maybe twenty minutes. My buddy will be there in the next hour or two. We have to stay for a while, to get him settled. To say goodbye to Aggie and Jason, temporarily. But we'll go together, do you understand me?"

She picked up a forkful the bright yellow eggs, trying to concentrate on his words and staring at the eggs. "Together?"

"Yes, together. You and me."

She stuck the eggs into her mouth without thinking, and her stomach growled. She blinked, chewing slowly. With Ryder. She didn't doubt he could keep her safe from the Harvesters. "Okay," she said at last.

He sighed, and it was clear, even over the phone line, the sound was filled with relief. "Good, smart girl. Are you eating your breakfast?"

"No, yours. I threw mine away." She stuck another bite of eggs in her mouth, trying to concentrate only on the act of eating.

He laughed.

Philomena smiled faintly. The eggs were cool now, not especially appetizing. But she was starved.

"We'll have to pack some things for you when I get back."

"Mm." She didn't want to think yet about packing, about leaving. No, just breakfast for now.

"Promise me, Mena."

She swallowed another forkful of eggs. "Promise what?"

"You'll be waiting there if I hang up now."

She considered. If she left on her own, it wouldn't take long before she found herself floundering without resources or a plan. She was smart enough to know that. If she waited for Ryder, infuriating as he'd proven to be even before she met him in person, she knew she had a better chance of staying alive and getting back to Jason and her mother in one piece. "Okay."

"Promise me."

She stuck her tongue out at the phone. "Fine, I promise." He didn't need to know she thought he might be her only chance. It would only make his head fatter.

"Good girl."

She rolled her eyes.

"I've got a little business to take care of now, so I'm going to hang up. I'll be there soon."

She thumbed off her phone when the line went dead, setting it beside the plate. She felt a tiny bit better now. Calmer. The man had other talents besides churning up her hormones and deliberately annoying her. She scooped up another bite of eggs, and another, until she'd finished his breakfast.

By then, she felt almost normal. Philomena finished clearing away the dishes, rinsing them and leaving them in the sink while she put away last night's dinner dishes from the dishwasher. She kept busy, not allowing herself to think of what might have happened earlier. Of what had happened to the Harvester. When Ryder let himself into the house nearly forty minutes later, she'd finished the website she'd been working on last night.

He looked grim, his mouth a tight line in his hard face, and her stomach twisted in anticipation of whatever was about to come out of his mouth.

Instead of speaking, he went to the fridge and took out a juice bottle, opening it and taking a swig before he sat across from her. "I went through his pockets and to his motel to have a quick look around," he said at last, setting his bottle down and meeting her gaze. "I found his laptop and some notes. Some weapons." Ryder studied her face for a moment. "It was always too much to hope he hadn't told anyone else where you were."

She closed her eyes and bowed her head, feeling goose-bumps raise on her arms.

"I don't think anyone will look for him right away, though I imagine if he doesn't check in, someone will come." He nudged her foot with his under the table, and she opened her eyes, reluctantly meeting his dark gaze. "We have a little time to plan."

That didn't make her feel better.

The knock at the front door made her leap up, shoving the chair backward into the fridge. Her pulse surged, too loud in her ears.

Ryder rose in a flash and set his hands on her shoulders to steady her. "It's all right. Just my buddy Danny. Breathe, smart girl." He brushed a kiss on her forehead, then moved away.

Philomena gulped in some air, willing her racing heart to slow down. She couldn't leap into the air at every shadow or whisper of sound. It would frighten Jason. She forced herself to take a slower, deeper breath, releasing it just as slowly.

Ryder smiled when he returned, trailed by another man, just as big, just as brawny, only with curly red hair. "Mena, this is Danny Rafferty. Danny, this is Philomena Gregory."

Danny stuck out his right hand, and she shook it. "Nice to meet you, ma'am."

"Nice to meet you, too." She glanced at Ryder, and he winked. Heat touched her cheeks.

"I'm just going to take a peek at the alarm system, if it's all right with you."

She nodded, though Ryder had apparently already given him permission, as he moved away, up the back stairwell. She folded her arms on her chest, still concentrating on breathing evenly.

"Better?"

She nodded. "If all the Harvesters know where I am, Mom and Jason can't stay here either."

He didn't look like he wanted to agree, but he nodded after a few seconds anyway.

That made her stomach clench tighter, but she kept breathing evenly. In. Out.

"We'll figure out what we're doing, Mena." He touched her shoulder lightly, then picked up his juice bottle and took a drink.

"What did you do with him?" She heard her voice shake, and steeled her spine, as though it would steady her voice, too.

His jaw tightened, making a muscle there jump, and he shifted his shoulders as if to ease the tension there. "No one will find him for a long time."

"We should let Kallan know."

Ryder pulled her against his chest, his big hands sliding up and down her back. "Okay."

She took another deep breath, inhaling the warm scent of him, spicy and male and oddly comforting.

"It's all right to be scared, Mena," he said, one of his warm hands cupping her nape.

"Well, that's good to know." She laughed, rubbing her forehead on his chest. She unfolded her arms and set her hands at his waist. "Thank you."

"See all the fun you've been missing by avoiding me all this time?" he teased.

She laughed again, lifting her face, and the sound caught in her throat at the intense look in his eyes. *Oh*, that *was dangerous*.

His melted chocolate eyes, deep and dark, warmed with desire and things she didn't want to think about. He held her gaze while he lowered his head, brushing his lips over hers, once, twice.

Heat slid into her belly, loosening the muscles there.

Footsteps on the stairs had her swallowing hard and moving away.

Amusement tinted Ryder's expression as he released her.

She retreated to lean on the edge of the sink, wrapping her arms over her middle. Breathing space seemed an excellent idea right now. Touching him made her brain turn to mush, made her forget why she couldn't indulge in things other women did. Why she didn't want to anyway.

Danny came into the room, rubbing one hand over the top of his head. "Lots of windows up there," he said mildly.

Ryder grunted in reply.

Danny shot her a questioning glance, and she shook her head. "Do what you need to do. I don't have a choice."

As the two men walked outside together, voices low, she realized it was the truth. Her choices were now limited, and she'd do whatever they asked of her to keep Jason and her mother safe, no matter how little she liked it.

Philomena shut her eyes. Life as she knew it was over.

She had a feeling her new life might suck even more than it had for the last eight years.

CHAPTER THREE

R yder helped Danny carry in spools of wire and tools from his buddy's truck. Mena had moved to the living room with her laptop where he saw a screenful of gibberish, so he assumed she was working on a client's website. Her face was pale but set. She wouldn't like his plan. He'd known that before he arrived. He didn't love it, but it was the best thing for all of them right now, especially since he knew other Harvesters knew her location.

He met Aggie and Jason at the back door, devoting several uninterrupted minutes to his son's chatter about the game he'd played with his grandma before breakfast. Gods, he loved this boy more than anything.

Mena had been right when she'd said earlier it wasn't safe for her to be with Jason or Aggie now that the Harvesters knew where she was. Even with an amped up alarm system on both houses, none of them were safe there. It would take the Harvesters some time to figure out Mena was gone, to figure out it wasn't even her house, but who knew what they'd attempt in the meantime. Kallan hadn't seemed to think they'd kill anyone else who happened to be in the vicinity, but his family had disowned him eight years ago when he got in their way to save his own Medusa. Things in the Tassos family might have changed drastically since then.

Which meant Ryder had to separate Jason and Mena. Indefinitely.

It was a strategy he knew would be difficult for everyone.

He didn't want to dwell on it right now, though, patting Jason on the behind as his son rushed to the steps to see what Danny was doing in his bedroom. "Stay out of his way, Jase," he called after the boy.

"I will, Daddy."

He stood there in the kitchen for a moment, putting off what had to be done for just a few seconds more. In the next room, Aggie spoke quietly as she took off her coat. Mena rose from the sofa to give her mother a heartfelt hug. Ryder took a deep breath. Now, while Jason was upstairs, he had to tell them.

He moved toward the living room. Tension tightened Mena's face when she saw him behind her mother, as if she knew and dreaded what was coming. Even Aggie's normally serene face wore worry lines when she glanced over her shoulder at him.

"We need to talk about what we're going to do, ladies."

Mena dropped back onto the couch, her gaze sliding away from his. The older woman sank onto the rocking chair, coat on her lap.

He sat on the sofa beside Mena, but he didn't touch. Tension rolled off of her in waves. He wished he could say something to make her feel better, but it would be quite a while before he could do it honestly.

"We have to go, too, don't we?" Aggie asked before he could decide where to start.

He met her gaze and gave her a little smile, ignoring Mena's soft sound of protest. "I'm afraid so, Aggie. But not with us."

The older woman didn't look surprised. "For how long?"

He hesitated. "I don't know," he finally said. Honesty was best. "You might not be able to come back."

Mena gasped, her head coming up fast.

Her mother just sighed. "I thought so."

"Mom, your job--"

She put her hand across the space between her seat and the sofa, touching Mena's knee. "It's all right, Philomena."

"It's not all right."

She shushed her daughter with a motion of her hand. "When this curse fell on you, everything became negotiable."

Mena dropped her chin again, and he saw her swallow several times, biting her lip.

"You probably have a couple of days to tie things up here, Aggie. I don't think anyone is going to come looking for our Harvester friend right away." He shook his head when Aggie opened her mouth, and she shut it, most of the color leaving her cheeks. "But I want to get Mena out of here today."

"Today?" Mena's head shot up once more. "I thought you said we had time." Her wide eyes were shiny.

He steeled himself against the impending tears. "Not time to dawdle. Time for you and I to get a head start." He knew the tightening of her jaw was a bad sign, so he kept talking. "We need to be far away from here before any more of them decide to join the party, or come to see what happened to him."

She glared at him, then averted her gaze, nostrils flaring.

He bit back a grim smile. "We're going to pack some necessities for you this afternoon, Mena, and be on our way. Danny will stay here with you, Aggie, help you get things settled and then away in the next couple of days." He met the older woman's gaze, gratified when she nodded her agreement. He hadn't doubted Aggie's cooperation. "Danny's brought some new identification along for everyone." He didn't look at Mena when she faced him once more, but from the corner of his eyes, he still saw the fear mingling with her annoyance now.

"When will it be safe for us to be together again?" she asked, her voice hoarse with emotion.

His urge to smile faded. "I don't know." He reminded himself--honesty. "I want to be sure they haven't picked up our trails."

Mena pushed to her feet and moved around the coffee table, and her mother's worried gaze followed her. She strode into the kitchen, her boots heavy as she paced the other room.

Ryder got to his feet.

"Let her be, Ryder," Aggie said softly. "Just for a few minutes."

He didn't want to do that. He wanted to wrap her in his arms and make her understand it was best this way. *His* way.

"She'll make up her mind to it. She knows she has to. If not for her, then for Jason and me."

He swallowed hard. Of course she would. She'd done a lot of things she didn't want to do since she'd become the Medusa--probably far more even than he knew about, more than he could imagine. He shifted his weight to one foot, watching when she walked past the doorway, her black skirt flaring out behind her. And he waited, instead of following her as he wanted to do.

He heard Jason's running footsteps in the hallway upstairs, and his attention shifted for a second. "Don't run on the steps," he called. Immediately the light steps slowed, and Ryder grinned. His son appeared a moment later, his dark eyes shining with excitement.

"Daddy, Danny let me cut the wires!"

"Really?" He scooped his son up and hefted him in one arm. "I thought you were going to stay out of the way."

"Danny said I could help."

From the corner of his eye, he saw Mena's skirt flaring as she circled the table. "How would you like to go on a trip, Jase?"

"Where? Where we goin'?" Jason's little fingers dug into Ryder's shirt, his eyes widening.

He pushed his son's dark hair away from his face. "You and Grandma are going to go somewhere with Danny, but it's a surprise."

"Wahoo!" His fist pumped in the air. "I can't wait!"

Ryder gave his son a quick, hard hug and pressed a kiss on his round cheek. "I thought you might like an adventure." When Jason squirmed, he set him down.

"How come you're not comin' with us?"

"Because I have to go somewhere with Aunt Mena."

"You mean Aunt Phila." Jason grinned at him.

He winked at his son. "No, I mean Mena." He felt her presence behind him before he heard her unsteady exhalation.

"It's Philomena, you clown," she muttered, pushing

around him to kneel in front of Jason. She caught Jason's hands in hers. "I wish I could go with you, baby."

His son tugged one hand free to touch her cheek. "I know. 'Specially since you just got back, and I know you missed us." He patted her face softly. "But Daddy'll bring you to us later, I bet."

Ryder could see her smile was forced, and, when he bent a little, he noted the sheen in her eyes. *Damn.*

"You're right. But you better not grow too much while I'm gone, or I'll be really aggravated." Her teasing was choked.

Jason's smile turned lopsided. "I can't help it I'm gettin' to be a big boy."

Mena wrapped her arms around him swiftly, shutting her eyes, and two fat tears slid down her cheeks. "Yes, you are."

Ryder's heart wrenched at her pain. He dropped to one knee beside them and swiped away her tears. Her eyes fluttered open, still filled to overflowing, her lashes wet, and she bit her lip. He gave her an encouraging nod, and she shut her eyes, squeezing Jason tighter. Ryder wiped away another tear that slipped down her face, so when she eased away, Jason wouldn't see it.

"You'll be a really good boy for Grandma and Danny, right?" She got to her feet, sniffling.

Ryder handed her a tissue from the box on the end table.

"Course I will," Jason said with a disgusted look at her. "I'm always a good boy."

She laughed, unsteadily, but a real smile touched her lips.

Ryder set one hand at the small of her back, offering his support. She gave him a quick, grateful glance, then wiped the tissue beneath her eyes. "You'll have to pick out your most important things to take along," she said after a moment.

Jason thought about it for a minute, his expression solemn. "You mean my *really* important stuff?"

She nodded.

"Huh. I might have to add a couple things to my box." The boy shot her a quick, sly smile. "Can I have a bigger box?"

The adults in the room laughed, and Aggie got to her feet, a tissue in her hand, as well. "Come with me, young man. Why don't you show me this box?"

Ryder watched them climb the stairs, and Mena shuddered at his side. She took a deep breath, but she didn't look up. "We need to go to your place soon," he said after a moment.

She nodded, and her spine stiffened under his fingers.

He patted her, then moved away, giving her a minute to finish pulling herself back together.

"This sucks," she said after a few seconds, but she didn't sound as if she were about to burst into tears anymore.

"Yeah, it does." He studied the photo collage over the sofa, which consisted mostly of pictures of Jason, from his birth until the last year or so. "We need to make sure everything that can be connected to you gets packed away." He swung around and found her glaring out the front window. Better than crying, he supposed.

"We should have set up a trust and bought the houses through it in the first place," she mused. "Nothing with names on it. We talked about it a long time ago."

He nodded. "It would have helped, I imagine."

"Can we do it now? In case we're ever able to come

home?" She turned to look at him again. "Set up something and sell the houses to it, I mean."

"I'll look into it." He didn't point out returning would only keep them in danger, no matter whether it was a week, a month, or even a year from now. As long as she was the Medusa, the Harvesters would hunt her.

Mena chewed on one corner of her lower lip as she walked past him.

He trailed after her, watching as she put together a couple plates with sandwiches on them, fruit cups in the center, some cookies on another plate. When she caught his gaze, she shrugged. "Jason's going to want lunch, and maybe Danny would like some, too."

He watched her climb the back stairs, the sway of her hips making her skirt float around her booted ankles. His imagination slid up further, recalling those long legs wrapped around his waist.

Blood surged downward, and he shut off that train of thought. Now was not the time.

As he spread peanut butter onto another slice of bread, he realized he hadn't actually *seen* her legs yet. Or the rest of her.

It was a problem he'd remedy later.

Grinning, he stuck the knife back into the peanut butter jar just as she returned. He winked. Something of his thoughts must have shown in his face, because pink washed up her throat and into her cheeks, where it deepened.

His grin widened. Definitely later.

Philomena refused to cry. Not now, when Jason could see her. After he'd eaten, she helped him sort through the things he kept in his 'most important things' box normally stored under his bed--a metal wind-up soldier she'd given him when Ryder was still in the Army, a picture of himself in between her and her mother from a couple of years ago, a couple of pretty rocks. Little boy treasures. Her heart hurt.

She bit her lip when Ryder jerked his head toward the door later, then gathered her laptop and purse and carried them into the kitchen.

"How much more does Danny have to do?" she asked when he followed her into the room.

"Most of the windows are linked. He just needs to finish the last bedroom, then wire it all into the main system." He leaned against the wall, folding his arms on his wide chest. "Are you ready?"

"No." She met his gaze. "But I have no choice, do I?"

He shook his head.

"Then I'm as ready as I'm going to be." She swallowed down the lump threatening to block her airway. "Let me say goodbye."

Jason sat on the couch with his box in his lap, and a small pile of other things on the cushion beside him. "It's too hard to choose, Aunt Phila," he complained.

She smiled at him, ruffling his dark hair. "I know. But everything won't fit into the box. That's why you have to decide which ones would make you very sad to leave behind. To never have again." She leaned closer and inhaled the clean smell of him, soap and peanut butter and fresh air.

He sighed. "I know." He lifted his head. "What's in your box?"

"You and Grandma."

He laughed. "Your box isn't big enough."

"Are you saying I'm too big, young man?" Aggie asked

from her rocking chair, where she was making a list on a legal pad.

He giggled some more. "No, Grandma."

Philomena wrapped her arm around him. "I've got to get going, buddy," she whispered. "I'll see you soon." *I hope.*

He pushed his box aside and slid his arms around her neck, tight. "I'll miss you the most."

She shut her eyes. "Nope. I'll miss *you* the most. You need to promise to take care of Grandma, okay?"

"Course I will. I'm the man of the house, right?"

"You bet. But maybe you can let Danny help, too." She released him before she squeezed him too hard. Or couldn't let go at all. "I'll talk to you soon."

"Every night?"

She nodded, her chest aching as she got to her feet. "You know it."

Her mother met her in the middle of the room and hugged her tight.

"I'm so sorry, Mom," she whispered around the lump clogging her throat.

"Curse that Athena," Aggie muttered.

Philomena laughed, as she was sure her mother intended. "I'll talk to you soon, too." There was so much more she needed to say.

Her mother leaned away. "I know, Philomena, my girl." She cupped Philomena's face in her hands. "Take care, and do what Ryder tells you to do."

She laughed, a little wildly. If her mother only knew...

He was waiting when she turned around, understanding in his face. He held out one hand, and she hesitated. This was the point of no return. Literally.

He waited, his hand steady.

Reluctantly, she slid her palm over his, only slightly

reassured when his warm fingers wrapped around hers. Dimly, she heard him tell Jason they'd call later, then give her mother a quick goodbye. She just kept thinking she might never see this house. She might not see her family again.

By the time they got outside, she was shaking.

Ryder touched her chin. "I need you to be able to drive your car to your place, Mena. Can you do that?"

She nodded, but she wasn't absolutely sure she could even stop her hands from trembling long enough to get the key in the ignition.

"I'm going to follow you there." He kissed her, hard, startling her back to the present, then searched her face. "Smart girl." A hint of a smile curled one side of his mouth. "Let's go."

She climbed into her car and fumbled the key into the ignition, relieved when the engine started. Inhaling slowly, she concentrated on the familiar ritual of reversing out of the driveway and steering along the narrow, winding road to her own house.

The cottage sat away from the road, only a few scattered trees near the house, though the forest wasn't too far across the meadow out back--just far enough so no one could find easy hiding. She pulled the car into the garage and climbed out, taking her things with her. Ryder waited at the door, and she hit the button to close it just before she walked out, for what she feared was the last time.

She pushed the thought away.

"Is your code still the same?" He guided her to the front door of her house.

She blinked. "The same as what?"

He smiled. "The same as it's always been."

"You've never been here." She'd made sure of it.

His smile widened. "Not with you, no."

Her eyes rounded. "With Mom?" She might have to kill her mother.

He didn't reply, just took her keyring from her, unlocked the front door, and punched in her alarm code.

She glared at his back as he moved further inside. "When?"

"We need to get your stuff and get out, Mena." He continued on to the kitchen.

She dropped her things onto the table in the entryway, annoyance surging through her. "How many times?"

He didn't answer, but she heard the refrigerator open.

Damn the man. She strode along the short hall and found him twisting the top off a water bottle. "Ryder."

He just shot her an amused glance as he took a long drink.

She growled and spun away, to her bedroom, where she shut the door, hard.

The man was impossible.

She fumed as she yanked a carry-on suitcase from the top shelf of her closet and opened it on her bed, then dragged open several drawers on her dresser.

When he strolled into the room, she glared. "Get out."

"Might go faster with an extra pair of hands," he said mildly.

She huffed out a breath and turned her back on him, yanking a handful of underwear from one of the open drawers.

"Mm, nice." He plucked a pair of blush-tinted lace panties from her fingers. "Is there a bra that matches those?"

She snatched them off his long fingers and dropped them into the suitcase, ignoring the heat climbing her cheeks at his question. Then realized she had indeed also grabbed the matching bra in her next handful. She shut the first drawer and lifted a couple sweaters from the next drawer.

"You do own jeans, right?"

She elbowed past him to get to her closet and heard his soft laugh. She took out a few of the long skirts she favored for the easy access to her dagger and dropped them into the suitcase on top of the sweaters.

"Mena."

She glanced over her shoulder and found he'd rummaged in another of her drawers to come up with a sheer, green, lacy negligee. Electra had sent it for one of her birthdays, years ago, and she'd tucked it into a drawer where it had stayed. Until now. It looked ridiculously feminine dangling from his big hand, and the images it brought up in her head were x-rated.

"You're packing this, right?"

She shut her eyes for a second, knowing from the heat in her cheeks that she was as red as one of the sweaters she'd put into the suitcase, then she snatched it from his grasp. "No." She dropped it into the drawer and instead pulled out a long flannel nightgown with buttons to the chin.

He laughed when she put it into the suitcase, but she didn't care.

She did pull a few pairs of jeans from another dresser drawer, and then returned to the closet for another pair of boots, a calf-high pair of soft brown leather ones that had a sheath for her dagger along the side of the right one.

When she got back to the bed to drop the jeans into the case, the negligee lay on top of the flannel nightgown, and she growled.

Ryder just smirked.

"If you can wear it, you can take it," she ground out.

When she put her boots on the bed beside the suitcase, he caught her wrist and tugged her closer. "Smart girl, you know *I'm* not wearing it," he whispered, brushing her lips with his before he released her.

Philomena whirled away and stomped into the bathroom to gather necessary toiletries. And make her racing pulse slow the hell down.

Her reflection in the mirror over the sink confirmed the high color in her face she'd felt with the rush of heat a few minutes ago. She realized her eyes were dark, the pupils enormous against the green outer rings. She ran some cold water and splashed it on her face.

As she dragged the hand towel over her face, she paused, catching her reflection's gaze.

He'd pissed her off on purpose.

She straightened, considering, and rehung the towel, her pulse easing a little. Just when she was getting ready to flip out over having to leave her home and her family, he had pissed her off to distract her.

She turned away from the mirror and picked up the small handful of things she'd taken out of the medicine chest, feeling a reluctant smile tug at one corner of her mouth.

"Bastard," she said clearly when she stepped back in her bedroom and found him sprawled over the double bed, making it look very, very small.

He blinked. "What?"

She smiled. "Thank you."

After a moment, his expression cleared to a blank slate. "I don't know what you're talking about."

She just hummed her dissent, and then set about repacking the suitcase more neatly. She did, however, drop the negligee onto the bed. He didn't need to see her in a skimpy piece of lingerie. He was tempting enough when she was fully clothed.

Too tempting.

"Have you got everything?" He propped his head on one hand, dark eyes following her around the room.

She made one last trip to the closet, removing the small metal box there. Her own 'box of important stuff'--birth certificates, family photos, passports, more than one for her. Just in case. She tucked it into the carry-on, and then stood for a moment, hands on her hips. Had she forgotten anything else? Anything desperately important? She didn't think so.

When she turned around, Ryder had sat up and zipped her bag. "I think that's it," she said.

He nodded. "Let's go, then." He got to his feet and hefted her suitcase.

"What will happen to everything?" She paused in the entry to gather her coat, purse, and laptop bag.

"Danny will have a crew come in and pack anything personal, anything with direct links to any of you. Store everything else separately. Then we'll figure out what to do with the houses and cars." He gave her a reassuring smile. "It'll be all right, Mena."

She noticed he didn't promise she could return, however.

It was best he didn't make promises he couldn't keep.

RYDER GLANCED OVER PERIODICALLY TO CHECK ON HER as he drove. They'd been on the road for three hours, and dusk had given way now to the winter's night, the dark sky dotted with stars and a sliver of moon. Mena had sat quietly, mostly staring out the side window of the truck, occasionally shifting position. By now her busy brain had probably conjured up a million ways this could go very wrong.

"We're nearly there."

She started, looking over at him. "Nearly where?"

"Where we're going." He flashed a quick grin when she rolled her eyes. "A nice little resort with honeymoon cabins."

Her eyes widened. "What?"

He couldn't help that his grin widened. "I didn't think it would be nearly as easy to secure an entire hotel without having to talk to management as it will be to secure an individual cabin."

She stared at him for a long time. He could feel it, even after he shifted his gaze back to the road ahead. He'd steered them off the interstate a while ago, and now they wound into the Pocono Mountains toward their destination. Finally, she sighed and put her head on her hand, elbow resting on the truck door.

He still grinned, though to himself now. It was true. He'd made the reservation yesterday, before he'd taken her up against the side of his truck, before he'd had to kill the Harvester. Not because the setting would be romantic, but because it would be safe. Now, though, he wasn't especially unhappy about the romantic part either.

He steered the truck off the road when he saw the sign illuminated by the headlights, then followed the winding drive to the main lodge. The structure was impressive, built of enormous logs, and standing two stories high, the front side mostly glass. A stone chimney towered along one side of the building, issuing steady puffs of smoke. He turned the truck off. "Let's get checked in, Mrs. Michaels." He pushed open his door, not waiting for her response. He met her at her door and touched her chin. "We're newlyweds, baby. You're supposed to look happy, not like this is the worst day of your life." He bent and kissed her quickly. Hard. It was enough to put a hint of color in her face and make her eyes darken.

Catching her hand, he towed her along, up the three wide steps to the lodge porch and in the double doors to the registration desk. While he took care of checking in, Mena stood quietly at his side, looking at the enormous stone fireplace on the opposite wall, her gaze sliding over the golden logs of the walls. She even summoned up a pretty good smile for the older man behind the desk when he spoke to her, but Ryder could see she'd just about reached her limit for the day.

Outside, he put her back in the truck, then drove along the lane at the side of the lodge to their cabin. It was a smaller, less-windowed version of the main building, with a stone chimney reaching past the pointed roof, though no puffs of smoke emitted from this one. Not yet, anyway. "Come on," he said. "We'll take our things in, then call Jason and get some dinner."

She nodded and pushed her door open.

He met her there, tugging their bags from behind the seat, then caught her hand to tow her along to the cabin door, lit by a small lamp overhead.

He flipped on the light switch just inside the door, illuminating a nice little room. If you could ignore the giant heart-shaped bed with a shiny red cover on it that dominated the space.

Mena's eyes widened, then she started to laugh, covering her mouth with one hand.

Ryder felt his lips curve as he kicked the door shut behind them. He continued into the room with their bags.

It got worse, he discovered, his gaze drawn to the clear, wineglass-shaped tub in the opposite corner with curved stairs leading up to it.

He dropped the bags beside a cushy-looking armchair and glanced at Mena, who gasped for breath between bursts of laughter. He set his hands on his hips, his gaze flitting over the oversized couch near the fireplace, the tiny television in the front corner, and a small table with two chairs opposite them, then the door at the back of the room. He stuck his head in, relieved to see a real bathroom with a shower.

Not that he'd mind getting Mena into the glass tub. His brain obliged him by summoning up images of her in a froth of bubbles.

His blood heated.

When he turned around, she'd sunk onto the sofa, still giggling as she wiped tears away.

"Looks like fun," he said gruffly, moving toward her.

Her laughter spiked again. "You're kidding, right?"

He stopped walking at the end of the sofa, his gaze sliding over her face. At least there was some color in her cheeks now. "No. There's quite a selection of scented bubbles on the vanity in the bathroom, too." He winked at her when she collapsed back once more, her giggles uncontrollable and probably bordering on hysterical.

He wondered if she realized how pretty she was this way, fully relaxed at last. He stuck his hands in his coat pockets to keep from touching her. He had plenty of time for touching later. "We should call Jason."

She swiped at her wet cheek with one hand, straightening and nodding, while she tried to stop laughing.

He dug his cell out of his pocket and pushed a button

on it, only half-listening as it dialed the number. "Hi, Aggie, how're you guys doing?"

Just like that, Mena's shoulders tensed again.

He stepped around the end of the couch and sat beside her, setting his free hand on her knee. "Really? I bet he loved it."

Mena frowned at him, and he gave a tiny head shake. "Well, good. Can I talk to Jason?"

Mena leaned closer, and he kissed the tip of her nose, startling her. "Hey, buddy. How are you?"

"Hi, Daddy! I helped Danny with the alarms."

"Really?" He tilted the phone so she could hear, too. "You didn't touch anything you shouldn't did you?"

"Course not. He said I was a big help."

"I bet you were." He nudged her elbow with his own, just because.

She narrowed her eyes.

"What are you doing now?" he asked his son.

"We're havin' pizza. Danny got *three* of 'em, Daddy. We couldn't decide what to put on 'em, so he said we'd just get 'em all! I didn't like the one with pineapples on, though. It tasted funny."

He listened to his son chatter on for a few minutes, then cleared his throat. "I have someone here who wants to talk to you, buddy."

"Aunt Phila!"

She heard the shout, and a little smile curved her lips.

"Yep. Hang on, bud." He held the phone out, and their fingers brushed when she took it.

"Hi, baby. How are you doing?" she asked, sitting back against the sofa.

He pushed to his feet, giving her some privacy while he checked the cabin. All three windows locked securely from inside, and the only entry was the front door. His gaze slid to the bed, and he tried to imagine sleeping on it.

It was heart-shaped, for fuck's sake.

Then again, he didn't imagine sleep would be the first thing on his mind when he got her in it later.

He turned around in time to see her lean forward, her elbow resting on her knee and her forehead on her hand. Her expression was somber now, so he guessed she was talking to her mother and not Jason.

He waited until she finished her conversation before he returned to her side. "Let's get some supper. I'm starving." He took his phone when she held it out. "We passed some restaurants on the way in. I bet we can find something good." He didn't wait for a response, just pulled her to her feet and rebuttoned her coat.

Philomena let him seat her at a corner booth in the bright, busy diner he found and didn't protest when he told the waitress they both wanted the dinner special. She just kept thinking of her mother and Jason and the danger they were in because of her. Because if she didn't think about that, she'd be thinking instead of the coming night and the monstrous bed in the tiny cabin she was about to share with Ryder. And that was unsafe territory after the past twenty-four hours, just as dangerous as the Harvesters, but in a much different manner.

"You're thinking way too hard about this, Mena," he said softly, stroking the back of her hand where it lay on the table.

She glanced up from her mound of mashed potatoes,

aware of the warmth climbing her arm from where he touched her. "How can I not?"

"Danny will make sure they're safe." His low voice was soothing, though it sent shivers up her spine for far different reasons. "They'll be getting ready to travel tomorrow, then hit the road the following day."

"Jason should be in school." She didn't let herself think of the other thing.

He smiled, setting his hand more securely over hers. "It'll be fine, baby. I promise."

She set her fork down. "You shouldn't make promises like that. You can't know for sure."

His dark eyes went serious in a flash. "I *will* keep the two of you safe, Mena."

Her stomach twisted at his words. "You should worry about keeping Jason safe first."

"And how do you think he'd feel if I let something happen to you?" His grip on her hand tightened.

She looked away, swallowing. She didn't want to think about the possibility.

"For all intents and purposes, you're his mother, Mena. You've raised him since he was born. No--" he held up his other hand when she opened her mouth to protest-- "just because she gave birth to him and sends him a birthday card if she thinks of it, that means nothing. Desi is a lousy mother, but you aren't, and Jason knows it. He'd be devastated if I let something happen to you." He shot her a hard glance. "And even if I didn't want you so bad my zipper's about to burst, I'd need to keep you safe just because you're family."

His argument didn't make her feel better. "So you have control issues and a knight in shining armor complex," she said, lifting one shoulder.

He tugged on her hand, regaining her attention. "I may work well in protector mode, Mena, but I'm no knight in shining armor." He held her gaze this time, his own heated. "And having a sheet of solid metal between us is my idea of torture."

"Ryder, it's sex," she said, keeping her voice low, pleased when it didn't shake. "Good chemistry doesn't mean you should put your life in danger. Not when you have a child to think about." Still, the warmth from his fingers around hers had spread, all the way up her arm, to her face, her breasts, into her belly, lower.

His jaw hardened. "I don't think there's another woman I've ever made love to before you, or a woman I've slept with that I'd ever risk my life for. Just you," he whispered.

His words made her breath catch. *Too scary.* Too soon. *Too impossible.* And, in her experience, a big fat lie. She tugged at her hand, but he refused to let go, his dark gaze searching her face. Her heart pounded crazily, and she wanted to go. *Needed* to go. Somewhere. *Anywhere,* as long it wasn't this close to a man who'd just made such a claim. Her pulse tripped over itself.

"You should eat a little more of your supper," he said at last, his tone gruff. "I plan to exhaust you into oblivion on our heart-shaped bed when we get back to the cabin."

Just like that, heat exploded in her core to obliterate the fear. For years, she'd managed not to let any man too close. They couldn't be trusted to keep their word. She'd learned it when her father abandoned them when Desi was two. She'd relearned it in high school when her true love decided he'd rather sleep with her wild younger sister than date Philomena, who wouldn't put out.

And now Ryder had bulldozed his way into her life and

her bed. At least now she knew better than to believe pretty words.

But her mouth went dry with the images her brain summoned up at his words, and she lifted her water glass with her free hand, ignoring the slight tremor of her fingers to take a quick drink.

"I realized earlier you've seen all of me, but I haven't seen you yet," he continued, his eyes growing darker as he spoke. "So we need a big fire in the fireplace, and all the lights on."

Philomena shut her eyes against those images, but it didn't work. She remembered all too well the ways he'd touched her last night, first outside and then later, in her bed.

She thanked all the Gods she wasn't getting ready to PMS, or her wild hormones would have her leaping over the table to get at him now.

"Then I can spread you out on the bed and take my time with you. The way I should have last night. Taste every inch of that pretty body, tease you to the brink and back again."

Her breathing hitched, and she realized she was shaking. With desire. Lust. Need. For Ryder. Apparently men weren't the only ones with big brain-little brain issues.

"I could almost lay you on this table now and take you," he rasped, "I'm so hard. But I'm going to take very, very good care of you tonight." His thumb slid along the outside of hers, slowly. "It's going to be so good, Mena."

She swallowed back a tiny moan when he nudged her knee under the table with his, and she forced her eyes to open. She tried to focus her gaze on the plate of half-eaten food in front of her, but he kept stroking her hand, and her imagination kept supplying her with other places and ways he could touch her.

"Are you wet for me, Mena?" he whispered, leaning nearer.

She couldn't stop herself from meeting his gaze this time, and she swallowed hard at the dangerous expression on his face. Predatory. Hungry. She wouldn't admit it, not here, but her panties were drenched.

"Wet enough for me to slide deep?"

Her breath rushed past her lips. How did he know? Or did he know his words would have just that effect on her?

"Let's go." He freed her hand and took out his wallet, tossing some money on the table, then pushed to his feet and grabbed their coats.

She got to her feet, willing her wobbly knees to hold her up. He helped her into her coat and then guided her out into the cold night, one big hand low on her back to steer her to the truck.

She wasn't going to stop him, she realized.

Or herself.

Dangerous or not, while she had the chance, she was going to indulge just a little.

CHAPTER FOUR

Ryder steered the truck back to the little cabin in five minutes flat, going too fast for the winding, snowy roads.

When they'd left the restaurant and he'd kissed her, she lifted into his arms with no hesitation, and his body hardened even more at the soft feel of her. During the short drive, her fingers warmed his on the seat between them.

He parked just outside their front door, shutting the truck off, and he heard her swallow in the sudden silence. He shoved his door open and went around to hers.

Her green eyes were enormous in the soft light from over the door, and he wished for more illumination to see the emotion in them. He lifted her out of the truck, sliding her down along his body, torturing himself. And her, judging by the strangled sound she made when her belly rubbed over his erection. He wanted to hear that sound again. He didn't kiss her, though, much as he wanted to. No, he wanted her inside and naked.

Now.

He pulled her along, up the two steps to the door, and

shoved the key into the lock. He'd left the light on when they went to get supper, and the room looked exactly as it had an hour ago. Not that he expected trouble here. No one knew where they were, not even Danny. He shut and locked the door behind them, releasing her hand as he dropped his coat onto the armchair on his way to the fireplace.

There were logs, kindling, and matches all within easy reach of the big fireplace, and in just a few minutes, he had a fire crackling in the hearth. He sat back on his heels, feeling the warmth as the flames licked into the bigger pieces of wood. Now, to Mena...

She still stood inside the door where he'd left her, though she'd removed her coat and had her arms folded over her middle, protectively. Cheeks pink, she'd fixed her gaze on the fireplace, avoiding him.

He wasn't allowing it. He pushed to his feet and strode to her, tugging on her sleeve until she let her arm fall away from her belly. He caught her hand and drew her along to the sofa. "Sit with me, Mena." He'd told her over dinner exactly what he intended, but he didn't have to rush right to the main course.

He sank onto the couch and patted the cushion beside him. She sat, stiffly. He rubbed his hand over the back of her sweater, felt her tense even more. He ignored that and kept stroking, massaging lightly.

"You smell good." He gave one of her curls a light tug. "Is it shampoo or something else?"

He studied her sober profile until she turned her head a little toward him. "Probably a combination," she said at last.

"Come kiss me, Mena." He slid his hand up her spine, then down again. "Please."

Her head turned further, her green eyes considering.

After several long heartbeats, she shifted on the sofa, drawing one knee up, then the other, so she knelt beside him. The tight peaks of her nipples showed against the soft wool of her sweater. His mouth watered in anticipation. *Patience.*

She touched his lower lip with her forefinger, lightly. Skimmed from one side to the other.

His breath came faster.

Her lashes lowered when her gaze dropped to his open mouth, shielding her eyes.

When she set her hand on his chest to brace herself and leaned nearer, his heart bounced off his ribs. The enticing scent of her surrounded him, something sweet and spicy, the musk of her desire. His dick ached.

A little closer. A breath between them.

Finally!

When her mouth settled over his, his inner caveman rose up, demanding he take charge. He reined in the urge, letting her tease him with brief, soft kisses from one corner of his mouth to the other, her warm tongue sliding out to taste him several times. His fingers flexed on her back.

The heat from her mouth spread all through him, making his heart pound harder, tightening his groin even more.

Then she deepened the kiss, slanting her mouth over his.

He slid his fingers into her hair--soft curls like silky ribbons against his palm.

Her nails pressed harder into his chest as she moaned into the kiss.

He lifted his other hand to her waist, slid higher to cup her breast.

When she arched into the gentle caress, he stifled a

shout of triumph. He had plenty of time to get her to the bed.

Ryder's breath caught when she shifted over him, straddling his thighs, and his fingers tightened on her breast, tugging at the tight tip. Her hips rocked down then, right along his aching cock.

"Yes, just like that, baby," he breathed roughly against her lips.

Her fingers slipped into his hair, and her mouth slid over his, cutting off further words.

He felt her heat through the light wool of her skirt, the heavy denim of his jeans. And he wanted to sink into it. Over and over again. Forever.

He forced his concentration back to her mouth. Sweet and warm, she explored his lips, his mouth with her tongue. He pinched her nipple, gently, and swallowed her moan. The sound tasted delicious.

Her hips shifted over his, in a small, circular motion this time, and he slid his other hand from her nape to her hip, pressing her closer.

Mena lifted her head, her breaths coming roughly, her green eyes unfocused.

"Do it again," he whispered.

She rocked her hips, harder this time, and he heard the gasp that escaped her.

"How wet are you, baby?" He rolled her nipple between his thumb and forefinger.

She tried to focus her gaze on his face, but he lifted his hips, wedging his cock hard against her. Her head dropped back, eyes sliding shut as her mouth opened on a soundless cry.

He wrestled several yards of wool out of his way to find one of her bare thighs, sliding his fingers higher until he reached the lace of her panties. Another couple inches to the heat between her thighs, and he found his answer. The fabric was drenched. Sweat beaded on his forehead. "Jesus," he ground out, rubbing his fingers over the wet crotch of her panties so her hips moved toward him.

He'd promised her slow. Somehow, he had to deliver on that, no matter what his dick thought.

Moving carefully, he eased his fingers under the elastic at her leg, then down into the scalding wetness. "So nice." He slid his fingers over her clit, and she jerked in his arms. "Easy." He kept going until he could ease one finger into her slippery folds, deeper, into her sheath.

"Oh, Gods," she moaned, her chest rising and falling quickly with her breathing.

"You like?" He stroked deep, then withdrew to repeat the caress, over and over, gritting his teeth when she met his strokes eagerly. He slid a second finger inside her, rewarded when her body convulsed on his digits. His brain obliged him by bringing up the memory of how she'd felt around his cock last night.

He pushed that away and tried to concentrate on making this about her. Teasing her with shallower strokes, occasionally rasping his thumb over her clit and making her gasp.

Mena shifted nearer, her tight nipples rubbing his chest as she wrapped her arms around his neck. "Ryder."

He smiled and nipped at her lower lip. "Right here, Mena." He cupped her jaw with his free hand and kissed her once more, slowly. Deeply, mimicking the strokes of his fingers inside her with his tongue in her mouth.

When they parted this time, both breathless, he slid his hands under her and pushed to his feet. If he didn't get her onto the bed now, his legs would never get them there later.

She tightened her grip on him.

"It's okay. Just need to get you naked." He smiled. "Wrap your legs around me."

She did, her lower lip caught in her teeth.

"Ah, Gods." He ground his teeth together for a second, steeling himself against the heat pressed to his belly. "You feel incredible, Mena." He inhaled deeply, then moved around the sofa toward the bed.

When he set one knee on it, the bed shifted, rolling, startling him. A waterbed. He grinned, easing her onto her back.

Her eyes widened when she realized the bed was moving.

"Just imagine," he rasped out, settling over her and shutting his eyes for a second. "The waves in the bed will make it go on forever." He rocked his hips into hers just once to set the bed in motion.

Her breathing hitched, drawing his attention again to the taut nipples pressing into his chest.

"You really have on too much clothing," he muttered, easing to his knees between hers. He stepped off the bed and tugged her boots and socks from her feet, sliding his hands up her pale legs to where her skirt was still bunched above her knees. He pushed it higher, higher, his heart pounding harder in anticipation. He paused, catching her gaze for a long moment, then slid it far enough to reveal ivory panties, wet at the core of her.

His mouth watered, and he bent nearer. "Smell good," he managed. "Bet you taste even better." He inhaled deeply of the musky sweetness, then licked over the wet lace.

Her hips jerked toward him as a startled sound escaped her.

"Delicious." He caught the sides of her panties and

tugged them down, down, revealing swollen pink folds glistening in the firelight. "So pretty."

He got her underwear off, tossing them somewhere behind him as he bent back to her. Parting her outer lips with his thumbs, he exposed the deeper pink inner lips, slick with wetness. "Gods, I have to taste," he said, hearing his own guttural tone. The first lick made her cry out, made his eyes close with the pleasure of her taste. The second had her shivering under his mouth. And then he lost count. He speared her with his tongue, teased her clit with his lips and teeth, slipped his fingers deep inside her to stroke over a sensitive spot that made her sheath contract on him.

"Come for me," he whispered, his teeth gently scraping over her clit as he pressed his fingers deep again. "Now, Mena."

She came apart, her cry echoing in the room, her hips arching into his strokes. When she finally relaxed back onto the bed, he was dying.

Instead of focusing on the throbbing of his groin, however, he eased to his feet, helping her to a sitting position so he could tug her sweater up and off at last, revealing a bra that matched the discarded panties, ivory lace barely veiling the dark rose nipples he very desperately wanted to taste. He paused long enough to kiss her, loving the bite of her nails at his nape when he staked his claim. While he withdrew from the warm depths of her mouth, he unhooked the bra and peeled it away from her swollen breasts.

"Look at you," he breathed, one forefinger lightly skimming over the creamy upper slope, lower, to the tight peak. "Beautiful." He bent and sucked the tip into his mouth, lightly at first, teasing her with his tongue until she arched toward him, a soft moan reaching his ears.

He eased her backward, his mouth busy at her breast

while he fumbled with the button and zipper at her hip so he could remove her skirt, too.

Finally, *finally*, he had her naked.

When he released her nipple a long time later, she shifted restlessly on the blanket, her hips rocking, begging silently. He propped himself up on one elbow to look at her. All creamy curves, tinted now with a rosy glow from her rising desire and the flickering firelight. His gaze skimmed over the tattoo low on her hip, intent on more intimate places now.

He slid one hand down over her belly to the nest of crisp curls between her thighs and dipped his fingers easily into her slippery folds. "I love that I can do this to you, Mena," he whispered, catching her gaze when her lashes fluttered up. "And I'm dying to be inside you."

"Has anyone ever told you you're too slow?" she whispered, her eyes shutting again for a second when he thrust three fingers inside her.

He chuckled. "No, I don't think so. I don't think you would have said that last night, either." He twisted his fingers on the next stroke, so his thumb rasped over her clit, and a keening sound escaped her. "You're so close."

"Please, Ryder." She forced her eyes open, the green irises only a thin circle around pupils dilated with need.

"I can't resist such a lovely plea." Reluctantly, he withdrew his fingers from her sheath and sat up. He swiftly stripped off his shirt, then pushed to his feet and unbuttoned, unzipped his jeans. He had to pause to kick off his boots before he could free himself of the jeans, and then he stopped, standing beside the bed to look over her again.

She was incredible. And he was incredibly lucky. He knew it.

He also knew she was nowhere near ready for him to be

talking forever as he had that morning. Or for their dinner conversation.

But he needed her to know he meant it.

He climbed onto the bed, his knees parting her thighs even more, and planted his hands on either side of her shoulders. "Take me in, Mena." He kissed her lightly.

Her warm fingers found him, paused to stroke, to squeeze.

"Mena." He heard the warning in his tone, and knew she had, too, because her fingers stilled for a moment on his shaft, before continuing their slide up to the sensitive head of him.

He clenched his jaw against the pleasure of her fingers there. Hell, anywhere on him.

He bent and nipped at her shoulder, making her fingers tighten on him just a little. "You're playing with fire."

She shifted, one knee bending at his side, and she finally obeyed, guiding his erection, so the tip glided into slick folds.

His breath hissed out against her skin, and he heard hers catch in her throat. "In, Mena," he ordered.

Her fingers eased him to her pussy, and he jerked his hips toward her, dislodging her fingers as he wedged himself halfway inside her before stopping.

"Oh Gods, don't stop," she whispered, her fingers sliding around to grip his ass.

He dropped to his elbows, pressing closer so her tight nipples burned his skin. "I'm not going to stop, baby." He stroked her damp hair back from her flushed face with one hand. "I promise." He slipped forward another inch, feeling her flesh tighten, then relax around his cock. "You feel so good, Mena." He nudged her nose with his. "Are you okay?"

"I will be," she teased, a hint of a smile touching her lips.

Ryder groaned, then jerked his hips, hard, so he seated himself fully inside her.

Her gasp made his pulse quicken.

"Like that?" He shifted his hips from side to side, rubbing her clit with the motion.

"Gods, yes." Her fingers dug into him.

"Good." He caught her mouth with his, demanding everything she had to give.

And she gave.

When he grew conscious again of what they were doing, his thrusts were quick and hard, harder. Her body shook around him, skin slick with sweat. *Mine,* he thought, *she's mine.* It became a silent chant in his head with each thrust into her wet, clutching sheath.

When the climax broke over her, he caught her scream in his kiss, his own body demanding its release as well. He tried to resist, to draw out the pleasure a little longer, but with her trembling beneath him, her inner muscles milking and clutching at him, he failed, groaning as his orgasm exploded.

Philomena didn't want to move. She thought she might have been lying beneath Ryder for hours, and she didn't care. Her breathing moved at a normal rhythm at last, and her heart nearly so.

Ryder's long fingers slid through her hair, slowly, his body still inside her and stirring with interest once more.

Heat touched her cheeks. She didn't think she could do that again. It had been *intense.* More intense than anything she could recall. Far more intense than an indulgence or distraction should be.

He rolled to his back, keeping her tucked tightly against him, and the move wedged him deeper inside her.

"Oh." She blushed, putting her face against his damp throat.

His low chuckle warmed the top of her head. "Are you all right?"

"Fine." She shut her eyes. Better than fine, judging by the way her body felt suddenly slick and hot around him again.

One of his big hands slid down her back, then up, all the way to her nape. "That was amazing." He kissed her hair. "I think you killed me."

"Apparently not," she said before she could stop herself.

His laughter shifted his chest beneath hers.

She blushed hotter, and when he cupped her chin in one hand, she resisted for a moment, then let him raise her face.

The wretched grin curved his lips, but his expression softened as his dark gaze met hers. "Come kiss me, Mena."

Her gaze dropped to his lips, and her mouth watered. her nipples tightened once more against his chest. It was a really good thing the Medusa couldn't get pregnant, she thought absently as she stretched to drop a soft kiss on his mouth. With chemistry like this, any normal couple without birth control would have a brood in no time.

When she would have lifted her head, he caught her nape and drew her down, his tongue sliding along her lower lip.

His other hand wedged between their bellies, his fingers sliding low enough to rub over her suddenly aching clit, making fresh heat burst in her middle.

When he released her mouth long moments later and her breath came raggedly again, he met her gaze. "That's better," he rasped. "I still haven't managed to touch and taste every inch of you yet."

Philomena blinked. "I don't think I mind," she admitted.

The cocky grin tugged at one corner of his mouth, and the finger stroking her clit paused. "I hate to break a promise." With that he lifted her off of himself, and she stifled a moan of protest.

When she glanced down, she found him fully erect, glistening with the evidence of her own desire, and she swallowed. Hard.

Her attention was so distracted by the tempting sight of his erection that when he flipped her onto her belly and straddled her legs, she let out a yelp of surprise. His knees pinned her thighs together. "Ryder?"

"Shh." His warm breath teased through her curls before he swept them away from her nape. He kissed her there, gently, his tongue flicking out over the same spot, and goosebumps lifted on her skin.

He teased her forever, his wet, open mouth sliding all over her back, her shoulders, even her butt. When he closed his teeth on her ass, she jerked beneath him. He laughed softly, then licked the spot to soothe her.

It had the opposite effect.

Her inner thighs were slick with wetness, and when she tried to lift against him, he simply held her still with his strong hands at her hips.

"Not done," he hummed along her skin.

"Please."

He kept kissing his way down the back of her leg, all the way to her heel. When he breathed over the sole of her foot, she jerked reflexively. He laughed, shifting to her other leg. He worked his way slowly up, nipping at her calf, licking the back of her knee, scraping his teeth along her thigh as he neared the spot where leg joined ass.

She tensed beneath his mouth.

"Are you nervous or impatient?" he asked, licking that spot.

Shocking heat jolted into her core, and she shut her eyes. "Both."

He hummed a reply, then nipped the curve of her ass again.

Right before he wedged his hand between her thighs and into the wet folds there. "Ah, Gods," he breathed against her skin. "How can I resist?" His fingers slipped inside her, three of them, stretching her as he pushed deep.

She whimpered. She didn't want him to resist. She needed him to *not* resist. Her body lifted into his strokes without any effort on her part.

When the first wave broke, she lay panting and sheened in perspiration atop the blankets. When he pushed her thighs wider and lifted her hips to push into her from behind, she rocked back to meet each hard, desperate thrust, silently begging for the next release.

Ryder withdrew when she was on the very edge, her entire body shaking with the need, and she sobbed a protest.

He flipped her over, then pulled her astride him, jerking her hips down to sheath himself inside her aching body.

Philomena cried out at the deep thrust, bracing herself with her hands on his strong shoulders.

His jaw was set, his skin gleamed with sweat, his hands hard on her hips. "Come again, Mena. For me."

She couldn't resist him, or her own wild need, rocking

her hips to meet his each time he jerked his up, seating his cock higher, harder inside her.

Gods, she was *so* close.

Ryder's hard finger on her clit pushed her over the edge, and a ragged cry escaped her. Her entire body tightened, clutching at his, intensifying the scalding wash of his orgasm inside her.

She collapsed on his chest, dimly aware of the sobbing breaths rushing past her lips, of the way her body shuddered in the aftermath.

Ryder kept her secure in his arms, murmuring to her, one big hand brushing her wet hair away from her face.

Philomena nuzzled his chest, feeling the slickness beneath her cheek, and smiled a little. His heart still pounded too quickly under her ear, and she inhaled unsteadily.

If he kept this up, she'd never survive.

Her smile spread. He was definitely attentive to her needs, that was for sure.

His mouth slid over the top of her forehead, just at her hair, warming her.

The bed had finally stopped rocking, too, she realized. Who knew waterbeds were so much fun?

Ryder kissed her. "Sleep, baby."

She considered that. She was tired, but not sleepy. Too much arousal still buzzed in her veins. She shook her head.

"Not ready to sleep yet?" He tipped her chin up.

She swallowed at the look in his eyes. And at the feel of his cock thickening inside her. Shook her head once more.

"What a shame." He bent to kiss her, lazily.

The kiss warmed her all over again. A slow heat inched along her skin, thickened the blood in her veins, dampened her inner thighs.

It occurred to her much, much later, when her brain had finally shut down after two more spectacular orgasms that left her wrecked, the Harvesters wouldn't have a chance to kill her: she would die of pleasure in Ryder's bed.

It didn't seem a bad alternative at the moment.

IN THE LOW LIGHT FROM THE FIRE, RYDER WATCHED her sleep. He'd gotten out of bed earlier to shut off the overhead lights and the lamps. Now, he lay awake, exhausted, but not ready to sleep.

He'd worn her out at last. For the moment.

Getting past her emotional barriers was going to be a whole lot harder than getting her into bed had been.

He glanced around the room, a smile tugging at his lips. The heart-shaped bed wasn't so bad. Somehow, he'd missed the waterbed mention on the website when he'd made the reservation. Probably because he hadn't anticipated sharing a bed with her quite so soon. He'd also missed the mention of the wineglass tub, but that didn't mean he wouldn't enjoy it with her, too.

He had not yet, however, studied the tattoo on her hip. He knew it had started as a snake-shaped birthmark. Aggie had told him all of the Medusa's descendants had one somewhere on their bodies. But only the woman who became the Medusa would gain the tattoo when the curse fell on her.

He didn't want to disturb her to pull back the blankets and look now that she finally slept, though. It could wait till morning for closer inspection.

Still, it took him a long time to relax. He may have gotten her safely away, but he knew the Harvesters didn't give up, and now they knew who she was, there was no safe place for her.

Not as long as she was the Medusa.

And eventually, she would refuse to keep running, demand to make a stand.

The thought taunted him, even in his dreams. When he woke, he was alert but didn't feel rested. Good thing he could fall back on his years of military training, nights with next to no sleep while on a mission. He inhaled slowly, exhaled even more slowly.

Mena slept beside him, her breath warming his chest.

He slid his hand down her spine, curving around her ass, and pulled her nearer. His body was already on alert, and when her belly brushed it, his cock went fully erect.

He grinned in the dim light of early morning. Maybe he could wear her down simply by keeping her brain too wrecked to continue protesting his protection.

His smile faded.

Mena was way too smart for him to get away with such a ploy.

And he knew the barriers she kept around her emotions would take a long time and a lot of effort to breach. They had taken years to build up. He couldn't expect to demolish them in a matter of hours.

But he was persistent. And patient. He'd learned the skills as a child. Honed them as an adult.

He brushed a kiss on her forehead.

Determined.

She stirred, shifting closer to him in her sleep.

And he'd waited long enough for his Medusa.

Philomena Gregory was his, one way or another.

CHAPTER FIVE

Aristotle Tassos dropped to his knees beside his desk and bowed his head, heart racing. "My Lady," he murmured.

"Your nephew is dead, Aristotle."

His head jerked up, and he stifled the urge to blanch under the steely grey gaze of Athena. "My nephew?" He had a terrible feeling he knew to which nephew She referred.

"Yes. That fool Nestor. He was killed at the Medusa's home." She glared down at him. "Why did he not kill her?"

Another dead nephew. Ari swallowed, his mouth dry. Beneath his seventy-eight-year-old knees, the plush carpet was not plush enough. "I'm sorry, My Lady. I know he intended to--"

"Intended to." Her lip curled with distaste. "It seems to me the Tassos family is only able to intend to do their job these days." The tall woman in the flowing white gown folded Her arms over Her chest. "I grow weary of the lack of results."

He bowed his head under Her furious gaze. "I am so

sorry, My Lady. I vow to You, we *will* kill the monster." He shut his eyes.

"Perhaps I should remind you," She said after a moment, "there will be repercussions if this task is not carried out, Aristotle. I will vent my frustration with your family on you if this monster is not killed."

He bowed lower. "I promise, it will be done." He tried to slow his too-quick breathing.

When there was only silence in response to his words, he dared to lift his head a few inches.

The Goddess was gone.

He struggled to his feet and braced himself on the edge of his desk, his heart pounding too quickly. He concentrated on breathing evenly, trying to make his pulse slow. Perspiration dripped into his right eye, and he brushed it away, noting the shake of his fingers.

He moved carefully around the desk and dropped into his chair. He fumbled in the top right drawer until he found a pill box, popping a small white tablet into his mouth and swallowing it. After a moment, his heartbeat began to ease back into a more regular rhythm.

In a few more minutes, he felt better, though worry still pulsed along his veins. He'd done all he could over the years to teach his nephews the importance of fulfilling this task for the Goddess. Surely it couldn't be so difficult now there were so many modern technologies at their fingertips. Not to mention the special abilities the Goddess had gifted them with.

He straightened in his chair, setting his jaw. They would do this job, by the Goddess. He would make certain of it.

He glared at the photo on the front of his desk, an old black and white picture of a young man. "You fool, Iphis.

Look what you have brought us to. The Goddess would kill you all over if She knew what you'd done. All these years later, and I am still cleaning up your mess."

He reached for the phone on the corner of his desk.

These boys would come to heel, and they would do it now.

Several hours later, Aristotle glared down his nose at the younger Tassos men seated in front of him. "I'm depending on you two to do this job properly."

"Of course, Uncle Ari."

He studied Baltasar for a long moment. His nephew sat erect in the chair, fully at attention, his dark gaze focused on Aristotle's face. Unlike his older cousin, Georgios, who lounged in the next chair, looked far more relaxed. However, his gaze was also focused on his great-uncle Ari. His talents were far different from Baltasar's--he was currently the best tracker in the entire Tassos family. Georgios had more technological abilities, as well as a very handy talent with locks, even better than his late cousin Nestor.

"I know your cousins understand the importance of finding and eliminating this Medusa," he said after a minute. "But I am going to trust you two to lead the hunting party into Pennsylvania. While the rest scour the houses, I expect you will find leads to her present location. If you can find her nephew, use him. Or her mother. I don't care how, but we must kill her. And we need that amulet." His mouth pinched. "Do not disappoint me." He did not add, "as your cousin Kallan did." Everyone in the family knew of his treachery, and he was now as hated as the vile monster Medusa.

He waited while they made all the appropriate noises of agreement, then dismissed them. After they'd left the room, he sank into his chair and reached for the pill bottle again. His heart raced too fast.

His nephews had to find her this time and kill her. The longer the Medusa lived, the more likely it was someone in her family would discover the secret he kept about his own family, a secret that would cause the Goddess to sever all ties to them, perhaps even wipe them out. He couldn't allow such a thing.

He reached for the phone. "I am ready for him." He glanced at a sheet of paper on his desk, then looked up when he heard footsteps. "Ah, Elek, come in. Have a seat."

The younger man who entered moved purposefully across the room, easing onto the chair Aristotle had indicated. "I came as quickly as I could, Great-uncle."

Aristotle smiled a little and sat back in his own seat. "Thank you." He studied the other man for a few moments. "I don't believe I can stress enough how vitally necessary it is for us to eliminate this monster," he said finally. "The Goddess is still very angry about your cousin's betrayal with the last Medusa. Our failure thus far to kill this monster does not help our cause."

The younger man's somber expression didn't alter. "I understand, Great-uncle Ari."

Aristotle shook his head. "I'm not certain you do, but I believe you grasp the urgency better than your cousins, which is why I have chosen you for further training and to more closely assist me."

Elek lifted one eyebrow. "Assist you with what, if I may ask? I thought you wanted me involved in the hunt."

"I am thinking more of you coordinating the search. Your skills will be useful to that end."

A hint of disappointment flashed over the younger man's face, but then he nodded once. "As you wish."

Just as he'd thought--moldable.

"I want you to collect as much information about this monster as you can, including her extended family. Also, this man who killed your cousin. He clearly knows about us, and I want to know about him, too. Everything." Aristotle clenched his fingers tight, tighter. "If he is so willing to kill one of ours, we must be willing to kill him to get to the Medusa."

Aristotle intended to make sure they got this Medusa, one way or another. One man would not stand in their way.

PHILOMENA SAT ON THE SOFA IN FRONT OF THE fireplace, staring blindly into the low flames.

She'd been cooped up here for four days already, and it was driving her crazy. She wondered how her cousin Andi had managed weeks in hiding from the Harvesters after they'd found her eight years ago. While she wondered it, she sent off a quick email to Andi to ask. Just for a distraction.

Not that Ryder had failed to distract her. He had kept her much too distracted to think of the trouble they'd left behind, and she'd let him. She ached in places she'd never imagined aching. Still, there were moments when her head wasn't clouded with desire and the danger to her family returned the forefront of her thoughts.

Behind her, his heavy footsteps sounded on the wood floor as he paced. She resisted the need to turn around to look. He was on the phone again, speaking too low for her to hear.

He'd had several of those calls the past few days, and she suspected they had to do with her.

She scowled into the fire. Of course they did. What else could it be?

His footsteps drew nearer, and she forced herself to clear her expression. "How would you like a day trip tomorrow?" The cushion beside her sank under his weight.

She shot him a wary glance. "A day trip? Like getting out on work release for good behavior?"

One corner of his mouth turned up. "It's not your bad behavior keeping us here, Mena." He touched her knee, lightly. "I was thinking you've got to be stir crazy by now, so we should get out for a while."

She narrowed her eyes to study him, trying to figure out if this was a trap of some sort.

His smile widened. "No strings, I promise."

"Where?"

"Philly."

She shifted her gaze back to the fire, trying to keep her excitement from showing. Out of the cabin. Somewhere away from a bed and too-close proximity to Ryder for a while so she could think. "What's in Philly?"

"Lots of historic sites, shopping, food, my new office."

She slanted another glance at him, resigned. She *knew* there was a catch. "You need to go to work."

He shook his head. "No. The office is fine. But I was thinking maybe you'd create our website for us, and you might like to see the office."

Intrigued, Philomena leaned forward to prop her elbows on her knees, displacing his warm fingers. "You want me to do your website?"

"Mm-hm. I've seen your work. I like it. I'm sure you'd come up with something just right for us." He mimicked her pose, elbows on his own knees, shifting close enough so their shoulders brushed. "Right now, we're mostly getting new clients from work of mouth, but we'd like to increase our visibility. What do you think?"

Her pulse quickened. She wanted to do it. She needed something to do. She'd managed to finish off two smaller websites for other clients already in the last few days, and now she didn't have another job due for over a week. And if she wasn't working, her busy mind circled around two subjects: the Harvesters who were hunting her and her very sexy relationship with Ryder.

She caught her lower lip in her teeth, her gaze following the flickering flames behind the screen. "I'd need to know exactly what you're looking for. What kind of info you want out there. What style."

He nudged her shoulder with his. "I'll take you to the office tomorrow, and you can see for yourself. Then we can sightsee if you want."

She couldn't resist any longer, turning to look more fully at him. "Really?"

He smiled, the slow, sexy grin that made her blood heat in her veins. "Really."

"Okay. But I make no promises on the website." He didn't need to know she already wanted to do it.

He swooped in and kissed her, hard. "Deal." He pushed to his feet. "What do you feel like for supper?"

She didn't care, really. Already, her brain had shifted to work mode and was considering possibilities for his security firm's website. "Do any pizza places deliver out here?" she asked after a moment.

"I don't think there's a pizza menu in the stack." He moved to the table in the opposite corner, flipping through the small pile of restaurant menus. "Nope."

She realized she was staring at him and shifted her gaze away, heat that had nothing to do with the fireplace warming her cheeks. "It doesn't matter." *Work.* She'd been thinking about work. Needed to be thinking about work. Not Ryder.

His booted footsteps crossed the floor to her side, and she tried to concentrate. Coding. He blocked her view of the flames, and she lifted her gaze from his groin at her eye level to his face, forced to tip her head back.

A wicked grin curved his lips, making her want to shift her focus to eye level once more. "How about we get room service, and eat in bed?"

"Will you tell me what the phone calls have been about?"

His smile vanished. "Work."

She sighed and sat back, away from him. "Paying work, or me?"

He squatted in front of her, his expression sober. "Both." He touched her knee, and she ignored the heat of his fingers seeping through the heavy denim of her jeans. "Mena, there's no news. The Harvesters don't know where you are, they don't know where Jason and Aggie are." His dark gaze held hers.

"And have they come looking for the first guy yet?" She watched him carefully.

Something flickered in his eyes, and he hesitated.

"Yes." Her heart beat a little faster, this time in fear. "How many of them?"

His mouth tightened. "Two."

She considered that. Two more men on the hunt for her now. Two more men in her mother's house. Probably in her house, as well. Her stomach wrenched.

"The crews already cleared the houses of anything related to your family, Mena. They have no clues to where you are."

But they'd already found her once. And now they'd been in her home. She shut her eyes, nauseous.

One of Ryder's hands stroked over her head. "I'm sorry."

Even if somehow she wasn't the Medusa someday, she'd never feel safe there again. It would remain tainted, since she knew would-be murderers had been there. She bowed her head, but his hand stayed there, warm and comforting. It annoyed her that he could distract her even when she felt so lousy.

Still, she didn't move, letting him stroke her hair, while she tried not to think about the loss of her safe haven.

"Come on," he said after a few minutes, catching her shoulders and drawing her to her feet.

She opened her eyes, and he steered her away from the fire. "What--"

He snagged a bottle of bubble bath from the vanity and then guided her to the stairs leading to the glass bathtub.

She laughed. "You're kidding, right?"

"Am I laughing?" As they climbed the steps, his expression remained serious, though his brown eyes gleamed.

"I...you're crazy." She shook her head.

He smiled at last, releasing her arm to turn on the water and dump in some of the liquid from the bottle he carried. "Maybe. But I am also willing to try new things, and I'm willing to get in this tub with you and give you a back rub." He set the bottle on the ledge and yanked at the hem of her sweater.

"A back rub, huh?" She lifted her arms when he pulled her sweater up, up, feeling more excited about this than she should.

"Yes, and I am very good at them." He dropped her sweater behind her, catching her gaze. "So pretty," he murmured, sliding one finger over the blush-colored bra she wore. Her nipples tightened, both because of the cooler air washing across her skin and because of his warm finger teasing her.

She tried to concentrate on his words. "How do you know?" She swallowed a moan when he tugged at her nipple, sending a bolt of heat rushing into her middle, leaving her panties damp.

He bent and dropped a quick kiss on her open lips. "Jason told me."

She laughed, then sucked in a quick breath when his other hand eased to her waistband, fingers slipping between denim and her skin as he undid the button, then slid the zipper down.

"If that's not a testimonial, I don't know what is." He flicked the front clasp of her bra open and peeled the sheer garment away from her flesh, making her shiver. "Nice." He cupped her breast against his hard palm. "Soft."

Philomena tried to concentrate, but her mind had given up and let sensation take over. Her knees turned to water when he gave her jeans a shove, sending them down around her ankles. Then he slipped his other hand inside her panties, squeezing the handful of her bottom that he got, before gliding his fingers lower, lower until he found slick, hot flesh.

She heard a high, soft sound coming from her throat, and she didn't care. Ryder knew just how to distract her from her worries.

~

RYDER KNEW THEY NEEDED TO GET OUT OF THE TUB before the warm water went cold. But with Mena resting against him, relaxed finally, dozing, he didn't want to disturb her.

Yeah, he could stay here a while.

But that wasn't what she needed.

He got them out of the tub and dried off, then carried her down the steps to bed. He climbed in behind her. "We didn't get supper yet," he murmured, settling one hand on her belly to hold her close.

She rolled her head to look at him when she opened her eyes. "I'm not hungry."

He smiled. She was clearly exhausted. He touched her lower lip. "Go to sleep, baby. I'll wake you when it's time to call Jason."

Her eyes closed, and she snuggled nearer, one hand over his on her abdomen.

Ryder's smile faded as he listened to her breathing even out as she drifted off to sleep. He'd successfully distracted her for now, but he knew she'd think about it again, and eventually he'd have to let her deal with the fear.

When he was certain she was sleeping, he eased out of the warmth of the bed and pulled on a pair of clean jeans. He added some wood to the fire, then called the lodge to order dinner for them. Mena might not be hungry yet, but when she woke later, she may feel differently.

While he waited for their meal, he sat on the over-stuffed armchair and watched her sleep.

Whether she liked it or not, whether she fell in love with him or not, Philomena Gregory was a part of his family, and he intended to keep her safe.

She'd asked him who'd keep her safe from him. He should have countered with who would keep him safe from her?

Absently, he rubbed the heel of his hand over the scar

on his ribs. She had touched it earlier, her warmth seeping into his chest as her fingers glided over the old knife wound, but now his heart hurt.

Yes, indeed, who would keep his heart safe if she didn't fall in love with him?

~

Elek ignored the curious, disgruntled and outright hostile gazes of his cousins and uncles and studied the pages in front of him for several more minutes. While he finished collecting himself to speak, he listened to the hushed sounds of movement. Finally, he took a measured breath and exhaled slowly, raising his gaze to the men in the room.

"This man with the Medusa is well-trained, but his military background, his training will be fairly standard. Nothing we don't also know how to do." He focused on Petr, slouched in a chair in the far corner. "And we outnumber him tremendously, so our chances of locating him are much better than Odysseus's chances for a quick trip home from Troy."

Petr flushed and looked away, probably embarrassed to have his words parroted back at him in front of the room. As he should be.

"A small group will be going from here to the Pennsylvania properties to do a more thorough search. This man is too meticulous to work without a plan. We simply need to decipher his method for creating that plan." Elek scanned the room again. "Petr, Demos, and Vasily, you will return with Baltasar and Georgios. Great-uncle Ari also wants us to look for her immediate family. Chances are good they haven't gone far. An older woman and a young boy--" He paused, his gaze skimming his family once more--"if we get the opportunity to use them to get her, we will."

Several sets of eyebrows lifted around the room, while some of his cousins narrowed their eyes at him. Elek sat back in his chair. "Phillip, Cyril, Gregos and Doran, we would like you to stay. The group heading to the house should move out within the hour. Everyone else, that is all for now, but don't go far."

Ari nodded once, and Elek felt a surge of satisfaction. He *could* do this.

He reined in his satisfaction, though, watching his cousins and uncles filing out of the room. Except for the four he'd called out.

Ari waited until the door shut behind everyone else before he cleared his throat. "I have another task in mind for you," he said, his sharp gaze covering all of them. "I want you to find out all you can about this man, this Ryder Ware. Then I want you to keep an eye on his interests, his apartment, his business. Everything. He has killed one of ours, and I want him stopped."

Elek watched the comprehension in his cousins' eyes.

"I will expect a report after you complete your investigation. The sooner, the better," Ari said, settling back in his chair. "You can be in Philadelphia in a couple of hours if you leave now."

His cousins understood it was a dismissal, and they rose almost as one and left the room.

Elek looked at his great-uncle again. "What would you like me to work on now?"

"Take a break. Get some fresh air, a meal. I know you have closeted yourself in your office for the past two days. You need a break."

He nodded once, though he thought of the notes on his

desk with a pang of longing. "All right. I will get something to eat before I return to work." He nodded and headed for the open door.

Aristotle remained at his desk after Elek left the room. He'd chosen well. Elek reminded him of himself at the same age--just uncertain enough to stay humble despite the trust placed in him, but determined to do the task they'd been chosen for by the Goddess.

For the first time in several years, Aristotle felt more confident in the outcome of their current hunt.

This Medusa would *not* escape them again.

CHAPTER SIX

Philomena fidgeted in her seat as they neared Philadelphia. After so long in the cabin, she'd been more than ready to get out, even if it meant Ryder did some work.

She touched the dagger hilt beneath her skirt, almost absently, as she watched the other cars on the highway. They'd missed rush hour, but residual heavy traffic on the expressway heading into the city slowed them down.

She tapped her fingers on the armrest.

"Mena."

When she glanced over, she found Ryder wearing a lopsided grin. "What?"

"We're nearly there."

She stopped tapping.

"Give me your hand." He held his out.

She shifted her gaze from his palm to his face, trying to read his expression. Finally, sighing, she lifted her hand to his. "Talk to me."

Warm fingers curled around hers, and he set their

joined hands on his hard thigh. "What do you want to know?"

Philomena swallowed. "Tell me about your family."

"Ugly story. Mom eventually hated the idea of staying a military housewife, so she bailed when I was eight, then died of a particularly nasty cancer when I was eleven. By then, Dad was out of the service, so he drank himself stupid every night. I'm sure he felt guilty for not being there when she needed him, and then it was too late."

She'd wanted a distraction, but this wasn't exactly what she'd imagined. She tightened her fingers on his reflexively.

He shot her a half-smile. "I started doing odd jobs a couple years later so I had food to eat and clothes to wear. When Dad lost his job because he went in drunk one day, he found my stash of money and drank it all. I had to keep finding new places to hide it. When I hit high school, I had a teacher who helped me open a bank account so Dad couldn't drink my money away anymore."

"I'm sorry, Ryder," she murmured, horror and pity tightening her chest.

"Don't be. That very messy upbringing sent me into the military, gave me the order I needed to function." He squeezed her hand. "I never wanted a family, though."

She blinked, thinking of her first call to him about Jason. "Then why--"

He grinned at her across the small space in the cab of the truck, warming her from head to toe. "How could I not, after you demanded I take responsibility? Just because I never intended to have a family didn't mean I would relegate a child of mine to an even worse life than I had. Clearly Desi had no intention of parenting, and I had no idea what to expect from you."

Philomena blushed, recalling that first phone call. "You must have thought I was insane."

He lifted her hand to brush his lips along the back of her fingers. "I thought you were right. I should be responsible for my child. Every man should take responsibility for his child."

She shut her eyes, wishing she'd kept her mouth shut. Her own father hadn't felt that way.

He rubbed his thumb along the side of hers, making warmth slide up her arm, distracting her. "What do you want to do first?"

She dragged her mind away from his warm fingers and what they did to her, and back to their trip. "Lunch."

He nodded. "Then what? Sightsee?"

She considered for a moment. "I've never seen the Liberty Bell," she said at last.

"Okay. We'll go there after lunch." He squeezed her fingers. "Anything else?"

"Then the office."

He frowned, as if he'd expected something different, but nodded. "All right."

She wouldn't admit it to him, but she was curious about his work space. What kind of place would it be? Utilitarian? With three men running it, it might just be a rented room with a couple of desks. But she was curious. And seeing it would help her to figure out the best website design for them.

Might even give her a few more clues to the man himself. Aside from the terrific dad, the sexy bad boy, the bossy ex-military man who still thought he was the commander.

She relaxed over lunch. He took her to a little hole in the wall place downtown with the best pizza she'd ever eaten. They lingered over the gooey cheese and greasy pepperoni for nearly forty-five minutes. Then they walked the few blocks to the Liberty Bell. Because of the enduring cold weather, there weren't many tourists, so they strolled slowly through the building, checking out each of the exhibits. They sat through a movie, too, before they finally got to the bell, which she decided was both more and less impressive than she'd expected, and far smaller than she'd thought it would be.

When he suggested walking up the hill, she opted to skip the Constitution Center, so he swung their joined hands between them as they strode back toward the restaurant and truck. About two blocks from there, he steered her into a sleek, modern-looking building.

The office.

Her attention piqued, Philomena studied their surroundings. A security desk dominated the main lobby, with a burly, uniformed young man behind the desk. He nodded at Ryder when they passed by.

He whisked her into a shiny, silent elevator, and they rode to the third floor. The door opened onto a bright lobby where a grey-suited young woman with sleek blond hair sat behind a curved desk.

"Good afternoon, Mr. Ware," she said, looking up from whatever she was doing on a computer. "I didn't realize you were stopping in today."

He stopped at the desk. "I brought Ms. Gregory in to see the office. She'll be designing our website. Mena, this is Carys." He failed to mention that Philomena hadn't yet agreed to do the website. Arrogance, or confidence? she wondered.

The young woman stood and offered her right hand. Philomena shook it, then realized Carys had noticed Ryder was holding Philomena's other hand. She blushed as the young woman's lips quirked.

"I've been nagging these guys for months about getting a website up and running. I'm glad to see you've been more successful than I have." Carys turned her attention to Ryder. "And Ken's in his office, in case you wanted to talk to him."

Ryder nodded and turned, pulling Philomena along. "Thanks, Carys."

She strode along at his side, willing the heat to fade from her cheeks. "She thinks we're dating."

He lifted one eyebrow.

She raised their joined hands.

His other eyebrow winged up. "Baby, in case you hadn't noticed, we're way beyond dating," he said in a low, sexy rumble that made her pulse race faster.

She bit her lip, wanting to point out their relationship wasn't permanent, something most dating couples usually considered a future goal. But she didn't speak. Not here.

Ryder stepped in her path to stop her. "Mena, I don't care if the whole world knows we're together." He dipped down to catch her gaze. "If it weren't for our pesky Harvester problem, I would rent a billboard and tell all of Philadelphia."

She frowned at him, a flutter of nervousness in her middle. "Why would you do that?"

Something flickered in his dark eyes, gone so quickly she couldn't decipher it. "Because I somehow think small gestures might not be enough to convince you."

Her mouth dropped open. "Convince me of what?" she managed, though her mouth had gone dry and a little voice in her head shrieked 'don't ask!'.

Ryder swallowed, his gaze sliding over her face. "This

isn't the time or place for this discussion," he said at last. "Come on." He turned and towed her along the hall.

Philomena's stomach churned. He was serious. The conversation over dinner their first night away... Dear Gods, what was she supposed to do with *that?*

She tried to refocus her attention when he stopped in an open doorway midway along the hall.

"Mena, this is Ken Robards. He does some surveillance work for us. Ken, this is Mena."

She shook the tall man's hand when he came out to greet them. "Nice to meet you." Work mode. *Think about the website.*

Ken's gaze slid from her to Ryder. "Keep this guy on his toes, all right?" he said at last.

She blinked.

He winked at her, and she blushed, averting her gaze. "So, boss man, I didn't know you were in town today."

The two men chatted for a few minutes about work. She looked around, trying not to pay too much attention to their conversation, in case there was anything she shouldn't hear. The office was bright, as the lobby had been, with a nice, functional space, the desk perpendicular to the window, a low bookcase and filing cabinet behind it, and a pair of comfortable-looking chairs in front of it. No artwork hung on the walls, but with nearly an entire wall of windows overlooking the city, there was no need.

Ken wore a shirt and tie, his sleeves rolled nearly to his elbows, a dark blazer draped across the back of his chair. Like Ryder, he was a big man, tall and broad, his curly black hair close-cropped, though Ken wore a wide gold wedding band on his left hand.

She turned to study the hallway, where there were a

few frames hanging on the walls, prints of local sites, it appeared.

Her overall impression so far was of a friendly office, with a competent staff.

And secure, judging by the small cameras at either end of the hallway, another in the middle, all sweeping back and forth silently. She looked around Ken's office and found another at the ceiling on the window side of the room, so it could catch everything in its arc.

She imagined every office was arranged similarly. She didn't know how to work the notion into a web design yet, or even if she would, but she'd figure it out. Something about keeping watch, maybe.

Her brain was so busy considering possibilities, that when Ryder gave her fingers a squeeze, she jumped.

"I said, are you ready to see the rest?" he said, giving her a grin that let her know he was aware of her wandering attention.

She nodded. "Just thinking about the website."

"I know, smart girl," he murmured as they walked away from Ken's office, "I could see the wheels turning." He shifted nearer so their arms brushed.

Philomena focused on her surroundings to distract herself from the warmth of his hand on hers, but it was a difficult task, especially when he stepped into a large, dark office at the end of the hallway, pulling her inside as he flipped on the lights. He nudged the door with his foot so it closed soundlessly behind them.

"My office." He swept out his free arm and gave a half-bow.

She shook her head and pulled away. "The corner office, of course," she teased, moving to the windows with blinds between the panes, only halfway down, to study the bustling street below.

He stepped up behind her. "Of course." His hands settled on her shoulders. "What do you think?"

"Nice place." She swallowed when he massaged her shoulders a little through her coat.

"And you'll notice my office doesn't have one of those security cameras." His warm breath brushed her ear.

"Don't even think about it," she said, turning to face him, as warmth rose in her cheeks.

He laughed. "Can't blame a guy for trying, can you?"

"Has anyone ever told you you're insatiable?" she asked when he wrapped his arms around her waist and pulled her loosely against him.

His smile faded. "I never have been before." One of his hands stroked up the middle of her back.

Philomena's heart beat faster. How on earth could she possibly respond?

He studied her face for a long moment, making her pulse quicken even more. "Why don't you look around?" He released her and went to sit in the big chair behind the glossy wooden desk, picking up a small remote and adjusting the blinds so they slid up further.

She watched him, her fingers curling into her palms to keep from reaching out for him. Ryder was temporary. She couldn't have permanent. Clearing her throat, she forced her gaze away from him, sliding it around the room. His office had a second door, and she moved toward it.

It opened into an office almost exactly the same as Ryder's though not on a corner.

"That's Danny's. The door on the other side of his opens into Joel's office, and his is another corner room," Ryder said from behind her.

She nodded, closing the door. "Why doesn't Danny have a corner office?"

He grinned when she turned around. "He's afraid of heights. Getting him to take any of the outside wall offices was a real battle."

She smiled reluctantly. "Why not let him have an office without windows?"

"He's a partner, he's got to have a big office."

She shook her head. "Men are so dumb sometimes," she muttered, sliding her fingers over an empty shelf on the bookcase in his corner.

"I heard that."

She didn't reply, her mind turning possibilities. She sat in a chair facing his desk and crossed one leg over the other. "Nice place."

He folded his forearms on the edge of the desk. "Are you coming up with ideas?"

She nodded. "Yes. I'll have to think about it for a while, though. And you'll have to let me know what kind of style you prefer, what sort of info you want on the site."

Ryder's dark eyes studied her for a few moments. "Okay. Have you seen enough?"

"Yes." She pushed to her feet, pausing when all the fine hairs at her nape stood on end.

Someone was out there watching her.

She shifted her gaze to the two walls of windows, her heart beating up into her throat.

"What's wrong?"

She shook her head. "I'm probably being stupid, but I feel like someone's watching." *A dangerous someone.* There were far too many windows.

Ryder rose in a flash, his sharpened gaze shifting from one nearby building to another. "I don't see anyone."

Neither did she. But that didn't mean there wasn't a Harvester out there watching her. Waiting.

He grabbed the remote from his desk and closed the blinds completely. "Let's go." He moved around the desk, taking her arm to steer her from the office.

Philomena's breath wanted to come faster, and she had to force herself to inhale slowly, evenly, then release the air. Repeat.

Downstairs, they paused at the security desk just long enough for Ryder to murmur something to the guard, and then they hit the sidewalk, walking quickly.

"If I tell you to run, can you find your way back to the truck?" he asked, his gaze darting around.

She tried to think. "Maybe." Gods, how could they have found her?

He pressed a key into her hand. "Good. If I tell you to run, you go. Get to the cabin and I'll meet you there."

"What about you?" She felt an irrational urge to run now. To get as far away from here as possible.

"I'll get there. But if I have to stay behind to deal with anything, I don't want you to wait around." His fingers tightened on her arm. "Your first priority is to get to safety."

She swallowed as she nodded. Fear tried to squeeze her lungs tight.

They were within sight of the truck when he swore under his breath. "We need to move, baby." He started to run, and she quickened her own pace, her boots thumping faster on the sidewalk.

From behind them, she heard people shouting. "Hey, watch where you're going, buddy!" and "Yo, asshole, that was my foot!"

A Harvester. And apparently, he didn't care they were on the street in a very big city with an audience.

Philomena sucked in a quick breath and ignored the stitch in her side, moving faster when Ryder did. He unlocked the truck with his remote and pushed her in through the driver's door.

"Get down." He slid into his seat, almost on her heels, and started the truck.

She wedged herself into the space between the seat and the dashboard, closing her eyes for a second. *Gods, please don't let me die.*

Ryder stomped on the gas pedal, whipping out into traffic to the sound of honking horns. He drove too quickly, and she saw his mouth tighten when he glanced in the rearview mirror. "Son of a bitch," he muttered, pressing harder on the accelerator.

Philomena closed her eyes again, chest aching. She so wanted to see Jason one more time.

"It's Ryder."

She opened her eyes and found him with his cell to his ear.

"I need a rental car waiting when we get back...No, I don't care what kind...Thanks." He tossed the phone onto the seat.

"How did he find me?"

"Lucky timing for him, I think."

"What do you mean?"

"Kallan told me there are usually one or two Harvesters in the big cities along the east coast. I figured Philly is big enough we wouldn't run into one or two people. My mistake." His jaw tightened. "I'm sorry, baby. My fault."

"What are you, psychic?" She shook her head. "Just drive, Ryder. I don't want to die today."

"I won't let you." He flashed her a cocky grin and whipped the truck around a sharp corner, tires squealing.

Philomena put her head on her knees, hoping his assurance was justifiable.

He sped around a few more turns, still muttering curses under his breath, then she felt the truck gain a lot more speed. Highway.

She lifted her head far enough to see the close-set buildings dropping away as he merged onto the interstate. "How many red lights did you run?"

"Just a couple." Strain bracketed his eyes even though he smiled.

She put her head back down. "If I die today, make sure Jason knows I love him."

"You're not dying, Mena," he snapped, "today or any other day for a long, long time." Then he looked into the mirror. "Bastard."

Under her, the truck vibrated as it gained more speed. "Promise me anyway."

"Fine. But you can tell him yourself tonight."

She smiled into her lap and took a deep breath. "Just drive, would you?"

His short laugh made her relax a tiny bit.

Until something pinged off the roof of the truck.

"Son of a bitch," Ryder growled, accelerating even more.

She tightened her arms around her knees, turning her head to look at him. "Is he shooting at us?"

"Keep your head down."

She stifled a cry when something hit the back window, cracking the glass in a fine imitation of a spider's web. She pressed her face hard against her legs.

Ryder whipped the car into another lane, accelerating so the engine rumbled louder.

Philomena shut her eyes and prayed to all the Gods.

It seemed a very long time that they wove in and out of traffic, off the interstate, then more city driving, before Ryder slowed.

Philomena turned her head to look at him.

"We lost him." Some of the tension had left his face, but not all. Not enough.

The knot in her belly tightened. "Then what's wrong?"

"He was close enough behind us to get the license plate number. If they have the resources to track that, he'll know about my business. Or they already knew, which is how he found us so easily. Fuck, I'm so stupid."

She considered that. Of course they already knew. They would have researched her thoroughly.

"Which is why we're getting a rental car. Carys should have one for us by now." He slid a card from a spot on the dashboard and rolled down his window as he pulled into a parking garage entrance.

Philomena eased up from the floor, her cramped legs screaming a protest as she slid onto the seat.

"Our personal parking garage," he said as he scanned the card in the machine at the entry. "For the business." He slanted a quick grin at her.

She waited until he parked, then slipped out, stretching her legs and her back.

"You okay?" He set one big hand on her shoulder, rubbing a little.

"I'll be fine, as long as I can sit on the seat for the next leg of this trip," she said lightly.

He gave her shoulder a squeeze. "I'll see what I can do about that." He shut and locked the truck, then steered her to the elevator.

Upstairs, they came into the lobby from the far side.

Carys smiled at them when they emerged from the elevator. "Good timing. Abe said the car just arrived."

"Excellent. While we're gone, the truck is going to need some work. We got winged, and the back window needs replaced." Ryder tossed her the truck keys. "Anything I need to know?"

The receptionist shook her head. "We're good here. Be careful." She waved at Philomena. "See if you can't make him behave while you're at it."

Startled, Philomena shot him a quick glance, finding him wide-eyed as well. "I wouldn't know where to start," she managed after a second.

Ryder guided her this time into the main elevator, down to the front lobby, where the security guard rose and held out a set of keys. "First spot outside, sir."

"Thanks, Abe. I appreciate it." He grabbed the keys and hustled her out the door and into the nondescript rental car waiting.

Philomena sank into the seat and buckled up, closing her eyes. Her heartbeat had finally returned to normal, but her head throbbed.

Ryder slid in and started the car. For such a boring looking sedan, the engine revved pretty loudly. She opened her eyes and turned to look at Ryder. He shrugged. "Our rental agency knows we sometimes need speed."

She smiled.

"Rough day, huh?" He eased into traffic this time, unlike their earlier rush.

"Kind of. At least he didn't start shooting while we were running for the truck." She wasn't sure her heart could have taken that.

Ryder grunted in reply, and she took a deep breath, shifting to find the most comfortable position. If she took a nap now, maybe she could head off the stress headache building at the back of her skull.

Except behind her closed eyelids, she kept imagining what might have happened if the Harvester *had* caught up to her. Her pulse quickened, and her mouth went dry.

"Don't think about 'what if'," he said gruffly after a few minutes.

She worried the inside of her lower lip with her teeth. Easier said than done.

Her head pounded harder.

"How would you like a change of scenery?" he asked a little later.

She forced a laugh. "This one didn't work out so well. Maybe not." She kept her eyes closed, concentrating on making her headache go away.

"That's not exactly what I meant." He caught the hand she had resting on her leg and laced their fingers. "I meant, let's check out of the cabin tomorrow and go somewhere else."

Philomena opened her eyes to look at him. "Where?"

"Somewhere farther away from Philly than the Poconos."

She couldn't argue with that. If there was more than one Harvester in the vicinity, it was bad for her, and she'd bet they could call in reinforcements to help them fan out to look for her outside the city. The mountains weren't nearly far enough away from Philadelphia right now to suit her. She shuddered and pulled her coat tighter around her.

Ryder squeezed her fingers, but it didn't make her feel better.

She wondered if they could get far enough from here to stay out of the Harvesters' reach.

ELEK REFRAINED FROM PUNCHING GREGOS IN THE face, but his fingers still curled tight at his side. "Explain to us exactly how you lost them," he managed. Anger rushed along his veins, heating, settling in his gut. Burning like lava.

Gregos shifted his gaze from Ari to Elek, a dull flush climbing his neck. "Something spooked them. They were already running when I reached the building." He looked away.

"And you didn't shoot them."

Gregos's face turned redder. "It was lunchtime and there were people on the street."

"Or disable their vehicle." Elek could feel the edges of his nails biting into his palms.

His cousin shook his head. "I did get off a couple shots at the truck, but it was too fast," he muttered. "And he drives like a maniac."

Elek really did want to punch Gregos. His muscles quivered with the fury coursing through him. "Get out," he managed. "We will deal with you later."

Gregos didn't wait to see if Elek changed his mind, pivoting on his heel and striding from the room, head down.

"You exercised far more restraint than I believed you had, Elek," Ari said. "Well done."

Despite the praise, he still couldn't unclench his fists.

"Go to the workout room. We can talk later about our next step." Ari patted his shoulder. "Go. You'll feel better."

Elek went, mind spinning as he changed into shorts.

He wouldn't have let the monster escape, no matter how crowded the street. And if he had to go to prison, even died himself, it would be worth it.

Gregos? He was unworthy.

Elek went directly to the heavy bag in the corner and slammed his fist into it, imagining his cousin's face. Again. Harder. Over and over until he couldn't see through the sweat burning his eyes, until he couldn't breathe. Until he sank to his knees on the mat, then dropped flat on his back, swiping his wet forearm across his brow, not that it did any good.

As he caught his breath, he realized his hands throbbed. He hadn't taken the time to put on the sparring gloves, or even to wrap his knuckles before attacking the bag. He opened his eyes and lifted his hands.

Scraped, swollen and bruised. As Gregos should be.

Elek growled and slapped his hands on the mat. His cousin was an imbecile, not clever enough or brave enough to fully participate in the hunt for the Medusa, so he would be removed, given a non-essential assignment to serve as punishment for this monumental failure.

He took a slow breath, then released it, feeling some of his anger dissipate. Uncle Ari believed he could do this, and he would. Somehow.

CHAPTER SEVEN

Ryder didn't like the pallor in Mena's face. She'd been quiet for the duration of their drive back to the cabin, where she'd kicked off her boots, popped a couple of aspirin, and curled up on the sofa beneath a heavy blanket.

He left her alone, starting his computer to look for a new refuge. It only took him fifteen minutes to find somewhere within driving distance, someplace they could blend in. Then he fired off emails to Danny and Joel to let them know what had occurred that afternoon and to tell them he was taking Mena to a new spot in the morning. When he finished, he shut down and moved to stand behind the couch.

Mena still lay with her eyes closed, but she wasn't sleeping. A faint frown marred her brow, and every once in a while, she rubbed her temple.

He'd done a shitty job keeping her safe today. If she hadn't felt like they were being watched, the Harvester might've killed them both. He had to do better from now on. Much better. "Sit up," he said finally. He walked around and helped her upright. He sat behind her and started massaging her shoulders and neck, lightly at first, then pressing a bit harder into the tight muscles there.

When he hit a particularly tender spot, she made a soft sound. "You need to relax, honey." He kissed the back of her head. "Don't you have anything stronger than the aspirin?"

She shook her head.

He made a mental note to find something. "What are we going to do for supper tonight?"

She sighed. "I don't care."

He returned to the spot that had made her wince before, gently working the knot there until her shoulders relaxed a bit. "I'm thinking we ought to try the Chinese place we passed on the way in earlier."

"Okay."

He frowned. She was being rather agreeable. "Maybe after, we can come back and try the bathtub again." He waited.

One of her shoulders lifted in a shrug.

He stopped his massage, frowning. "Talk to me."

"I don't want to talk right now."

"Talk to me anyway." Ryder started to stroke her nape next, feeling her muscles there gradually relax as well. "Are you still imagining what might've happened?"

"How can I not?"

The tension in her voice was echoed in her shoulders once more. He sighed. "We had a little brush today, Mena. I won't lie to you. But it wasn't nearly as bad as what we almost had at your mother's." It wouldn't help to tell her he was imagining it, too.

She jerked under his hands, a quick tightening of her body, a defensive gesture.

He pulled her against his chest. "The thing is, you've lived with this threat for years. You just never had any close calls." He wrapped his arms around her middle to keep her from fleeing as she seemed to want to do. "Now you have, and you've got to be prepared for more."

"It sucks."

He smiled at the back of her head. "I know. There's nothing I can say to make this better for you, Mena, but you need to stop thinking about it. Stop thinking 'he might have killed me today' and think instead 'he didn't get the chance to kill me today'."

She bowed her head. "I suppose you want to take the credit for that," she said after a moment, her voice strained despite her effort at a light tone.

"I'll share, since your instincts told you we were being watched." He frowned. "He got lucky today."

"Or they really did already know about you and were watching the office in the hope we'd show up eventually."

He didn't like that idea. He should've thought of the possibility already. How could he have missed it?

Mena sighed deeply. "I need to call Jason."

"Okay." He didn't release her, though. "Then we'll go get dinner, and when we get back, I'm going to strip you naked and see how long it takes to make you scream."

She shot him a quick glance over her shoulder. "Why is everything a competition with guys? Why how fast? Why not, how long can *you* last instead?"

His body hardened at the images in his head now. "Are you complaining about my technique?" he growled.

She shook her head. "Just making an observation."

"Bet I can hold out longer than you."

"There you go with that competition thing again." Her lips curved finally. Just a little, but it was something.

He kissed her lightly. "Fine. No keeping track for tonight? Better?" He released her.

"Great." She pushed to her feet, then turned around and braced herself on his shoulders. "Thank you, Ryder. For keeping me alive today." She bent and brushed a quick kiss on his cheek.

He let her go, watching the sway of her hips as she made her way to her purse, where she took out her cell phone and dialed her mother. He didn't tell her he hadn't wanted to keep her alive just for Jason, or for her mother.

He needed to keep her alive for himself, too.

PHILOMENA TRIED NOT TO THINK ABOUT YESTERDAY AS she folded her belongings into her carry-on bag in the morning. Her headache was mostly gone, but there were still faint twinges every now and again that warned her not to think too hard. So she attempted to keep her mind on her packing. And wondering where they were going, since Ryder hadn't told her. She hoped it was somewhere with a laundromat, because she'd nearly run out of clean clothes.

Ryder was on his cell, talking in a low tone on the other side of the room.

Those calls were starting to annoy her. It couldn't be he didn't trust her with the information. After all, who would she tell, the Harvesters? Not so much. She felt pretty certain he just didn't want her to be any more stressed.

She ought to tell him she couldn't possibly get any more stressed than she already was. Unless an armed Harvester was in the room with her.

She folded a sweater into the bag, then went to the bathroom to make sure she hadn't left anything there. The mirror over the sink reflected a pale face surrounded by untidy curls. Philomena tried to finger-comb her hair into some sort of order, but it didn't work, so she gave up and pinched her cheeks instead. Even that didn't help, so she collected the tube of toothpaste and toothbrush sitting there and went back to the main room.

Ryder was waiting, arms folded on his chest as he studied her. "You should take a nap when we hit the road."

"Is that your way of telling me I look like crap?" she asked dryly, putting her things into her suitcase.

"Maybe it's my way of saying I've been keeping you from your sleep too much the last few nights."

Warmth rose into her cheeks, and she bent to zip the bag, avoiding his gaze. "Sounds like the same thing to me."

He stepped nearer, catching her wrist when she started to lift the suitcase. "I'm sorry about yesterday, Mena."

She frowned. "You didn't know we'd run into a Harvester, Ryder. It isn't your fault."

His dark eyes were troubled, and she realized he had faint smudges beneath them from lack of sleep. Her protector was tired, too.

She touched his face with her free hand. "You aren't responsible for them." She patted him, then pulled away, taking her bag to the front door.

"But I'm responsible for keeping you safe, and I didn't do a very good job yesterday."

"I'm still alive."

He glared at her. "That isn't what I meant."

She sighed as she straightened. "Fine. You'll do a better job today then." She set her hands on her hips. "Where are we going?"

His mouth pursed a little as he watched her. "North."

She rolled her eyes. "Fine. Keep it a secret. As long as there aren't more heart-shaped beds there."

He smiled, though it wasn't his usual cocky grin. It was a start, she figured.

～

Ryder parked in front of the drug store, frowning. He hated to wake Mena, now she'd finally fallen asleep. But she needed something stronger than the aspirin she'd taken last night for her headache, so he'd had Carys find a doctor to call in a prescription for a stronger painkiller, and this was where they were to pick it up. He debated with himself for just a couple seconds more, then touched her shoulder, lightly.

She startled awake, pushing herself upright in her seat. "Are we there yet?" she teased after a second, her voice husky with sleep.

It made him think of the way she sounded in bed at night, and his blood heated. He cleared his throat. "Almost. I need to get a couple things." He jerked his chin in the direction of the store.

"Oh." She frowned for a second, then her expression cleared as her cheeks pinkened. "I should, too, if we're going to be gone too long."

He considered that. "How's the stress level?"

She swallowed. "Pretty high. It's been less than a week, but Andi said it didn't matter if the stress level was high enough. 'Worse than perimenopause' was what she said."

"Okay. Let's go." He grabbed the keys and pushed his door open, taking a moment to stretch when he climbed out of the car. Mena did the same on her side of the vehicle, bending from the waist to her right, then to her left, and rolling her shoulders.

He considered her statement. Kallan and Andrea had

told him the same thing, a long time ago. His gaze slid to her hair, and he wondered how she dealt with that aspect of the curse every month.

He followed her into the store, one hand at the small of her back. "Lead the way." He scooped up a basket when they passed a small stack.

Mena blushed faintly again, leading the way into an aisle he'd never before had occasion to visit.

He grinned as she selected the items she wanted, avoiding his gaze. When she would have taken the basket from him, he kissed her lightly instead, holding tight to the handle. She lifted wide eyes to his face. "It's all right," he whispered.

She caught her lower lip in her teeth and shifted her gaze away. "We should find a couple other things, too."

"Like what?"

"Hot water bottle. Heating pad." She searched the aisle directory signs until she found the one she wanted.

His grin faded. His conversations with her cousin had given him a pretty good idea how much suffering was involved. He wondered how big this prescription was he was about to pick up, if there would be enough for that, too. If it was even strong enough.

"What did you need?" She put the heating pad box in the crook of her arm, and the hot water bottle into the basket.

He studied her face, not quite as pale now as she'd been earlier, green eyes guarded. "Come here." He caught her arm and drew her close for a brief kiss. It didn't sate his need, but it would do for now. He released her, gratified to see a bit more color in her cheeks. "We just need to hit the pharmacy counter and I think we're good."

They snagged a few other things along the way--water

and soda, some snacks--and Mena paused in front of a display of hair accessories, her expression sobering. She took a card from a hook--bands designed to wrap around ponytails and added them to the basket, her lower lip in her teeth again.

He steered her to the pharmacy counter, where he paid for their things, giving her a hard look when she tried to hand him some cash.

"You've paid for everything," she said quietly. "For days."

He held her gaze. "Don't worry about it."

She frowned at him. "I have money."

"I know you do. So do I. You should keep yours in case of an emergency. Or in case you see something you really, really want when we're sightseeing."

"More sightseeing?" Her mouth twisted. "That didn't work out so well last time."

He grinned. "This will." He took their bags from the woman behind the counter and steered Mena out to the car.

She sat in silence, brooding once more, as he turned the car toward their destination. He patted her knee. "Almost there."

She frowned, searching for a road sign as he drove. "Niagara Falls?" she said several minutes later.

He eased the car into the parking lot at the hotel. "Have you ever been?"

She shook her head, her gaze shifting from the sign in front of the hotel to his face.

"Neither have I. It'll be fun."

"It's another honeymoon spot." Pink tinted her cheeks.

He shrugged. "We'll blend in just fine."

She lifted one eyebrow in disbelief.

"People still honeymoon over the winter, Mena." He

took the key from the ignition and shoved his door open. "See?"

Her attention shifted to the couple coming out of the front door, arms wrapped around one another, oblivious to her scrutiny.

"Come on, baby. Let's get checked in. I'm beat. And hungry."

She climbed out of the car, gathering their shopping bags while he grabbed the suitcases, and then she followed him into the lobby.

This hotel was pretty swanky, compared to the rustic charm of the last place. Lots of gleaming, dark wood here, elegant furnishings in the lobby, again around a fireplace. Further, the formal dining room filled with white-covered tables was visible.

Mena kept her mouth shut while he checked in, though he could tell by her expression she was mentally calculating how much this place cost.

He didn't care. It had been a long time since he'd spent money on anyone besides Jason, or anything beyond work and necessities. It had been even longer since he'd had a vacation. He'd saved plenty of money, enough to partner with Danny and Joel, plenty to put away for Jason's future, and plenty more in case of emergency. This didn't quite qualify as an emergency yet, since they'd managed to ditch the Harvesters yesterday, but it qualified as necessary travel. If he turned it into a vacation opportunity at the same time, well, he had a beautiful woman at his side, one he'd been trying to get his hands on for years. He wouldn't waste his chance.

Their room was on the ground floor, as he'd arranged, for easy exit if necessary, and he led the way around the corner from the registration desk to the hallway leading to their room.

The room wasn't just a room, but a suite, he discovered when they stepped inside, the outer room a sitting area with a small gas fireplace and cushy sofa and chair, a large television in the corner.

Ryder kicked the door shut behind them and then led the way to the bedroom. It was twice the size of the sitting area, a king-sized bed in the center of the room, flanked by matching glass night tables and facing an enormous window that overlooked the wooded area behind the hotel. The bathroom opened off to the side, an enormous jetted bathtub in one corner.

He set the suitcases on the luggage rack in the open closet, then took the bags from her. Her gaze had caught on the big bed, and he hid his grin.

She shook herself a little, forcing her gaze away from the bed, and avoided his gaze as she turned to the windows. "Pretty view."

"It is. Let's find a laundromat, get some supper, then call Jason, so we can relax." He slid his hand up her back to her warm nape. "Okay?"

She nodded and let him steer her out of the room once more

Laundry time was interesting. He averted his gaze from an obviously newly-married couple wearing shiny new wedding bands and groping one another in front of their dryer. An older man seated in the far corner couldn't seem to take his eyes off of them, the newspaper in his hands forgotten. Mena glanced at them, a faint, sad smile curving her lips again, then focused her attention on her task of folding jeans and ignoring his minimal attempts to engage her in conversation.

Dinner was quiet, and he let her be, not trying to tease her out of her brooding, or even to irritate her. Instead, he commented on the meal, touched her every chance he got, and bided his time.

Her phone call to Jason had her eyes shiny with tears by the end of it, and something twisted in his chest at the sight. At the knowledge of how much she loved his son. So much that she'd leave him to keep him safe, not knowing when or if she'd see him again.

He gathered her in his arms when she hung up and felt her trembling against his chest, trying to keep her emotions in check. "It's okay, baby," he murmured over the top of her head.

"It's not okay." She grasped his shirt tight in one hand, shuddering. "It is definitely *not* okay."

He let her hold on, stroking her back, her head, until her shaking eased and her breathing evened out once more. Then he stepped away and dropped onto the sofa, pulling her across his lap.

Mena kept her face against his shoulder.

"You need to relax." He glanced at the small table beside the couch and saw the remote for the fireplace. He lifted it and hit the button to start the fire burning.

The soft whoosh made her jump, and she glanced over to see what had made the sound, then relaxed.

"There's a start." He found the television remote and turned that on, too. "Maybe we should have picked out some wine."

She shook her head.

"No?" He flipped through channels until he found a station playing music, no video, something new agey and soothing, then put the remote on the table. "You don't like wine?"

"I like it just fine, but it's not a good combination with my PMS or aspirin."

He filed that away for future reference. "Okay. So you think soon?"

She nodded. "Very. Do you suppose there are any adult stores around here?"

His eyebrows shot up. "I'm sure we can find one, but do you really think you need toys when you've got me here?"

She lifted her head at last, her cheeks bright red. "I need one for during. The cramps get so bad that not much helps besides heat, either a shower or the heating pad, and...an orgasm," she whispered. "I didn't think about it while we were packing. I should've, but wasn't thinking in terms of how long we'd be gone or how much the stress would mess with me."

Ryder thought about all of that. He'd been distracting her while she packed, plus she probably hadn't wanted to admit then just how long it would take to be safe from the Harvesters. "I can still help." He watched the color in her cheeks deepen further as she averted her gaze, and he smiled. "I'll find a store." He eased her onto the couch, giving her a moment to collect herself while he went in the other room and got his laptop.

In a few minutes, he'd found three stores within a thirty minute drive of their hotel. Probably for all the honeymooners. "We have choices," he announced, turning the screen toward her.

Mena's jaw was tight and her cheeks pink, but she took the laptop and studied their options. "This one," she said at last, turning the computer back to him and pointing.

"Okay. Do you want to go tonight, or can we wait?"

"Tonight, I think." Her expression was serious, no hint of embarrassment now.

He cupped her face in one hand. "Okay." Her skin was soft against his rough palm. "It'll be all right, Mena," he promised, leaning close enough to brush her lips with his.

She wanted to believe him. He could see it in her eyes. He could also see that she didn't quite.

He'd make sure it was all right. If it was the last thing he did.

~

Philomena couldn't believe she was wandering through an adult toy store with Ryder. Or at all. She'd made all her previous purchases via the internet. Why on earth hadn't she packed something?

Probably because Ryder was there, stretched across her bed, already teasing her with the negligee. Distracting her.

She took in a fortifying breath and glanced at the table beside them. She thought her face must be glowing, it was so hot. The display at hand was a selection of S&M toys, leather floggers and paddles, gags and whips. Not exactly what she was looking for.

Ryder's eyes gleamed with mischief when he caught her gaze.

Oh, no. She moved away, dragging her gaze to the next display. Vibrators. Just what she needed.

And just what she didn't want to shop for with Ryder looking over her shoulder.

"This one looks interesting," he murmured, his tone gravelly in her ear, as he pointed to a bright green one covered in tiny knobs.

She sucked in a sharp breath when his fingers settled low on her back. "I don't think so."

"You don't like your toys fluorescent?" He chuckled.

"How about that one?" He indicated a curved pink one with a small piece jutting out near its base, designed to stimulate her clit while penetrating to her g-spot.

She tried not to think of Ryder 'helping' with that. Failed. Heat rushed through her. "It's a possibility," she admitted after a second.

"Hm." His breath warmed her cheek as he shifted nearer. "And this one?"

'This one' was enormous. Flesh-toned, with thick ridges. The box claimed it thrust on its own. *Dear Gods.*

"Perhaps not." She instead lifted the last box on the table, a smaller vibe, smooth except at the base where tiny nubs jutted out all the way around a protrusion to stroke her clit.

"Why don't we get both?" Ryder took the box from her and picked up the one she'd said was a possibility. "We need a shopping basket."

She turned to look at him, alarm mingling with the desire simmering in her veins. "We don't need a basket."

He slid her that slow, sexy grin, and her temperature rose about twenty degrees. "We do." He brushed a kiss on her mouth and steered her toward another display.

Blindfolds.

Her heart stopped for a few seconds. She hadn't considered he was in danger by being with her during her period. She never had to worry about it at home, as she was always alone. Ryder was in grave danger just by being with her for the next few days. How could she not have realized?

While she stared at the vast arrangement of blindfolds, in various colors and sizes, hung on the wall, Ryder found a shopping basket. And had added to her two vibrators already, with silk scarves in several colors and a couple tubes of something. She tried to focus her gaze on the contents of his basket, but he distracted her by selecting one of the blindfolds.

"I think leather would be too hot," he mused, replacing it on its hooks.

"Leather?" She stared at him, trying to ignore the pulsing low in her belly.

He winked at her. "Too hot for what we need." He picked up another. The front was black satin, the backing soft cotton. "Hm, this might be good."

She blushed. She was going to have to let him blindfold her. For three days.

She shut her eyes for a second. *Wow,* this *might be awkward.*

He added the blindfold to the basket.

"I think we're covered," she said tightly, pointing toward the front of the store.

Ryder grinned at her. "We haven't looked at everything yet."

She sighed, resigned, and followed him around the rest of the shop, grateful that at least they were the only shoppers there at the moment.

By the time they got to the counter, Ryder had added lube and toy cleaner to their items, as well as flavored massage oils and batteries. She couldn't even look the woman behind the counter in the face while they checked out.

Ryder tucked her into the car with the bag, then went around to his side. He leaned across and kissed her, just a feathery brush of his lips on hers. "It'll be fun."

She shook her head. "You're impossible."

"The drill sergeant kept telling me the same thing during boot camp." He winked at her and started the car.

"We should find a grocery store to stock up on snacks

and drinks, before this really kicks in," she said, as much to distract herself as to distract him.

"Okay." His grin didn't waver.

So much for distraction.

He kept his arm around her during their quick trip through a grocery store on their way back to the hotel, never letting her break contact. While they chose some fruits and other snacks that didn't need to be chilled or heated and drinks, her brain wouldn't stop inventing new ideas about what might happen later. Forget 'might'. What *would* happen later. The musky scent of his cologne teased her nose, made her knees weak. Gratitude mingled with the desire when he guided her to the car and let her slide into her seat.

She shut her eyes and leaned her head against the seat. Sex toys. The man had bought her *sex toys*.

Heat swam along her veins. And he intended to use them on her.

Her nipples tightened, making her glad she had her coat buttoned up tight to her throat.

"Are you wet yet?" he asked, his tone conversational as he set his hand on her knee.

A helpless laugh passed her lips. Of course she was. But she wasn't going to tell him.

His fingers slid higher, into the space between her thighs. "Mm. Should've bought the paddle, too," he murmured, stroking along the damp seam of her jeans.

Philomena bit her lip, torn between laughter at his outrageousness and setting loose the moan trying to escape. "I don't think so." Even she heard how ragged her voice was.

"Open yourself to new experiences, Mena," he teased, stroking her harder, so her hips lifted into his touch.

"I think I can live without that one, thanks." She shut her eyes for a second at the rush of heat between her thighs.

"I don't know, seems like you might be interested." He shot her a dangerous glance in the light from the dashboard. And pressed right on her clit.

A startled moan passed her lips.

He whipped the car into the parking lot, driving around to the side of the hotel so they were as close to their room as he could manage, then eased his fingers from between her legs to shut off the engine. "Let's go find out."

She sucked in an unsteady breath and pushed her door open. Her knees didn't want to hold her weight when she stepped out, so she braced herself on the car for a second, taking another deep breath, but the frigid air did nothing to cool her down.

Their bags dangled from Ryder's fingers when he met her at the door to the hotel, then set his free hand at the small of her back to guide her to their room. Her heart beat much too fast.

She was sure it had nothing to do with the idea of spanking and everything to do with Ryder.

That certainty didn't make her pulse slow, however.

Inside, he shut the door and steered her right into the bedroom.

When his cell rang as he was dropping the bags onto the low dresser, she breathed a silent sigh of relief, moving away to unbutton her coat. She needed a few moments to get herself under control. The mirror over the dresser showed her flushed cheeks and darkened eyes. She shoved her hair away from her face, then paused, studying her curls.

She'd have to deal with her hair tonight. Or very early tomorrow morning. Her heartbeat slowed a little, knocking painfully against her ribs.

She turned away from the mirror to look for the bag from the drugstore. She rummaged through it until she came up with the elastic bands.

"What are you doing?" Ryder set one hand on his hip.

She shut her eyes for a moment. "I need to braid my hair."

He dropped his phone on the dresser and took the comb and elastic bands from her. "Not yet." His fingers slid into her hair, tipping her head back so he could catch her gaze.

"Andi used to chop hers off every month." She swallowed hard, thinking how difficult that must have been for her cousin. "So short the snakes couldn't...." She bit her lip.

His fingers massaged her scalp as his dark chocolate gaze slid over her face, pausing at her mouth, lifting to meet her gaze again. "It would be a shame to cut it off." One of his hands cradled the back of her head, and the other slipped forward to touch her cheek. "It feels really nice on my skin," he whispered.

Philomena blinked up at him. She'd never considered that. His fingers eased down to the corner of her mouth, and when one tugged lightly at her lower lip, she opened, letting him slide in. Her tongue tasted him, almost of its own volition. The crotch of her panties was soaked in an instant, and she shifted a little, weight moving from one foot to the other. He tasted good, tempting.

He hummed his approval, easing his finger almost out, then back in, mimicking what her body was already screaming for him to do with other parts. Damned PMS-fueled hormones. When he withdrew this time, he replaced his fingers with his mouth, his tongue, and she lifted against him, feeling his erection notched against her belly.

She knew some of this was her out-of-control hormones. But not all of it, and knowing that scared her.

"Touch me, Mena," he breathed into her mouth, his hand cupping her breast through her blouse.

She obliged them both by tugging his shirt up and sliding her hands over his chest, feeling his breathing hitch when she found his tight little nipples and pinched them.

"Damn." He released her hair to catch her ass, lifting her against him, grinding his hips into hers so her breath caught, too. "I keep thinking I'm going to get to take my time with you, and you keep rushing me," he complained as he turned to the bed, planting one knee on the blanket, then carrying her down beneath him.

Philomena smiled, rocking her hips against his and enjoying the friction of his body over hers. "I'm not rushing you, Ryder."

He barked out a short laugh, and bent to nip at the side of her neck. "I'll never last long enough to try body oils or new toys at this rate."

She slid her hands around him, feeling his muscles flex and relax beneath her touch. "We have all night," she whispered, her lips grazing his forehead.

Ryder reared back, onto his knees, and he dragged his shirt off, then undid his jeans, shoving them down to release his straining erection.

She lifted one hand to stroke over the smooth head, feeling how damp it was already.

He shot her a glance that scorched the blood in her veins and the air in her lungs still more, then eased away, wrestling with his boots so he could kick off his jeans. "You need to be naked, Mena mine."

She eased to a seated position, reaching for the buttons on her blouse and trying not to think about what he'd just said. *His.* She'd gotten halfway down the front when he tugged impatiently, and several buttons went flying.

"I'll get you a new one," he muttered, catching her breast, then apparently decided her bra was in his way, too, because he yanked it down and rubbed his thumb over the tight, dark peak.

She leaned into the caress, eyes sliding shut. Then his mouth sucked in the same bit of flesh, and she had to brace herself on the mattress to stay upright.

Ryder teased her mercilessly, lips, tongue, teeth, and just when she thought she might explode just from his mouth on her breast, his fingers slid into the front of her jeans. She hadn't even noticed him unzipping them. She'd been too busy with all the other sensations rushing through her, making the desire coil tighter in her middle.

His fingers slid easily into her slick folds, higher.

Her hips came off the bed to meet them.

"Damn." He released his breath, his fingers slowly stroking in and out of her, his gaze slipping down to watch.

Philomena forced her eyes to stay open, watching the dark flush that bloomed on his face, the way his eyes looked nearly black now, the pupils so big. "Come inside me, Ryder," she whispered.

His gaze shot up to hers, and his fingers paused in their caressing.

"Please."

He nodded once, then eased his fingers from her body to shove her jeans and underwear the rest of the way off. When he'd finished, she undid her bra and slipped it off, tossing it aside and holding out her arms.

He didn't require another invitation, sliding her toward the pillows before he forced her thighs apart with his own, the crisp hair on his legs erotic against her smooth skin. Then the wide tip of his cock wedged into her, and her breathing faltered.

"You're wet enough for me," he rasped, bracing himself on his elbows so he could stroke her face, her breast.

"Yes." She knew it. He'd made sure of it.

He pressed deeper, his body stretching hers as he inched his way inside. "Gods, so hot and tight." His eyes shut for a second. "I love the feel of you around me, Mena." He opened his eyes again, his gaze fixed on hers.

"You feel pretty good, too," she said with a shaky smile, wrapping her arms around his neck. That was a serious understatement.

Another shimmy of his narrow hips and he was fully inside her, throbbing and hot. Thick. Hard.

Her breath caught as she felt the mini-explosions deep inside her already.

Then, just as slowly, Ryder began to withdraw, rubbing against sensitive tissues along the way so her trembling spread. To her fingers, her thighs.

"Just to take the edge off," he muttered.

"Okay, Ryder." She braced her feet and lifted into his next thrust, arching hard as the first orgasm bloomed.

HE REPEATED THE SLOW MOVEMENTS FOREVER, HIS arms shaking on either side of her, while she moaned and thrashed beneath him. He caught her mouth with his, not to stop the sounds of her pleasure, but to absorb them.

He muffled his own shout of triumph against her shoulder a little while later, his hips jerking one last time into hers. He collapsed over her, feeling her fingers slipping in the sweat along his spine. His breath came rough, unsteady. And her body still quivered all around his.

He grinned into the spot where her shoulder joined her

neck, also slick with sweat, and realized when her hormones went wild, they really went wild.

Good thing he'd been waiting such a long time for her.

"What's so funny, Ryder?" she asked, still breathless.

"Not laughing. Just enjoying." He nipped at her throat, felt her inner muscles clutch around him again. "Mm."

He was far too old to be so easily aroused, but his body twitched in anticipation.

"Are you all right, baby?" He licked the spot he'd just bitten, felt her shiver.

"Hm." Her fingers slid higher, into the wet hair at his nape.

He groaned, then took a slow breath, levering himself up onto his elbows. "Are you dying of thirst?"

She shook her head, green eyes fluttering open. "Not yet." Her fingers slipped along his shoulders, lower, to his biceps.

His cock was back at full attention already, so when he eased his hips away a little, he had to stifle a wince. Her body was so wet and hot around him, he really did think he might want to stay there forever.

So he shoved inside, hard, making her gasp. He let his gaze drop to her breasts, still flushed from her last few orgasms, the tips tight and dark.

"Shoulda got the nipple clamps, too," he teased, bending to pull one of the taut buds into his mouth and sucked, hard.

Her shoulder came up off the bed so he could have more of her pliant flesh.

He smiled as he released it, loving her whimper of protest. "I'll be right back." He groaned as he withdrew, fully this time. He eased away, until his foot hit the floor, then pushed himself upright. He found the items he wanted in the first bag, then turned back to the bed, where Mena lay as he'd left her, sprawled over the dark green comforter, her inky curls spread around her head, glinting in the light, wet around her face. Her thighs remained parted, her sex exposed to his gaze. Wet folds flushed with her release, slick with it. His mouth watered.

He'd get there eventually.

"Roll over, Mena." He brushed the arch of her foot with one fingertip.

She opened her eyes, then they opened wider when she saw what was in his hand.

He waited.

She licked her lower lip, her gaze shifting from his hand to his face. And she rolled, slowly, until she lay face down.

He smiled. Even her back was slick with perspiration where she'd been sandwiched between him and the blanket.

He stroked the back of her leg, noting the tiny shift of her hips. His cock stuck straight out, knowing where it wanted to be.

He ignored it for now. Instead, he clambered onto the bed at her side. He set down his toys and used both hands to scoop her hair away from her shoulders, her nape. Perhaps he should have let her deal with it already.

That would have meant waiting for this. Not happening.

When he had it situated so it wasn't too much in his way, he flipped the top on the tube of massage oil and squirted some into his palm. It smelled of cinnamon. Spicy. And warm on his skin. He grinned as he rubbed his hands together and set them on her shoulders.

"Oh." She jolted as the oil heated her skin.

"Okay?"

"Mm-hm." She settled again.

He stroked over the soft skin of her shoulders, her back, her upper arms, leaving a warm trail everywhere he touched. His hands tingled with it. He squirted more directly onto her skin and heard her gasp. He watched it pool in the shallow dip at the small of her back, then slid his hands into it, spreading it over her skin, along her sides so his fingers grazed her swollen breasts, down over the curves of her ass. Everywhere he touched, her skin turned pink after a few moments as the heat warmed her. He kneaded gently, feeling the few tense muscles in her shoulders relax under his massage. Her hips shifted against the blanket, and he slid his fingers lower on the next pass, over her ass, between her thighs. She parted them for him, then sucked in a sharp breath when his slick fingers skimmed over sensitive flesh.

"Gods, it's hot."

Exactly the idea. He found her swollen clit and rubbed over and over and around it with his oiled fingers, until she was trembling beneath him again, her hips rocking.

"Not without me, honey," he murmured, nipping at her ass.

She tasted good.

So he bent back to the same spot and licked her. Warm cinnamon spice on his tongue made him imagine how other parts of her were going to taste now.

Just thinking about it made his dick harder.

He took a deep breath, trying to push that thought out of his head for a while longer, then returned to massaging her, occasionally slipping his hands beneath her to cup her breasts.

When he rolled her to her back finally, her breath came quickly, and the scent of her arousal mingled with the spice. Ryder put some more oil on her belly, then swept it higher with his hands, all over her breasts. The tips were tight, oh, so tight. He had to taste one after teasing it with the oil, to suckle it, hard. Mena cried out then, her hips lifting off the bed. Her skin flushed even more, with a release that had tiny shivers rushing over her.

Ryder had to take several steadying breaths to resist the need coursing through him now. "Soon, baby," he rasped. "Soon." He counted to ten. Twenty. Thirty. Finally, at forty, he felt like he had a better grip on his control.

He dipped his fingers in the tiny pool of oil left in her navel, then slid them down, down, through the crisp black curls, lower, into her wetness. Her hips lifted into his touch, pushing his fingers inside her.

"Oh, Gods," she whispered, her head shifting on the blanket as her hips rocked into his thrusts. "Ryder."

"Right here, Mena. You should see how pretty you are." His gaze was fixed on the flushed wet folds he'd slid his fingers into. Her swollen clit gleamed with the oil he'd rubbed on it, tempting him. Teasing.

He bent nearer, needing just one taste. He licked her clit as he curled his fingers inside her, stroking over a spot that made her cry out again, body arching hard.

She tasted so good. He sucked on the tender bit of flesh, feeling her pussy clamp on his fingers.

His cock ached with the need.

Ryder licked his way all around her clit, his breath coming faster.

"Please, Ryder," she whimpered, her thighs trembling on either side of him. "Oh Gods, please."

He shut his eyes. He couldn't resist her begging, not when his body already demanded the same thing.

He took a shaky breath and slid his fingers free of her enticing heat, replacing them with the head of his cock.

Spasms still shook her, making her sheath tight, oh, Christ, so tight, as he tried to ease inside her.

"Ryder!" She lifted toward him, her hips slick when he tried to grasp them to slow her down. The movement forced him into resistant muscles another few inches.

"Easy, baby." He gritted his teeth.

"It's so hot."

"I know." He bent to kiss her, lightly, knowing the cinnamon oil was on his lips.

"Mm." She licked her lower lip when he lifted his head.

"That's how you taste." He smiled when she opened her eyes. "Spicy and hot."

A tiny smile curved her lips. "Your fault."

He eased a little farther into her heat now that she'd relaxed a bit. His cock was ready to go off, his balls tight up against his body. "I won't last," he warned her, sliding further. *Almost there.*

"I didn't wait," she pointed out with another smile, the tip of her tongue sliding along her lower lip again.

He groaned, closing his eyes for a second. "I know. I didn't mean for you to wait, honey." He finally settled all the way to the root. *At last.* "Gods." He leaned down to kiss her, bracing himself on his hands beside her shoulders. "You are amazing."

"So are you." She wrapped her legs around his waist, and he gained another fraction of an inch. "Oh Gods, it's hot." Her eyes shut and her head dropped back, exposing the pale column of her throat.

He set his mouth on it, sliding, open over damp skin, tasting salt and woman. Cinnamon.

He smiled, hungry for more.

"Don't wait, Ryder," she breathed, her fingers digging

into his shoulders. Already, her sheath clenched on his cock, and he hadn't even started to move.

Ryder let her have her way, withdrawing just a little before pushing back in, hard. Over and over, until her startled scream hit his ears, and his own release exploded.

This time when he collapsed, he rolled to his side, pulling her with him.

"I love you, Mena," he breathed against the top of her head when he could speak.

Good thing she was asleep, he mused, stroking his hand down her damp spine. If he'd said it when she could hear, she'd likely run right out the door, forgetting about the danger waiting.

No, that was one thing he couldn't say to her. Not yet. Probably not for a long time.

He kissed her cheek. But one day...

One day, he was going to tell her exactly how he felt.

Maybe he should have bought the fur-lined handcuffs, too, to make sure she stayed put when he *did* tell her.

CHAPTER EIGHT

Philomena leaned against the shower wall, exhausted. Panting. Aroused.

Having Ryder around to keep her safe was quite possibly more dangerous to her health than the Harvesters. He was going to kill her with pleasure.

His big body pressed tight to hers from behind this time, the hot water beating on them, though he shielded her from most of it. His erection throbbed inside her, and he showed no sign of giving up the iron grip he held on his self-control.

They'd had to shower twice to get all the edible oil off of themselves, laughing and teasing the first time, and then not so teasing the second. His strong hands left soapy trails all over her, slowly, purposefully.

Now the oil was long gone, but Ryder had taken her against the wall again, after setting his mouth on her sex, his wicked tongue leaving her breathless and shaking just before he rose and slid deep.

On the other hand, her hormones hadn't stopped doing a happy dance, ever-more-heated desire racing through her veins every time he looked at her with his melted-chocolate gaze. Or when one of his long fingers skimmed over her skin.

She'd much rather die like this than at the hands of the Harvesters.

Ryder began moving, his breathing raspy and irregular now as he withdrew, then shoved deep.

Philomena braced herself on the cool, wet tiles, her tight nipples drawing tighter when the tip of his cock rasped over a spot deep inside her to set off a mini-climax.

"Come again, Mena," he ordered roughly.

To help her obey his order, he wedged one hand between her belly and the wall and set his thumb over her clit, pressing hard.

Stars exploded behind her closed eyelids, and her breathing stopped for an eon.

He moved faster, harder, grunting with his own explosive release moments later.

"Jesus," he breathed, the word puffing out against the side of her face.

Philomena managed to lift one hand to touch his cheek, patting it gently.

"You're going to kill me," he teased, nipping at her earlobe.

Another rush of heat slid along her veins.

"That's another reason I keep a collection of toys."

"No need for toys when I'm able and more than willing," he growled, scraping the edge of his teeth along the sensitive skin just below her ear.

She huffed out a laugh and turned her face far enough to kiss him. It was the gentlest kiss they'd shared in hours, she realized.

Ryder winced as he eased his hips backward, slipping his semi-hard cock out of her.

She turned to face him fully, putting her face on his shoulder when he gathered her close.

"Tired, baby?"

She nodded. "But I need to deal with my hair before I sleep." If she didn't, he wouldn't be safe in the morning. Pleasure wasn't the only thing in her belly now. The first painful twinges signaled the onset of her period in a few more hours.

He hummed his understanding and reached out to shut the water off.

Philomena watched him grab two towels, wrapping one low around his lean waist, and her gaze dropped to the tight muscles just above the towel.

He held out the second towel to her, and she stepped into it, letting him dry her off. He even toweled her hair so it no longer dripped down her torso.

"Thank you, Ryder." She touched his forearm when he would have turned away with the towel.

His smile was gentle. "No problem." He tossed the towel onto the hook. "Let's get you combed out." He caught her hand and tugged her out of the steamy bathroom.

Her chest ached, watching him rummage through the things on the dresser to find her comb and the elastic bands he'd made her forget about earlier. He was being awfully understanding.

She pulled an oversized shirt from the small mound of clothing in her suitcase and tugged it on over her head, then held out her hand for the comb which Ryder now held.

"Sit."

She blinked.

"Sit. I want to do it."

Her eyes stung. Damned hormones. She blinked harder,

but her vision remained blurry. She sat on the foot of the rumpled bed rather than argue.

Ryder climbed behind her and began easing the comb through her tangled, wet curls. He was careful when he found knots, using his fingers to loosen them before sliding the comb through again.

Philomena shut her eyes at the burn there. This was bad. Very, very bad.

She hadn't meant to get so involved with him. Not like *this*. He was Jason's father, so there had to be some relationship, though she'd done her very best to keep it long-distance before now.

But this...this was something else entirely, and it had nothing to do with Jason. It had a little to do with the fact that a bunch of murderers were after her.

Mostly it had to do with some serious chemistry.

She tried to think of the last time she'd slept with a man she'd dated.

Tried harder.

"Okay." His hands settled on her shoulders. "I think you're knot-free now."

Philomena swallowed. "Thank you." She opened her eyes and turned to look at him over her shoulder.

He leaned in to brush a kiss on her mouth. "Go ahead."

She inhaled unsteadily and took the comb from him, shifting so she could see the mirror over the dresser. She parted the hair on top of her head. "Can you get the back?" She wasn't sure why she asked. Usually she just did it. It didn't matter if it was parted straight, as long as she got it all braided.

His eyes lit with his smile as he took the comb. "Sure."

Another squeeze in her chest. This was so, so bad. She

shut her eyes and steeled herself as his warm fingers slid through her wet hair, comb following.

"There you go."

"Thanks." Really, she could have done it herself. She should have. She did it at home every month. But he was sitting there watching her with a dangerous swirl of emotion in his dark eyes, heat and caring, making her wish for things she'd ceased wishing for after she'd become the Medusa. Things she'd given up hoping for long before then, if she were honest.

She stopped that train of thought dead in its tracks. Far too dangerous. And impossible.

Instead, she turned her entire focus to the intricate braiding of her hair. She started with the left side, with small sections at the front, working her way to the back and adding more sections in as she went until the side was finished. She took the elastic band Ryder held out and securely fastened the braid, then moved to the other side.

When she'd finished, she didn't feel the usual satisfaction the task brought. Just nervousness. No one had seen her during her period since she'd become the Medusa. Not even her mother. It was safest for everybody.

Now she had no choice but to trust Ryder to keep her safe for the next three days.

He still sat behind her on the bed, his dark gaze watchful, and she swallowed back some of the fear.

He'd already saved her from the Harvesters three times. He would continue to keep her safe.

But why?

She frowned at the question. He'd told her why. She pushed to her feet and set the comb on the dresser with the extra ponytail bands.

"Stop worrying so much," he said from behind her.

Philomena forced a little smile for him as she turned around. "Easier said than done."

He held out one hand to her. "You should get some rest."

She studied his hand, the long, strong fingers, wide palm. He had a tiny scar across the base of his palm, and another on the side of his thumb. She wondered how he'd gotten them. Then she thought of the way he'd touched her with those fingers earlier, and her blood heated again.

At least this time, she could blame it on her cursed hormones.

She slid her hand over his, feeling the warmth bloom in her belly. "I'm not quite ready to sleep yet," she said, surprised by how husky her voice sounded.

His fingers wrapped around hers, and she noticed his towel tented out in a hurry. "Really?"

She gave him a little push backward with her free hand, and he let her, not protesting when she climbed astraddle him and tugged the end of the towel free at his waist, exposing that gorgeous erection to her hungry gaze.

"Mena?"

"Sh." She curled her free hand around his cock, sliding up to the tip, then slowly down to the base, giving it a squeeze as she went.

He groaned. "You're going to be very sore tomorrow, baby."

"It doesn't matter." Whether she did this or not, she'd be in plenty of pain tomorrow. She rather thought she wanted the pleasure first. She shifted on her knees so she hovered over the tip of him. Without sliding her fingers between her thighs, she knew she was wet enough to take all of him. She sank down slowly, though, drawing it out as long as she could.

He released her fingers and caught her hips. "Gods, Mena. You feel amazing."

"Will *you* be too sore tomorrow?" she teased.

His dark eyes crinkled at the corners with his wicked grin. "I think I can take anything you dish out, honey."

"Good." She braced herself on his chest, lifting her hips before she let him guide her down. Over and over, slowly. Then it was too slow to suit her, and her hips rocked faster.

Ryder let her have her way, shouting with his release when she collapsed over him, boneless and breathless.

And she was very afraid she wasn't nearly finished with him.

Ryder's fingers clenched into fists the next day when Mena moaned softly in her sleep. She lay curled in a ball in the bed, wrapped around the heating pad, the satin blindfold both blocking out the daylight for her and keeping him from looking her in the eyes and turning to stone.

He kneaded the tight muscles at the back of his neck, wishing he could do something else for her. Anything. Being this powerless sucked.

It sucked as much as when Jason had been a baby and teething, miserable and unable to understand why, or when he was slightly older and sick with the chicken pox which had happened to strike during Ryder's three-day weekend leave visit, and Mena's period, and his son had cried for her the entire time. Ryder felt absolutely awful when he had to leave to go back to his base, but Aggie assured him Mena would be home that night. And she had been.

Both of those times, he'd been unable to help his son, to

make him feel better. All he'd been able to do was hold him and get his meds into him.

He could do it for Mena, too, and more later. She'd told him in the wee hours that by late morning, she'd be more than ready to hit the shower to try to ease the cramping-- with one of the vibrators they'd chosen last night. He would take care of her.

If she could trust herself, he could do more.

He paced into the sitting room, not wanting to disturb her already restless sleep.

During his discussions with Kallan and Andrea, both at Aggie's and since then, via phone and email, he'd heard their story, parts of it more than once. The part that mattered most to him right now was the potential ending of the curse for Mena. Andrea had fallen in love with Kallan, and once she fully believed in their love and in him, the curse had broken for her.

He thought the same thing could happen for Mena, if she'd trust herself.

He didn't think it was him she didn't trust. He was posi-tive it was herself. All those guys she'd dated who were temporary companions, she hadn't trusted them, and rightly so. But she'd chosen men she wouldn't have to trust fully. She didn't want a real relationship with them. With anyone.

He wasn't sure she did now, either, but he wasn't going anywhere. Not now, not later.

When he heard her moan again, he turned and stuck his head into the bedroom. He found her trying to sit up, the heating pad discarded among the tangle of blankets, one arm braced across her belly and strain bracketing her mouth.

He turned off the heating pad, touching her knee so she knew he was there. "You okay?"

"I need to get to the bathroom."

He caught her hand and eased her to her feet, feeling her sway. "Easy." He slid his arm around her and guided her to the other room. "I'll be right outside." He released her and pulled the door shut behind him to give her a bit of privacy. And so he could grab the waterproof vibrator.

When he heard the sink running a few minutes later, he tapped at the door. "Incoming."

She'd just replaced the mask when he stepped inside, her hands dropping from the sides of her face.

"Shower time?"

She nodded. "Do you mind?"

"You don't need to ask me that," he said, hearing the sharp edge in his tone. He took in a slow breath. "Sorry. I just don't like feeling so helpless."

A ghost of a smile--a grim smile--touched her mouth. "This is my life, Ryder."

He knew and hated it. "Hang on, let's get the water running first." He moved around her to the shower, testing the water to make sure it wasn't too hot.

"When you think it's too hot, make it hotter," she said from behind him, her tone ragged.

Steam rose around him already. Ryder swallowed and turned up the heat a bit more. "Okay." He returned to where she'd braced herself on the vanity and lifted her over-sized t-shirt off, noting the way her mouth flattened in pain when she straightened. "Easy," he breathed, wrapping one arm around her waist to help her the short distance to the shower.

When she stepped in, she shivered. "Not hot enough."

He winced as he readjusted the temperature. Every place the water hit her skin, color bloomed, and she let out a shaky breath, her head dropping back.

Ryder clenched his jaw as she stood there, her white knuckles gradually relaxing on the tile wall. Her mouth was still set, though, and the muscles of her abdomen quivered with tension.

"Will you hand me the vibrator?" she asked at last, her voice tight.

He grabbed it from the sink and returned to her side. "How about I help with this part, baby?"

"Don't be gentle, Ryder. I need this hard," she whispered.

His body tightened in a flash, even though he knew he was keeping his pants on. He knelt beside the open shower and flipped the toy on low.

She braced her feet apart, turning slightly to lean against the wall.

He swallowed hard as he eased the toy between her quivering thighs.

"Just do it, Ryder," she ground out, rocking her hips toward his hand.

He slipped the toy inside her, feeling her body's resistance. "You're not ready," he got out through his clenched teeth.

"It doesn't matter." She set her hand over his and shoved the vibe deeper, a soft sound escaping her when it was wedged fully inside her. "Turn it up."

He obeyed, then let her withdraw the vibrator partway before slamming it deep again. He took over, maintaining her punishing pace.

Her skin flushed now, not just from the scalding water, but from the release building in her. Her hips met each thrust of the toy, and when he turned the speed to the highest setting, a startled cry passed her lips, echoing around the steamy room. Her body bowed toward his hand, trembling wildly, her breathing ragged.

She was the most beautiful thing he'd ever seen.

He eased the toy's speed down, then off, slipping it from her shaking body. He blindly dropped it into the sink behind him. "Better?" he managed.

She nodded, sagging against the wall, her cheeks flushed with pleasure, the color all the way to the tight peaks of her breasts.

His mouth watered. Instead of touching, however, he pulled a dry towel from the rack and turned off the water, helping her out and drying her off. When she was no longer damp, he pulled the sleep shirt over her head to cover her. "I'll be right back," he murmured, and stepped out of the bathroom. He leaned on the closed door, his heart pumping madly, his cock aching.

When she tapped the door, he inhaled deeply and straightened. "Back to bed, or are you ready for some food?" he asked, grateful his voice came out sounding pretty normal as he opened the door.

"I should eat, I guess, before I crawl back in bed." Bright color still tinted her cheeks. "Thank you, Ryder," she added, catching one corner of her lower lip in her teeth.

He smiled even though she couldn't see it. "Anytime, baby." He put his arm around her and led her to the sitting room. "I'll get breakfast." He settled her on the sofa with a blanket and called room service. "Fifteen minutes. Can you last that long?" he asked when he sat beside her.

She nodded. "I'm sorry about this."

"It isn't your fault, Mena." He caught her hand and lifted it to his mouth, brushing a kiss on her knuckles.

"You're right. It's the original Medusa's." A faint smile touched her lips.

"Has anyone ever considered begging Athena's forgiveness?" he teased.

"Actually, yes."

He frowned. "Really?"

"A long time ago, but yes, according to family legend." She linked her fingers through his, then sighed softly as she shifted in her seat. "Athena apparently wasn't willing to forgive and forget."

"So this is forever? Generations not even born yet?"

She nodded. "She's a vicious, grudge-holding bitch, evidently."

He laughed.

Mena shifted, her mouth twisting a little.

"Already?"

"Not nearly as bad," she said, her free hand rubbing her belly through the blanket.

He scowled. The relief hadn't lasted long. "Let me." He moved to sit behind her, then slid both hands beneath the blanket to lightly massage her taut abdomen. The muscles there already tightened under his fingers. Her breathing was slow, measured. Deliberate. He slipped one hand around to her back, and rubbed there, too.

Mena rested her head on his shoulder. "Your fingers feel good."

So did her ass in his lap, though he didn't mention that right now. She had her hands braced on his thighs, and there was enough space between them so his erection didn't press against her.

Ryder concentrated on evening out his own breathing. "How would you feel about a pain pill after breakfast?"

Her head turned a little toward him. "I've got aspirin."

"The prescription we got yesterday is for you, baby." He

kissed her cheekbone. "It should help with these cramps so you can rest a while."

She was silent for a long time, and with her eyes hidden behind the blindfold, he couldn't tell what she was thinking. "That was very sweet of you," she said at last, one corner of her mouth tipping up.

Sweet. Great. He was sweet.

Ryder smiled. It was a start.

Philomena woke up warm. And not in as much pain as she should be feeling. She touched the mask over her eyes, then released a slow breath.

Ryder lay wrapped around her, his chest her pillow, and one of his strong legs between her knees, his breathing deep and even. Sleeping.

She smiled, then realized the pain pill he'd given her after feeding her scrambled eggs and toast still dulled the pain of her cramps.

Thank all the Gods!

She relaxed, wondering how long she'd been asleep. Lying here in the dark, she couldn't tell. Her stomach gurgled. Long enough to be ready for another meal, but not long enough for the pill to have worn off yet.

One of his hands slid up to her nape, warming her even more. "Are you okay?" he asked huskily.

She nodded. "Better." She might even be able to forego the shower and vibrator this go-round. That had never happened before. "Tell me what's going on."

"Where?"

"At home. With the Harvesters." She shrugged. "I just want to know."

He sighed. "Joel said the guy he's been tracking has headed to Virginia. Apparently there's a big meet-up of Harvesters he's going to."

"Virginia?" She frowned behind her mask, trying to concentrate on this new puzzle.

"One of Aristotle Tassos's homes. Joel is going to stick with his guy and see what he can find out there. I'm just happy they're heading south and not north." His fingers stroked her nape lightly.

"So Kallan's great-uncle is still alive?"

"Ari? Yes."

She worried her lip in her teeth. "*One* of his homes?"

"He's apparently not trusting enough to stay in one place for long, I'm afraid. Even before Kallan went rogue, Aristotle Tassos didn't ever call one place home for extended periods, though the Virginia estate is probably as close as he's got."

Philomena sighed. Her brain just didn't want to function on a subject so intricate. Probably a side effect from the pain pill.

"How're your cramps?" His other hand slid to her belly, grazing it through her sleep shirt.

"Not as bad as they should be."

"Good." He sounded like he was smiling. "How about some lunch?"

"Soup might be good."

"I'll see what I can rustle up." He kissed her lightly and rolled away. "Stay put."

Philomena stayed there, warm in the cocoon of blankets, his body heat surrounding her, as well as his scent. She inhaled deeply. She thought she'd know Ryder anywhere if she could just smell him. A smile tugged at her lips at the silly idea. But the spicy, masculine scent of him filled her lungs, her head, as she took another deep breath.

"Chicken noodle okay, honey?" he called from the next room.

"Fine." She rubbed her belly when a stronger cramp seized her belly. It was still dulled by the painkiller, but that was beginning to wear off.

Ryder's weight pressed into the mattress beside her. "You're rubbing your stomach again." He set his hand over hers, the blanket between them. "As soon as you have your soup, you can have another pill."

"How long did I sleep?"

"Four hours. About as long as the pill is good for." He stretched out beside her, stroking over the top of her head. "Which means you'll get another nap, then be awake for supper and the call to Jason, before you get back to bed."

Philomena considered his plan. "I appreciate all this, Ryder," she said finally.

"Stop." He kissed her forehead. "Like it or not, my Mena, you're family. I take care of what's mine."

Equal measures of panic and warmth bloomed in her chest. *His.* She wasn't sure she liked that.

Yet another part of her really did like the notion. That she might be able to relax her guard occasionally and know someone else was watching out for her.

She frowned. Too risky.

Jason's dad. Desi's ex-lover.

Somehow, that argument didn't have quite the same effect it had previously.

Before *Philomena* had become Ryder's lover.

She swallowed, more panic welling up. How on earth had she let this happen? She couldn't trust him to stick around. Her father hadn't.

"You're thinking too hard again, smart girl," he said softly, his warm breath sliding over her scalp. His fingers at her nape massaged the tight muscles there.

"I'm fine."

He laughed, just as there was a knock on the door to the outer room. "Liar." He rolled out of bed. "I'll be back with lunch."

She rubbed her hand harder over her cramping belly and tried to concentrate on the pain, rather than the tangled knot of emotion trying to clog her throat. Her brain wasn't functional enough to deal with it right now.

"Uh-oh." She heard him set a tray on the dresser, and then his weight depressed the mattress beside her. "Bad?" His fingers stilled her frantic rubbing.

"Not as bad as it could be." Let him believe it was just the cramps. He didn't need to know the effect he was having on her emotions. Not when she knew this could only be temporary.

"I don't think I believe that." He drifted a kiss along her cheek. "Can you sit up?" He helped her, then stuffed pillows behind her. "All right. Lunch, then another pill." He moved away, then returned, and she smelled the soup.

It smelled good. Like her mom's.

Her eyes stung behind the mask.

"Open." The enticing aroma got closer, and she opened her mouth so he could spoon the soup into her.

Hot tears spilled over beneath the blindfold, and she swallowed hard. The lump in her throat would choke her while she ate her lunch.

"Hey, what's this?" He touched her wet cheek. "Mena?"

She shook her head. "Stupid hormones. It smells like Mom's soup." She swiped at her other cheek. She didn't think anyone would fault her for one small untruth. It did smell like her mom's, he just didn't need to know that wasn't the whole reason she was crying.

"Ah, baby." He kissed her, gently. "Don't cry."

"I'm fine. As fine as I can be." She lifted one shoulder half-heartedly.

Ryder sighed, and she tried to imagine his expression. Would he be frustrated at not being able to solve the problem, or would he doubt her words? He was so over-confident, frustration was a given. He exhaled again, then the spoon clinked against the bowl. "Open for me, honey."

Philomena let him feed her, feeling more tears slip down her face. She didn't try to wipe them away, not wanting to draw any more attention to them.

Finally, he set the bowl aside, and the pill bottle rattled.

"I need to go to the bathroom first," she said, sniffling.

"Okay." He set the bottle aside, then flipped the blankets off of her, catching her hand to guide her to the other room. "I'll be right here." He pulled the door shut, and she flipped the mask up, blinking in the bright light of the bathroom.

She wiped both hands over her cheeks, annoyed at herself, then moved in front of the mirror. She looked a fright, her face pale and pinched, though the tip of her nose was pink from crying, and her eyes were a little swollen. She grabbed a tissue to blow her nose, then took care of other business, like brushing her teeth. Her belly twisted painfully, and she ground her teeth against the moan trying to escape, gripping the edge of the vanity until the pain eased slightly.

She reached for the mask, then paused. The vibrator lay on the vanity, the tube of cleaner beside it. More tears welled up. She was being stupid. Damned hormones made her overreact to all kinds of things, but this was the dumbest thing ever. Of course he would have cleaned the toy after they'd finished with it. He was an adult.

She sniffed again, her eyes burning as two more fat tears slid down her face, hot against her skin. She swiped them away, then tugged the mask back into place, willing herself to keep the rest of the threatening tears at bay until she was in bed. Preferably alone.

She tapped on the door, and Ryder opened it. He took her hand, silently led her to the bed, then handed her a pill and a glass of juice. She took them and let him settle her beneath the blankets with the heating pad tucked against her aching belly.

"I'll be in the next room, baby," he murmured, his mouth sliding over her forehead, then her mouth, "if you need anything."

Gods, please go, she thought, the tears still scalding her eyes. She nodded once, biting her lip in an effort to keep the tears from spilling over.

Just a little longer.

Finally, he got to his feet and padded out of the room.

She curled onto her side, away from the door, hugging the heating pad close and stifling her sobs in the pillow, which quickly grew wet under her cheek.

"Ah, baby," Ryder groaned as he stretched out behind her.

Her breath caught in her chest.

"It's all right." He wrapped his arm around her, sliding his other beneath her head. "Go ahead and cry. I'll be right here."

That only made her cry harder, and panic bubbled up. She wasn't going to be able to stop. Not with him holding her this way.

He petted her, his fingers brushing her forehead, her

wet cheeks. His strong body curved around hers as if he could absorb some of the pain.

Philomena cried until she couldn't cry anymore. Her entire body ached, not just her belly. Her eyes burned, her head throbbed, and her throat hurt from the ragged sobs she couldn't contain. When it finally ended, she lay there limply, her heart pounding in her ears, her breath coming in hiccups.

Ryder still held her.

If she'd had any tears left, she would've cried again at that. She simply didn't know what to do with him. She hadn't let herself imagine a man in her life since she was in high school. Not one who would stick around.

"Go to sleep, Mena," he whispered, settling her nearer. "It'll be all right. I promise."

She was very afraid it was a promise he couldn't keep.

CHAPTER NINE

Ryder almost felt like crying himself by the time Mena finally passed out from a combination of the painkiller and sheer exhaustion after her crying jag. He didn't know why she was crying. Only that the sound was so wrenching, it nearly broke his heart.

Somehow he didn't believe it was just hormones, either, though they probably amplified whatever the problem was.

When her breathing evened out at last, not even anymore tiny hiccups, he took a deep breath, willing his heartbeat to slow. If he could've done anything more to make her feel better, he would.

He wondered if she realized that.

He finally eased upright, tucking the blankets closer around her before he stood. Her dark braids remained intact, which was good for him--one on top of the blankets, the other sticking out from beneath her chin on the pillow. No sign of snakes. Her cheeks were pink and tear-stained, her lips slightly swollen, as was her nose.

He went to the bathroom for a washcloth. He soaked it under cool water and then returned to her side to clean her face, hoping he wouldn't disturb her. When he'd finished, he resisted the temptation to curl up behind her on the bed again and went out to the sitting room and started his laptop. He needed to see what was going on in the rest of their world.

He scowled at Joel's latest email from Virginia. "How do none of the listening devices work?" he muttered. Obviously, the Harvesters meeting inside the estate had something to scramble any signals for anybody outside trying to listen in on their conversations. But who did they think was spying on them?

It was an intriguing question. Kallan Tassos? Probably not, since he was only one man--one man intent on protecting his former Medusa.

He paced the sitting room for half an hour, unable to scrape together an answer. He fired off emails to Joel and Danny to see if they could come up with anything, then composed another email to Kallan, to see if he might be able to figure it out.

He stuck his head into the bedroom, only somewhat mollified to find Mena sound asleep. He did turn the heating pad down a little, though, figuring the pain pill should have kicked in and dulled her cramps so the heating pad didn't need to be on full bore.

Then he returned to the sitting room and his laptop. *Where to next?*

That would depend on the Harvesters.

Still, he did some searching for ideas. Away from D.C. and Virginia obviously. Away from Philly and New York. Pittsburgh? He stared at the Chamber of Commerce webpage for a few moments. March in Pittsburgh was iffy, weather-wise. But it wouldn't require them to provide identification to get on an airplane. And driving wouldn't create a record someone could hack into, the way a plane reservation would.

He saved the page, scanned through a few more, but couldn't decide. Not yet.

Ryder glanced at the time on his screen. Nearly suppertime. That meant another pill for Mena soon.

How was he going to get her through two more days of this? Already, the very first day, she'd cried herself to sleep, and he'd been unable to do anything about it.

He wondered if this was what full-time fathering would be like.

He hadn't sprung that one on Mena yet and didn't intend to do so while they were on the run--and definitely not while she was suffering this way.

Since he was out of the military and had quit working intelligence to partner with his buddies, he wanted to be with Jason all the time. He could do it now, making weekly or bi-weekly trips to the office if he had to. He'd already given the matter plenty of consideration, long before he realized the Harvesters were closing in on Mena's location. But being with Jason would also mean being with Aggie and Mena full-time.

A few years ago, if he'd made the same decision about his son, he would've arranged to live some place near his son's aunt and grandmother so they could remain in his life as much as they wanted.

Somewhere along the way, though, he'd decided he wanted Mena, too, long before he'd greeted her naked in her mother's bathroom. Sometime after he'd realized the way she'd put her own life aside to raise her sister's child, the way she chose men to date who would never be strong enough for her.

Philomena Gregory was his.

Ryder sighed, glancing at the open doorway to the bedroom. He didn't know yet how he was going to convince her of that. In the meantime, he had to satisfy himself with keeping her alive and out of reach of the Harvesters.

Philomena sat wedged into the corner of the sofa, listening to Ryder talking to Jason and holding the hot water bottle tight to her belly while she waited for the painkiller to kick in.

Her conversation with Jason had been short, as he'd been jumping around the kitchen wherever they were and playing with a dog.

She suspected Danny had simply taken them to his house. Jason was having so much fun with the dog, he could barely speak to her, which made her feel teary again. She'd told him she loved him and held the phone out to Ryder, who apparently had an easier time getting his son to pay attention to him. Hearing their conversation didn't make her feel any better.

She shut her eyes behind the mask and rested her head against the sofa. She was not going to cry in front of Ryder again.

When he finished his conversation, his weight depressed the cushion beside her just before his hand landed on her knee. "How are you feeling?"

"Fine."

He chuckled. "I know that's a fat lie, Philomena."

She sighed. "I'm ready for bed."

His fingers tightened on her leg. "Already?"

"Yes." She ignored the stinging in her eyes.

"How about if you stay here with me for a little while?"

He shifted beside her, releasing her knee to slide his arm around her shoulders.

"I'd rather lie down. I'm tired." She hoped that didn't sound as whiny to him as it did to her.

He slid her onto his lap, careful not to dislodge the blanket tucked all around her. "How's that pill doing?"

Obviously, he wasn't buying it. "It's getting there." She bit her lip to distract herself from the ache in her chest.

She felt his fingers on one of her braids, then at her nape. "But you're tired already?" His warm breath caressed the side of her face.

She nodded. The burning had spread into her throat now, where a lump swelled, clogging her airway.

"I wish you'd let me hold you for a while." He nuzzled her cheek, his face stubbled.

She squeezed her eyes shut tighter.

"Are you going to cry?" he asked, sounding suspiciously like he was smiling.

She shook her head.

"It's okay if you do." He rubbed her back gently.

"I just want to go to bed." It came out a choked whisper.

"Ah, baby." He'd clearly heard the tears in her voice and hugged her tighter against his chest. "All right." He got to his feet, keeping her in his arms. His stride was easy, and a moment later, he set her on the bed.

But he didn't leave, damn him.

No, Ryder's boots thumped to the floor and she heard the soft whoosh of his clothing following, then he climbed in with her.

Philomena swallowed around the lump in her throat. Then again. "I'll be fine, Ryder." It was louder than a whisper, but still hoarse.

He gathered her close, so she could feel the heat of him

through her nightshirt, even around the hot water bottle. "I know. And I'll be here until then." He settled behind her. "Relax." He swept his hand up and down her arm, then over her belly.

She felt the stupid tears sliding under the bottom and side of the mask again and let them go, her breath coming unevenly.

Ryder just held her tight, soothing her, wiping away her tears, and massaging her aching back until she fell asleep. Where she dreamed of him. Making love to her. Hard and fast, slow and teasing.

When she woke later, her belly cramped hard, and her pulse thrummed from the pleasure he'd given her in her dream.

The pleasure still to come.

And there was pleasure, even in the midst of this hellish period--while she propped herself on the wall of the shower and he filled her with the toy he'd chosen for her, teased her with it until she came hard, screaming his name.

ARISTOTLE GLARED AT HIS COMPUTER. NO SIGN OF THE monster since Gregos had lost her and the man four days ago.

The Goddess would be livid if She learned of this failure. He had let Elek deal with his nephews, choosing to remain silent while Elek gave them new instructions and sent them back to Philadelphia. He'd had no choice, because his anger made his heart race too fast. Too hard. So much that he'd required more than one of his pills simply to sit through the short meeting. He would show them no weakness.

No, the weak one had been his brother Iphis, and <u>he</u> was gone long ago, taking his shameful secrets with him.

He frowned at his wandering thoughts and dragged his attention to the email on his screen.

Ware's computer system was impenetrable so far, as were his office building, which also housed his apartment.

Aristotle shut his eyes and sank back in the chair. Even if he did not tell Her, Athena would know of this latest failure by Her Harvesters, and he didn't know how much longer Her patience with them would last. He feared not long. Goddess help them then.

When she woke two days later and carefully stretched, Ryder slept beside her. No more cramps.

Thank the Gods.

Philomena eased the blindfold off, blinking in the dim light from the lamp on the night table. Better.

Even better than the way she felt was the way Ryder looked. Her heartbeat quickened as her gaze slid over his face, surrounded by tousled blond hair, his cheeks stubbled--three days' worth, if she wasn't mistaken. One of his arms was beneath her neck, and the other held her close to him, keeping her warm.

She closed her eyes and inhaled. He smelled so good.

She frowned. He couldn't be hers. Or, rather, he wouldn't want to be hers. Not forever. No man would want that, to be saddled with a monster like her.

Easing away, she tiptoed into the bathroom to unbraid her hair, then into the shower. She stood for several minutes with her face turned to the hot spray, eyes closed as she deliberately cleared her mind and concentrated on how much better she felt than she had for days.

"Hey."

She opened her eyes in time to see Ryder stepping into the shower. "Hi." Her pulse quickened.

"How're you feeling?" He picked up the soap and started to lather his hands.

"Better." Her brain went immediately to places best left alone.

"Good." He gave her a lazy smile, then slid his slick hands over her, from shoulders to her arms, over her back, her belly. Her breasts tingled in anticipation, but he skipped them for now, his fingers slipping through the bubbles he'd tracked over her skin. "I'm glad to hear it." He slid one hand to cup her breast at last. "I think we're going to check out of here today." His thumb teased over her nipple, distracting her from his words. "Head west a little ways." He treated her other breast to the same teasing caresses, then turned her to face him, catching her mouth roughly. "Gods, I've missed you, Mena mine."

Against her belly, she felt the evidence of that. She wrapped her fingers around his erection and squeezed. She'd missed him, too, even if she didn't want to admit it. The vibrator wasn't the same.

He grunted appreciatively, then pinched both her nipples at the same time.

Lightning zinged into her middle, dampening her inner thighs in a completely different way.

"I don't want to wait," he murmured, sliding his mouth along her jaw to her earlobe. "Tell me I don't have to wait, Mena."

She shook her head, unable to catch enough breath to speak.

"Good." He released her breasts and caught her ass, lifting her against the cool, wet tiles. "I want your legs around my waist. Now."

As always, the command in his voice made her heart pound harder, made her body wetter, and she obeyed him, locking her ankles behind him so the wide head of his cock could nudge into wet folds. Deeper, so tight muscles had to relax to allow him entry. *Oh, dear Gods.* All the way in, until there was nothing between them. No breath, no space.

She forced her eyes open and found him watching her, his gaze predatory and hot.

"You feel amazing all around me," he whispered, rocking gently against her so the top of his shaft rubbed along her clit with each tiny stroke. "I won't last long."

"It's okay." She managed a lopsided smile at him, threading her fingers through his wet hair.

One of his hands left her ass to slide up and catch her breast. Cupping, squeezing gently, tugging at the aching peak. "I want you to come, too, baby." His guttural tone told her he was already close. As did the pulsing of his cock deep inside her.

The knowledge made her pulse skip, her body tighten in anticipation of the rushing pleasure. "I will." She tipped his chin up, kissing him this time. When his tongue slipped past her open lips, she let him take over, moaning when he thrust harder into her on the next stroke.

She couldn't believe how quickly he stirred this need in her. The heat was enticing, like she might be the moth to his flame, unable to resist flying into the fire that consumed her each time he touched her.

His hips moved faster, and his fingers on her nipple tightened possessively, teasing, tweaking, twisting until she arched hard, her inner muscles clamping onto his erection in release.

"Yes," he muttered against her mouth. "Come hard, baby. Let me all the way in." He stroked faster, deeper, harder, until all she could do was hold on, trusting him to keep her safe. When his own orgasm broke, his shout bounced off the tiles around them.

He rested his forehead on hers while they tried to catch their breath, his chest working hard against her breasts.

Philomena kissed him, lightly, over and over. On his mouth, his chin, his cheeks, the tip of his nose, his forehead. She felt more tiny spasms tighten her body around his, and her breath caught.

"This is going to kill me," she gasped.

He laughed, nuzzling his way along the side of her neck. "Wouldn't be a bad way to go, huh?" His fingers squeezed her ass tighter for a second, then relaxed. He let out a long, slow breath. "Wow." He opened his eyes and met hers. "Good morning."

She couldn't help the smile that answered him. "It is." She slipped her fingers through his wet hair and felt him shiver. "I'm starving."

He huffed another laugh. "Are you telling me to get off?"

Philomena blushed. "No."

"Good." He shifted his hips, making her aware his cock was thickening again inside her. "I'm not quite ready for breakfast yet. You?"

She swallowed at the intensity in his eyes. Shook her head.

"Good," he repeated, easing his hips backward until he slipped free of her body and dropping to his knees in front of her. "I have another breakfast in mind." He lifted one of her legs over his shoulder and licked along her slick outer lips, then delved inside, his thumbs holding her open for him.

Philomena's head dropped back against the tiles with a thump as her breath rushed out. She saw stars, both from the minor pain and the incredible pleasure coursing through her from his mouth on her flesh. He used his lips, his tongue, his teeth, teasing her to the brink, and then easing back, over and over, until she shook in his hands.

"Please, Ryder." She was almost there. Again.

He caught her clit in his lips, lifting his dark gaze to meet hers. Flicked his tongue over it, once, making her jump, twice, making her gasp. Then scraped his teeth over it. She arched into his mouth, covering her own with both hands to keep in the scream as she came.

Wave after wave of pleasure bloomed in her middle, spreading outward until even her fingers and toes were tingling and numb.

Then Ryder got to his feet and turned her around, his cock sliding along the cleft of her bottom until he took himself in hand and bent his knees to drive up into her once more.

Philomena tried to hold onto the slippery tiles, but couldn't find any grip.

He was demanding this time, even more than the last. His hips worked hard, each thrust deeper than the last, harder, until she thought he must be permanently a part of her. His rough hands at her hip and breast stoked the need in her until all she could think of was him. Inside her. Around her.

He stopped moving suddenly, his breath coming hard.

She sucked in a quick breath, opening her eyes.

"I love you, Philomena," he said clearly.

She shot a startled glance back over her shoulder at him, but he'd started moving again, and she had to scrabble to keep her feet under her now, his thrusts punishing. Her body imploded after a few more moments, and he groaned with his own release, one of his big hands settling flat over her belly.

She panted into the wall for a long time, his body surrounding hers, his warmth seeping into her when the cooler water would have chilled her. Her heart wouldn't stop racing, and her decimated brain started to reform itself.

Ryder kissed the side of her face, then eased his hips backward, a soft sound of protest brushing her ear when he withdrew his semi-hard cock from her body.

She murmured her own protest, but he turned her around and caught her mouth with his, gently this time. She set her hands on his shoulders and hoped her knees would continue to hold her.

After a long moment, he lifted his head. "Let's get some breakfast and get out of here," he said, tilting his head toward the door.

She nodded, her pulse still moving too quickly.

If he'd meant what he said, she was in a lot more trouble than she'd realized.

Ryder wasn't a man to say things he didn't mean.

Her mouth went dry as they climbed out of the shower. What the hell was she supposed to do now?

RYDER DIDN'T PUSH HER TO TALK AS THEY PACKED their things. Just helped her fit everything into her suitcase around the small metal box in the bottom, then loaded it all into the car. Steered her into the hotel's dining room for the breakfast buffet after checking out.

Mena remained silent as she ate.

At least she was eating. He studied her over the small table. She had dark smudges under her eyes from not enough sleep the past few days, and worry lines on her forehead, no doubt from his declaration in the shower.

He wouldn't take it back.

No, he decided as he finished his orange juice, he wouldn't take it back. She needed to know it was more for him than just the serious chemistry they shared in and out of bed. It had started a long time ago, during conversations and emails about his son, in the way his son felt about her, and it blossomed the more time he spent with her. There was no controlling emotion like that. Not the way he could plan for most things.

She could spout any nonsense she wanted about not wanting a relationship, or about not wanting a relationship with her sister's ex, but he was here to stay. Period.

He smiled at her when she peeked at him over her teacup. A tentative smile curved her lips, and he relaxed. Just a little.

"How do you feel about shopping?" he asked, setting down his glass.

Her eyebrows rose. "Shopping?"

"Our next destination involves some shopping." He winked at her and snagged the last piece of his toast.

"Oh." She narrowed her gaze at him. "I thought we didn't want to do big east coast cities," she murmured after a moment, leaning nearer.

"We're not going to New York." He grinned.

"Oh." She frowned now. "Give me a hint."

"That was your hint." He leaned over and kissed her lightly. "I'll tell you when we're on the road."

Mena nodded, setting her fork down. "All right. I'm done."

Ryder laughed. "Impatient, are we?"

She shrugged, her expression easing. "I feel like I need to move."

He nodded, understanding. Running for one's life wasn't a lot of fun, and even when in a secure spot, it often felt unsafe. "All right, baby." He pushed to his feet. "Then let's hit the road." He held out one hand to her, gratified when she took it.

Ryder didn't fully relax, though, until they were on their way. There wasn't a direct route from Niagara, but that was all right. It wasn't as if they had a deadline, and a twisting route would make it easier to spot anyone following them-- though there was no way any Harvester could know where they were. Even Kallan had told Ryder not to share their location with him while they were emailing about possible reasons for the anti-listening devices at Ari's Virginia home.

They meandered south through New York state near the lakes and into Pennsylvania's northern reaches, winding through the hills. A snow squall hit while they were heading west, but it didn't last. Mena relaxed as they drove, too, her bright gaze flitting over the landscape around them. When he finally hit the turnpike north of Pittsburgh and headed south, she gave him a quizzical glance, but he shrugged innocently.

She rolled her eyes and started to pay attention to the signs along the road.

"Monroeville?" she asked with a laugh after a while. "That's your idea of shopping?"

He winked at her. "It's got a big mall."

"You're such a guy."

He felt a burst of warmth in his chest at the affection in her voice. It might not be love, but it was something.

Right now, he'd take what he could get.

They settled into a hotel not far off the highway, less than a mile from the mall, and he arranged for the rental car company to pick up the car at the hotel. He'd get another. If anyone tried to track his car rentals, it would be harder to do with multiple companies and under different names.

He shut off his phone and turned to find Mena stretched out on the bed, her chin propped on her hands as she watched him.

He ignored the way his body heated under her green gaze. "You ready for supper?"

"I suppose we should eat. Then call Jase." Her gaze stayed on him.

"What's going through that mind of yours, smart girl?" he asked, dropping the phone onto the dresser and setting his hands on his hips.

"This running around thing doesn't seem to faze you at all." She tilted her head to one side, a tiny frown creasing her brow.

Ryder relaxed a little. "There was always a lot of running in my previous jobs, usually from men with big guns." Among other things.

Mena didn't seem mollified by his answer.

He moved toward her, nudging her aside to stretch out beside her. "What else are you thinking?"

"I'm just trying to figure this out." She turned her head to look at him. "I'd have imagined you would rather stay and fight than run."

His heart beat faster, and he was afraid he knew where

this was heading. He'd wondered if she'd get there, and it seemed she had. Already. "There's a time for fighting, and there's a time to run," he said slowly. "Knowing which is which can be difficult sometimes."

"I'd rather go back and fight. This is my life, and they're screwing it up."

He knew it. Stifling a sigh, he shut his eyes for a second, then met her gaze. "And you can't risk it. You have people who depend on you, who love you, and having you dead wouldn't help them out at all."

Her mouth twisted. "But my family is out of there now, safe. If we timed it right, I could turn whoever comes back into stone."

"And if they bring a small army? You can only look at one person at a time."

Her frown deepened. "You could slow them down for me, right?"

He didn't bother trying to stifle his sigh this time. "No. Because we're not going to go back and make you a sitting target for a family bent on killing you. Do you have any idea how many of them there are?"

She shook her head, her gaze going wary at his tone.

"Thousands. All over the globe." He watched her digest that. "Ken emailed to tell me there was another, smaller meeting in New York City right before they headed to Virginia. These men aren't playing games, Mena. They plan to kill you." He didn't tell her what that would do to him. It was enough for now if she realized what it would do to Jason and her mother.

His phone rang while she was pondering his words. Ryder went to grab it, pushing the on button and sitting on the foot of the bed. "Yeah?"

"Danny here. We've got a problem." His friend's tone was grim instead of the joking one he usually had.

He shut his eyes tight, feeling the muscles at the back of his neck tighten. "What?"

"I just heard from Joel, who finally caught some chatter when a couple of these guys were on their way out of the house. They're willing to use her family to get to her, Ryder. I figure if they can track you from the business, to find the connections, they can track us, too."

"They can." He pinched the bridge of his nose, feeling Mena move beside him, her shoulder brushing his arm as she sat up. "Get them moved. Let me know where when you get there."

"Will do."

He ended the call and took a slow breath, trying to calm his whirl of thoughts. Get his concern under control. They had the situation well in hand. This was just a little wrinkle.

"What's wrong?"

He debated not telling her, but she needed to know, if only to understand why she couldn't go home. "Joel caught some Harvester chatter, and they're planning to use your family to draw you out." He caught her bright gaze. "Danny will move Aggie and Jason."

Her cheeks whitened, and she sat back on her heels, her pulse jumping in the hollow of her throat.

"We can't go back, Mena," he said more gently, touching her fingers where they gripped her knee, hard. "It isn't safe."

She blinked and nodded slowly, her green gaze sliding away from him.

Ryder forced her to relinquish the punishing grip she had on her leg, wrapping her hand between both of his. "They'll be fine, honey. Danny is one of the best. He'll get them somewhere even safer, and Jason will just think they're having a big adventure." He rubbed her cold fingers. "I promise."

Her lower lip trembled, until she caught it in her teeth.

He took one of his hands away from hers and wrapped it around her shoulders, pulling her into his side. "It's okay."

"No, no, it isn't." She pulled away and got to her feet. She strode across the room to the bathroom, then whirled, her green eyes shiny. "I'll do whatever you want if it'll keep them safe, Ryder, but this is definitely *not* okay. My mother shouldn't have to run for her life. That little boy shouldn't have to run for his life because of my incredibly bad luck in having this damned curse fall on me before he was even born." Her chest rose too quickly with her breathing, and she angrily swiped away a tear.

He pushed to his feet, his own chest aching. "That little boy loves you, Mena." He took a few steps in her direction.

Her breath caught roughly. "Which is why I'll do whatever you tell me, but it might just be easier to let the Harvesters have me."

He curled his fingers around her upper arms and gave her a quick shake, his own anger rising. "How would it be easier for Jason if you died?" He scowled down at her.

"He'd be safe," she whispered, green eyes wide as she gazed at him through her tears. "He could go back to just being a child, playing with his friends at school. He could have a dog. He wants a dog very badly, and it wouldn't be safe with me, any more than he is now." A sob escaped her, and she clamped her lips shut.

Ryder closed his eyes for a second, regathering a measure of control, then pulled her into his arms. "He would be devastated if something happened to you, Mena," he murmured into her hair, feeling her shake, tiny tremors which meant she was fighting her tears. "So would your mother. So would I." He kissed the top of her head. "Smart girl, you know better than this."

She burrowed her face into the side of his neck, and her tears heated his skin.

"You know they would do anything for you, just like you'll do anything for them." He maneuvered so he could sit in the cushy chair against the wall and drew her onto his lap, stroking her back as she shivered. "Remember? That's why you were in such a hurry to leave after the first Harvester came calling. To keep them safe." He rubbed his cheek along the top of her head. "Part of their well-being is them knowing you're safe, too."

A muffled sound reached his ears.

"It's all right, baby," he whispered. "It's okay to be afraid. Go ahead and cry."

She shook her head. "I don't cry. Leftover hormones."

He smiled, glad she couldn't see it. "Then let it come. Get it out."

She shook her head again, but he felt more wetness sliding down his neck, dampening his shirt. Her fingers gripped his shoulders tightly, and she shuddered against him.

Ryder settled into the seat, pulling her securely to his chest, and slid one hand along her spine to comfort her. He wondered when she had last cried, prior to their flight from the Harvesters. Probably a long time ago. Maybe after she'd become the Medusa? Perhaps she'd tell him someday.

After a few minutes, she sniffled, and swiped her hand over her cheeks, sitting back a little. "I'm sorry."

He sighed. "No need for apology. Haven't we talked about this already?"

Mena bowed her head, and her hair slid forward to hide her face from him.

He tucked several curls behind her ear, revealing a wet pink cheek and closed eyes, lashes clumped together from her tears. He slid his thumb across her cheek, wiping away more moisture. "I love that you're strong, Mena. But sometimes, you need to let go and let someone else be the one *you* lean on for a change."

She looked up at him, clearly startled. "I don't...I haven't leaned on anyone except Mom since this whole thing started, and I try not to lean on her much," she said finally, her voice rusty. "She's had a hard enough time, raising two girls on her own, and now helping raise Jason."

"Well, you've got someone else to lean on now. I think my shoulders are strong enough to take it."

She frowned, looking unconvinced.

He wasn't sure if he should be offended or not. He chose 'not' for now. It was clearly a new concept to her to have to accept help from anyone else. She'd just have to get used to it. "Doesn't look like you're quite ready for supper," he said lightly, cupping her chin and turning her face toward his so he could inspect her tear-stained cheeks. "How about we call Jason instead? Then we can think about dinner."

She nodded, pushing away to go into the bathroom.

He heard water running, then splashing, and he let her have a minute.

She returned, still pink-nosed, her gaze somber.

He dialed Aggie's cell number and held out the phone to her.

Mena took it, forcing a smile when her mother came on the line. "Hi, Mom."

Her mother surely knew her well enough to know the

smile and jovial tone were being faked. Even if he wasn't looking directly at her face, he'd know it, and Aggie knew her daughter a whole lot better than he did.

Ryder pushed to his feet and gestured to the chair. He went back to the dresser and took his laptop from its bag, booting up to check his email. Behind him, he heard her half of the conversation, or most of it, as she lowered her voice while she was talking to her mother.

There was the email from Joel about what he'd over-heard earlier. He scanned it, rubbing one hand over his chin. Danny was absolutely right. If the Harvesters had made the connection to him, they'd try to find out every-thing they could about his business, his partners, his employees. Might be time to call in a couple of favors from some other old friends to get a few extra pairs of eyes on this. He considered that for a moment, then turned to look at Mena when she laughed, a genuine laugh this time.

Obviously she was talking to Jason. Her expression had softened and a real smile curved her mouth. "You did not," she said, her tone teasing. "Not a real horse."

He shut the laptop.

A flicker of pain crossed over her face a moment later. "I love you, too, buddy." Her voice thickened around fresh tears. "You want to talk to your daddy?...Okay, hang on." She rose and held out the phone to him, avoiding his eyes.

He caught her wrist instead of just taking the cell, pulling her against him as he lifted the phone to his ear. "Hi, Jase, what's this I hear about a horse?" He rubbed his hand up and down her stiff spine, feeling his shirt dampen beneath her cheek.

"I rode a horse, Daddy! A real horse! Danny took me today. It was awesome! Can I have a horse instead of a dog?"

Ryder laughed. "Instead of a dog, huh? You know horses

can't live in the house, right?" He held on when Mena would have moved away, feeling her quiver under his hand.

"I know. They live in a barn. But I really want a horse. I'd go ridin' all the time. I'd feed 'im apples an' carrots."

He nuzzled her hair, inhaling the soft scent of her shampoo. "Well, we'll have to think about it. Horses need a lot of space to run on, buddy. So, are you being a really good boy for Danny and Grandma?" He felt her shudder, and held on tighter.

She pinched his side, startling him, but he didn't release her.

"I'm always a good boy, Daddy. You know that," Jason said, sounding very put-upon.

"I know. Keep it up, okay?"

"I will. I love you, Daddy."

"I love you, too, buddy." He heard her breath catch this time, then felt the tears on his shoulder, wetting his shirt still more. "I've got to go get your Aunt Mena some supper, okay? She's starving."

"Aunt Phila, you mean." His son giggled.

"I'll talk to you tomorrow, buddy. Be good." He waited until the line closed, then shut off the phone. He dropped it behind him on the dresser and scooped Mena into his arms. When she didn't protest the move, he knew the depth of her upset.

He carried her to the bed and stretched out with her, keeping her in the circle of his arms. "That's why we won't go back, baby," he murmured. "Because Jason loves you and you have to stay alive for him." He knew it was a low blow, but it worked.

She couldn't contain her tears anymore, crying softly into his shoulder. Her tears soaked his shirt, and her breath warmed his wet skin underneath.

It didn't take her long to cry herself out, though, and she lay breathing raggedly against him for a long time afterward. "That was a cheap shot," she said finally, pinching his side again.

"I know." He wouldn't apologize, though. Not when he was certain he'd finally made his point. She could bruise his side all she wanted as long as she was safe.

She inhaled shakily. "Now I'm a wreck." She sniffed and lifted one hand to wipe her face.

He leaned back. "A beautiful wreck," he smiled, touching her lower lip with his forefinger. "We can get room service."

She shook her head. "I'd rather get out for a while. I just have to wash my face."

He held on when she would have pushed away.

Mena frowned at him.

"Are we agreed then?"

Her mouth flattened. "That I won't go back and let the Harvesters kill me?"

He nodded.

She glared up at him. "Fine, bossy."

Ryder held onto her again when she tried to move away. "We'll find a way out of this."

She shut her eyes.

"I don't care if you don't believe me right now," he continued. "I know you don't believe I'll stick around. I'm not your father, Mena. I'm not whoever else let you down by not staying. I'm not going anywhere. And eventually we'll get to a point where you're safe from the Harvesters."

She bit her lower lip, her eyes opening. "That is definitely a promise you shouldn't make, Ryder."

He wondered if she knew everything Kallan and Andrea had told him about their own experiences. Surely she did. "I won't promise you anything I can't deliver," he said instead of asking.

She looked as if she might argue his claim.

He put his forefinger over her lips to stop her.

Clearly he still had some work to do to breach Mena's walls.

He grinned, and her expression changed to wary, her eyes narrowing a little.

Good thing he was up to the task.

CHAPTER TEN

R yder paced the room, watching the snow falling outside, and wished he'd made up his mind two days ago to move her. Now they were stuck.

Mena sat cross-legged on the bed, tapping at her keyboard and ignoring his pacing, as she'd been doing half the day. He knew she was working on his website, but he didn't know how she could concentrate so well.

"Glaring at it won't make the snow stop," she said mildly, fingers flying over her keyboard.

He clenched his jaw and continued to stare out the window.

"Ryder, sit down. Turn on the TV or something. You're starting to make me nervous." She paused her typing to shoot him a quick glance. "You could email Danny or Joel for an update. Maybe it's not snowing where they are."

He scowled harder. It was definitely snowing where Danny was, but not at Joel's current location. Not yet. She didn't need to know that, though.

She might need to know, however, that a team of

Harvesters had left the meeting in Virginia and headed to her house again.

But he hadn't worked out how to break the news.

Of course, they wouldn't find anything. Danny's team had been thorough in their scrub. Nothing related to Mena's family remained. Sure, there was a little bit of furniture left in both houses, but no personal information would be found. And nothing to give any clues as to her whereabouts.

He leaned against the window frame, staring at the piles of fresh snow covering the ground.

Mena sighed and set her laptop aside. "Come on. Sit with me." She held out one hand.

He studied her, noting the pen tucked over her ear, the way her gaze was still not quite focused on him. He moved toward her, sliding his hand over hers and feeling her shiver. He stifled a smile and sat beside her on the bed. Then he decided he didn't want to sit beside her, so he tossed aside the pillows behind her so he could sit there.

"It's fine, Ryder." She let him settle her with her back to his chest, his fingers locking together over her belly. "The snow is supposed to stop tomorrow morning. Where were you itching to go?"

He shrugged, silent. He hated to ruin her relaxed mood. She'd been much more at ease since their shopping trip three days ago. It was the most fun he'd ever had shopping, choosing dresses for her to try on, sexy dresses, then lingerie to go with them, and teasing her the entire time. Of course, he'd kept her in bed for much of the past three days, so there hadn't been many opportunities for arguments.

But if he'd taken her out of here two days ago, they'd be farther from the Harvesters. At least out of the same state.

"Are you going to tell me what's got you all broody? I

know it isn't just the snow." She slid one hand over his, her fingers warm against his skin.

"There's a foot of new snow on the ground."

"It's Pittsburgh. They know how to deal with snow in the winter here. What else?"

He sighed, debating with himself. "There was a team of Harvesters heading for your place." He felt her stiffen in his arms for a moment, and then she forced herself to relax, blowing out a long, slow breath.

"Okay. But we're gone. So that's not a problem."

"It's closer to them than I wanted to be with you."

"Ah." She nodded, her hair tickling his nose. "So when the roads are plowed, we check out and go somewhere else."

He frowned. That didn't sound like Mena. He leaned forward to look into her face.

"What?"

"That's too easy."

A tiny smile touched her mouth. "Maybe I'm tired of arguing with you."

He didn't quite buy her easy agreement. "If that's the case, how about getting the red and black thing we bought the other day out of the bag later so I can play?"

She laughed. "We'll see." She patted his hand. "First, I need to finish the website."

"Finish? Already?" He tightened his hold on her.

"The big stuff. Pending your approval. And, I guess, Danny's and Joel's." She tilted her head to look at him.

"You work fast."

"It's not like we have other pressing business."

The tiny mole at the corner of her mouth tempted him to taste. So he did, leaning forward to kiss the corner of her mouth. Then he flicked his tongue over the spot, and he felt her heartbeat quicken under her ribs.

"Um, Ryder."

"Mm." He nuzzled along her jaw, finding his way to her earlobe and sucking the soft bit of flesh into his mouth. She tasted so damn good.

A soft sound passed her lips, encouraging him to continue. He continued on until she was naked beneath him, wet with arousal and perspiration, her breathing ragged, and her hips lifting hard into his.

It was a pretty good distraction, for both of them.

But he knew it wasn't making her any safer.

Ryder stroked his fingertips along her side later, while her breathing gradually slowed back to normal. He propped his head up on one hand, his gaze following his fingers over her ivory skin. He traced the top edge of her tattoo, then frowned, leaning closer.

"What?" she asked, her voice raspy.

"The cup in your tattoo is a different color."

She frowned, eyes still closed. "I don't think so, Ryder."

He touched the bowl of the goblet. It definitely wasn't the same color. It had been gold the first time he saw it. It was more silver now. Everything else was exactly the same, the flowers, the snake. Just the color of the cup had changed. He sat up to study it better.

Mena opened her eyes and sighed. "Really?"

"Look at it." He traced the stem of the goblet with his forefinger.

She pushed onto her elbows and looked down to where he stroked her hip. Her eyes widened in shock. "Oh, my Gods."

He examined her expression for a moment before turning back to the tattoo. "I guess it's never changed before." His mind raced, trying to think if he'd heard anything about that and coming up empty. He'd email Kallan.

Mena moved out from under his fingers, and hurried to stand in front of the mirror on the door. "What's wrong with it?"

He stayed where he was. "I don't know."

She turned a little to look more closely. "Everything else is the same." She glanced at him. "This must mean something, Ryder."

"Probably."

The question was, *what?*

PHILOMENA COULDN'T SIT STILL. SHE'D FIRED OFF emails to her mother and her mother's great-aunt Lydia, the unofficial matriarch of the family.

Neither had replied yet, though it had been over twenty-four hours.

It was making her crazy.

At least the snow had finally stopped. She paused her pacing to stare out the window, where a caravan of plow trucks made another pass at the road past their hotel, toward the mall.

"We ought to be able to hit the road tomorrow," Ryder said from behind her.

"Have they made it to my house yet?" She didn't turn around, staring after the disappearing trucks.

He hesitated for a few seconds. "Yes."

She shut her eyes. She hated the idea of those killers pawing through her house, her mother's house. Again. It didn't matter if no one was there, if all their personal things had been removed already. They were intruders.

"Joel said they found their buddy, too."

She hoped it hurt them to find the man who'd come to kill her. Her heart beat faster. What was wrong with her? She'd never been so vicious before.

Oh, wait. She'd never been on the run for her life before.

Ryder's hands settled on her shoulders. "It'll be all right. I promise."

"There you go again, making promises you shouldn't," she said lightly.

His fingers tightened on her. "I don't make promises I don't intend to keep."

She bowed her head. "I'm sorry."

"It's okay. I know you're a little stressed right now."

The tattoo was still the silvery color, faintly gold just around the edges. She'd checked it compulsively every time she went past a mirror.

It was ridiculous, but she couldn't seem to stop. The tattoo had never changed before, not once since she'd acquired it. Before she became the Medusa, it had simply been a snake-shaped birthmark on her hip. Then one morning she'd gotten out of bed with cramps from Hades and snakes on her head, and it had been a fresh, bright tattoo, sore as if she'd sat in a tattoo artist's chair for hours to have it etched into her skin.

She let Ryder pull her back against his chest, while she chewed on her lower lip. His heartbeat was steady, and it made her feel slightly better. "Jason and Mom are safe, right?"

"You know they are. Danny is one of the best." He kissed the top of her head.

Philomena sighed and turned in his arms to rub her cheek against his chest. Hearing that did ease her mind a little. Now if she could figure out what the tattoo thing meant...

"Have you had any emails yet?"

She shook her head, sliding her hands around him to settle nearer.

"I have."

She frowned, lifting her head. "From who?"

"Kallan."

Her pulse skipped. Kallan. *Andi.* She'd forgotten about Andi when she'd fired off her emails yesterday. *Duh.* "And?" She narrowed her eyes at him.

"Andrea's did the same thing." He lifted one shoulder.

"When?"

"When they were hiding out from the Harvesters."

"So it's a protective thing? A stress thing?"

He shook his head.

She raised her eyebrows. "What is it?"

His throat worked as he swallowed, his dark gaze scanning her face for a long, long moment. "An emotional thing."

Philomena frowned again. "Emotional?" She thought about the meaning of 'emotional'. Fear was an emotion. Lust was an emotion. She wondered if either of those was a strong enough emotion to change the color of the amulet in her tattoo.

Probably not.

Her heart pounded harder inside her ribs, realization dawning. She shook her head. "*No.*"

He didn't say anything, just kept his hands at her waist and his gaze on her face.

She pushed free and paced the length of the room. She was not falling in love with him. She dragged her fingers through her hair, scooping it away from her face while her pulse galloped along, drowning out any logical thought that might have surfaced in her head.

When she turned around, he still stood at the window, his broad shoulders tense. "You can't really believe..." She didn't even want to voice the words. That would be even more dangerous.

He didn't say anything, but she saw the muscles in his arms tighten when he curled and uncurled his fingers at his sides.

"Oh, my Gods," she whispered, shaking her head. She couldn't be falling in love with Ryder.

She dropped onto the foot of the bed and covered her face with her hands. She could deal with lust. He inspired that in her, and often. But love?

She couldn't even wrap her brain around the idea.

She'd never imagined she'd be free to love a man not a member of her family. Not since she became the Medusa. Not even since before then. Surely Andi had been a fluke.

One of his hands drifted over the curls at her nape, then down her back.

"I'm sorry, Ryder," she said after a moment. "I just hadn't thought about...*that*."

His weight depressed the mattress beside her, causing her to lean into him, and he wrapped his arm around her shoulders. Despite the tension in him, his touch remained gentle, making her feel incredibly guilty about her reaction to his suggestion.

The man had risked his life to keep her safe from a horde of would-be-killers. More than once. Not to mention the amazing sex.

But love?

Philomena closed her eyes behind her palms and tried to slow the whirl of thoughts in her head.

"It's all right," he said softly.

She lifted her head, focusing on his face. Tension bracketed his mouth, and his dark gaze was shuttered.

Making her realize she'd hurt him. *Oh Gods.*

She lifted one hand to touch his cheek, and he shut his eyes. She swallowed, wanting to make him feel better, but not sure quite how to do it.

She angled herself so she could wrap her arms around him, resting her ear on his chest. His heartbeat raced.

His big hand stayed at her back, though his cheek came to rest on the top of her head.

Philomena squeezed her eyes tight against the stinging there. She didn't want to hurt Ryder. Even if she'd never imagined being in love with him, she didn't want to hurt him.

And she didn't see how she could avoid it now.

ELEK'S IRRITATION SHOWED ONLY IN THE SUBTLE squaring of his shoulders, Aristotle noted with some approval. He learned quickly.

"Nothing at all?" Elek asked.

"Half the furniture is gone. There's nothing useful in either house," Demos said, his own annoyance plain in his tone and his expression. "We looked through everything left there."

"What about the man?"

Demos shook his head. "His apartment is untouchable--there is an armed guard twenty-four-seven, but we have someone sitting on the building. He's just gone. Wherever the Medusa is, he's with her still."

"Can we get audio on the office?"

Demos moved his head in a negative side to side wag. "We tried."

Elek nodded. "Thank you."

"We'll have to give this some thought," Aristotle said. "Take the rest of the day to prepare for another trip."

Demos left the room, and Elek sighed, his shoulders slumping a little.

"We'll find them," Aristotle said, sitting back in his chair.

The younger man turned to face him. "How? The last encounter was completely random. I don't know how you can be so certain."

Aristotle smiled. "I am certain enough for both of us. We have not come so far to fail yet again."

Ryder resisted the urge to rub his hand over his aching heart. He hadn't imagined Mena's reaction to his suggestion would be so...shocked. And still so resistant. He should've known better.

But that didn't mean he'd let her go.

He steered the car along the interstate, keeping an eye on the traffic behind them out of habit, but knowing there was no one following. They couldn't.

Danny had emailed him yesterday that he was taking Jason and Aggie to Tennessee for a few days. No one had any family there, not even Mena, so the Harvesters would have to get very, very lucky to cross paths with them there.

Joel's email hadn't been as positive. The Harvesters had torn both houses apart searching for any clue to Mena's whereabouts, leaving quite a mess behind. He'd scheduled a cleaning crew come in, and would scout real estate agents for when she and her mother were ready to deal with selling. In the meantime, Ryder would keep his mouth shut.

Mena had her chin propped on her hand, staring blindly out the window as he mingled with rush hour traffic heading west.

He'd snuck a peek at her tattoo in the shower that morning, and the cup remained the same silvery-gold color, which made him feel a bit better. The revelation that the cup in her cousin's tattoo had changed color as she fell in love with the Harvester who'd come to kill her and instead protected her from his family shocked Mena. It wasn't enough, though, to make her let go of the doubts and fears she still had. He knew her father had left her family when she was young. That obviously made it harder for her to believe. He wondered what else might have made her feel that way, reinforcing her belief.

On the other hand, the goblet hadn't reverted to its original color.

She might not want to be falling for him, but she was.

The knowledge made him only a little happier, because he knew she'd fight it now. Even harder than she had been already.

He stifled a sigh and shot her a quick glance. Her green eyes were shadowed as she sat back in her seat.

"Where are we going?"

"I haven't decided yet. Anyplace you want to visit?"

She gave him a quizzical look, a tiny frown wrinkling her forehead.

"I suppose it's too cold to think about horse races, so maybe not Kentucky. Chicago might be a big enough city to harbor more than one Harvester. How do you feel about auto racing?" He waited for her reluctant laugh. "Okay, not Indy, then." He drummed his fingers on the steering wheel.

"Does it matter?"

"As long as there's a bed, we're good," he teased, winking at her, gratified to see the blush climb her cheeks. He'd actually considered flying out of the country, but figured there was a better than even chance the Harvesters would be watching airports. Same thing with any major harbors with cruise lines sailing out.

But there was plenty of space between the two coasts, and they couldn't cover every inch of it all at once. There were a lot of them, but not that many.

Mena settled back, looking slightly more relaxed.

"We'll see if anything looks appealing along the way," he said finally, patting her knee.

"You should let me take a turn driving once in a while, Mr. Macho," she said mildly.

He grinned at her. "Fat chance."

She shook her head, her lips curving up and making him want to taste that tiny mole again.

He forced his attention to the road ahead. There would be plenty of time later.

For now, he needed to find a safe place for them to stay while he figured out a longer-term plan.

Philomena squinted at the blinking neon sign behind the car. The Starlight Motel in Bellefontaine apparently had a vacancy. She'd guess more than one, judging by the parking lot's dearth of occupants.

Probably not a lot of tourists in western Ohio in the middle of the winter.

Ryder tugged her door open and then dragged out their bags. "This'll do for tonight."

She took her carry-on bag and let him lead the way inside.

Check-in took all of three minutes, just long enough for him to hand over some cash and scribble something mostly illegible on the registration log.

Philomena was exhausted. She hadn't slept well last night. And no wonder after his revelation.

She thought she might be able to pass out and sleep the whole night away tonight, though. They'd stopped for supper earlier and called Jason from the diner. He was having a fantastic time with Danny, who kept finding things a six-year-old boy would love to do.

It made her wonder if Danny had a son, or just wanted to still *be* a six-year-old boy. She believed it must be the latter. If he had a family, they'd be in danger, too.

She dropped her suitcase next to the low dresser and fumbled with the buttons on her coat.

Ryder shut the door and fastened the chain and dead-bolt, then crossed to her, setting his own bag beside hers. "You look tired, baby." His hands brushed hers aside and undid the buttons she couldn't quite manage. "Why don't you get ready for bed?" He slid her coat free of her arms and draped it over the chair in the corner.

She shifted her shoulders, trying to ease the ache in them from sitting in the car most of the day. "What about you?" She dug her toothbrush and toothpaste out of her suitcase.

"I'm not really tired yet."

"You drove all day." She turned to look at him from the bathroom door.

"I'll let you drive when we decide where we're going. How's that?" He grinned at her, flashing his dimples.

She shook her head on her way into the smaller room.

When she emerged, his coat was draped over hers, and he'd kicked off his boots to sit at the small table and start up his computer.

Philomena dropped onto the foot of the bed to untie her boots, watching his long fingers move over the keyboard. "Checking in?" she asked, standing to unbutton and unzip her skirt.

He glanced over his shoulder as her skirt whooshed to the floor. "Yeah." His gaze landed on the leather sheath still strapped to her thigh, and his eyes darkened. "Have I ever told you how much I love a woman with a weapon?" He pushed to his feet and took the four steps to reach her.

She smiled when he knelt in front of her, his fingers finding the buckles and releasing them so the leather sheath fell from her leg. "Not lately."

He kissed the spot where her dagger had rested. "I do."

She threaded her fingers through his hair as he moved, dragging his open mouth higher, until his tongue slid between her thighs.

Philomena sucked in a quick breath, shifting her feet apart to let him slip his fingers inside her panties.

It only took a second for her body to respond to his touch. Her heart pounded harder, her breasts ached, and her body grew wet around his hard fingers.

"Mm," he hummed against her clit. "You know, I think I am feeling tired, after all." He thrust his fingers deep.

Her hips rocked into his caresses.

Suddenly, she wasn't nearly as sleepy as she'd been five minutes ago.

Ryder eased her back onto the bed, and she dropped flat, arms over her head, her breath rushing out as he slid her panties down her legs, out of his way. He nibbled his way along her inner thigh until he could thrust his tongue inside her.

Her body jerked toward his mouth.

"Easy, love," he murmured into her wet folds.

She slid her fingers into his hair. "Ryder."

He nipped at her clit, and her breath snagged in her chest. "Patience."

She lost track of how many times he brought her to the brink and then eased back, teasing her with his fingers and mouth. When she was shaking with the need for release, he finally undressed and rose up over her, forcing the wide head of his cock into her tight sheath, pushing steadily until her body accommodated the entire length of him. Philomena took in a shuddering breath, feeling his cock pulse inside her, her body clenching on him.

He nudged her nose with his, sliding his tongue along her lower lip. "Yes?"

She nodded.

A slow, wicked grin curved his mouth, and he slowly, slowly withdrew from her, then thrust hard, deep.

The rush of release made her brain shut down completely. Fantastic colors flashed behind her closed eyelids. Every damp inch of her skin was hypersensitive as he shifted against her, sending more waves of pleasure into her core, gentler than those generated by the hot erection sliding along sensitive flesh.

When she could finally open her eyes, Ryder had rolled to his side with her in his arms, and their feet still hung off the end of the bed. They both panted roughly, and she shivered when his fingers slid along her damp spine.

"Are you cold?" His warm breath puffed over her temple.

She snuggled closer to him. "A little." She shut her eyes,

feeling her chest squeeze when he yanked the blanket over her. She couldn't fall in love with him.

But apparently, she had formed an emotional attachment to him already, because Andi had been pretty adamant in her email response to Philomena last night about the reason for the color change in the amulet when she'd fallen in love with Kallan.

Philomena tightened her hold on Ryder when he would have shifted away.

She'd known before finally meeting him that he was a great father. It was an attractive quality. But she'd had no idea how dangerous his determination would be to her plans. How devastating to her defenses.

Reading Andi's email about the cup changing colors as she'd fallen in love with Kallan was scary as hell. Even scarier? Realizing she'd known and refused to believe it. Surely the fact she was relying on Ryder to keep her alive had something to do with the attachment.

She couldn't call it anything else. That would make it too much of a real possibility, a possibility she hadn't believed in for a long time.

Taking that chance? Much too risky.

Sure, Ryder had stepped up when unexpected fatherhood entered his life. He'd taken on Harvesters to keep her safe, for her family. But that declaration of his?

Mena knew that was totally for them. And she didn't know if she was brave enough to give a relationship a real try.

Maybe falling in love had worked for Andi. But Philomena? She was pretty sure she had deeper issues that guaranteed failure. And maybe it had been a fluke, ridding Andi of the curse.

He smoothed her damp hair away from her face, his mouth sliding along her cheek. "It's okay."

She opened her eyes, staring at his shoulder. He couldn't know she was worrying about doing something stupid like falling for him. She hoped.

"Go to sleep, Mena. I'll keep you warm," he whispered.

She squeezed her eyes shut and realized her fingers were digging into his back. She forced herself to relax her grip, but she didn't let go. She didn't *want* to let go.

That scared the hell out of her.

ELEK STUDIED ARGOS FOR A FEW MOMENTS. HIS OLDER cousin lounged in the chair, one ankle resting on the opposite knee, his jeans faded, a band logo peeling from the front of an even older t-shirt, and he wore his long dark hair slicked into a ponytail, a few strands of silver glinting atop his head.

"How is your work coming?" he asked finally.

Argos lifted one shoulder slightly. "Not well, I'm afraid. I expected he might have found some friends among the government contractors for his system, but apparently, he went to real geeks. I have not found a way in yet, but I'm still trying."

Elek wasn't surprised. Ryder Ware had been very thorough so far. "What about credit cards, bank accounts?"

Argos shook his head. "No activity since before Nestor located her mother's house. Before that, he withdrew twenty thousand in cash from several accounts. Probably for pre-paid cards. He's smart, but we'll find him."

Elek liked his cousin's certainty. He wished he felt it, too.

RYDER SAT AT THE LITTLE ROUND TABLE IN THE morning, doing random searches on his computer while they ate breakfast from the diner down the street. Mena worked on her own laptop, and he wondered if she was making further tweaks to the website, or sending more emails to her family.

He wondered, too, if she'd noticed the color of the cup in her tattoo was completely silver now. He'd seen it earlier while they got dressed. No more tinges of gold at the edges. He was pretty sure that had something to do with last night, and her refusal to release him after they'd made love the first time.

He picked up his juice, smiling. Whether she would admit it or not, his Medusa was falling for him.

"Where are we going?"

"I don't know." He sat back, meeting her gaze over their computers. "Which direction would you like to go?"

She looked surprised by the question. "I don't know," she said after a moment. "We don't want to go too far west, right?"

He shook his head. "Pretty sure even though some of these guys have flown in from the west coast, there are plenty more left out there." Plus he really didn't want to be so far away from everyone else. Just in case.

Mena pondered for a moment. "I've always wanted to see New Orleans, but that probably qualifies as a big enough city to warrant multiple Harvesters, huh?"

Ryder studied her face. "I don't know." She had a hopeful glint in her eyes, but he could see she'd tamped it down. "We can give it a try," he said after a few seconds, loving the way her green eyes lit with pleasure.

"Really?"

He nodded. "It's going to be a long drive."

"I told you I'd drive." She nibbled on her lower lip, looking as though she were still trying to restrain her excitement.

He caught her hand up from where it lay on the table. "We'd better get on the road then."

Mena gave him such a beautiful smile then, his heart stuttered in his chest.

He tugged her around the table and into his lap. "Come here," he muttered, catching her nape to kiss her.

Her response was everything he could have hoped for, and his body reacted predictably to her tongue sliding along his lower lip. When he pulled her closer, her tightening nipples brushed his chest.

"Might have time to go back to bed before we hit the road," he breathed against her lips.

She laughed. "You're a very bad man." Her fingers slid to the button on his jeans, teasing him before she settled her palm over his erection.

It wasn't like they were on a schedule.

"WHEN DID YOU LAST LET SOMEONE TOUCH YOU, Mena?" Ryder asked, still stroking her back.

"Just a few minutes ago," she said on a breathless laugh.

"You know what I mean. The last time you let another man touch you."

She stilled beneath his hand and was silent so long, he thought she might not answer. Finally, she let out a long breath. "A long time ago," she whispered.

"Before the curse?"

She nodded.

Ryder considered that for a few seconds. He'd known she hadn't been intimate with any of the men she'd dated in recent years, but so long? "What did he do to you?"

She tipped her head so she could frown up at him. "What?"

"He hurt you, whoever he was, reinforced your belief that all men leave." He felt her quiver. "How?"

She looked away, then put her head back down on his chest. "It doesn't matter. It hasn't mattered in far more than eight years."

"Bullshit. You know it's not true for all men, but it's been an easy way to avoid a relationship." He rubbed his hand down her spine again and gave her ass a squeeze. "I told you I'm not going anywhere. I told you that the first night."

"I knew you were going to be trouble," she muttered.

He grinned and hauled her up so he could catch her mouth. "The best kind," he agreed, nipping at her lower lip.

They got checked out just before they had to, and Ryder let her drive. He'd navigate for a while.

And plot his next move.

If he had a better idea what the Harvesters were planning, he might be able to decide just what to do with Mena.

He rechecked his email, but found nothing new from either Danny or Joel, and only a status report from Ken, who was monitoring from a distance. The rest of his guys were on paying gigs.

Mena seemed happy to have something to do. She'd found a radio station that suited her and cranked the volume on some eighties rock and bopped along with the music as she drove.

Ryder hid his grin by bowing his head over his laptop.

He wanted more of these unguarded moments with her, when she didn't worry about running from would-be murderers or her family's safety. And a whole lot more of those moments like last night when she held him as if she didn't want to let him go.

To distract himself from the hopeful notion, he did a quick search on hotels in Knoxville for the night. They'd decided to avoid the bigger Nashville. Knoxville would be long enough drive for one day. They would make it into New Orleans the following day. "Hey, this place has waterbeds," he teased, glancing over.

Mena blushed. "It doesn't matter what kind of bed, Ryder."

"As long as there's a bed. And, really," he continued, "we don't even need a bed."

Color brightened in her cheeks. "This is true," she agreed after a moment.

Ryder ignored the way his body tightened. They'd just climbed out of bed a little while ago. He'd have to be patient now. Knoxville was a long drive.

A very long drive, as it turned out. They got stuck in traffic in Louisville, then traded seats after a late lunch stop in Lexington. Now Mena was the one searching for a place for them to stay. She reserved a room as they drove into Tennessee, so when they arrived, all they had to do was check in.

After checking in, before they even carried in their bags, they sat down in the lounge to eat a late supper.

Mena sighed over her soda, faint stress lines around her eyes. "I need to call Jason. It's already past his bedtime."

"Anytime you're ready." He put his hand over hers on the table.

She nodded, then lowered her gaze to the table. "I don't want to spend the rest of my life running, Ryder."

He didn't tell her the one way she could avoid that. She must have heard from Andi by now, so she already knew. He didn't think reminding her would make it easier for her to let down the walls she kept around her heart. Reminding her might only make it harder for him to breach those barriers.

"You won't." He squeezed her fingers. "So are you going to show me the website yet?"

She smiled. "I have one or two more tweaks to make, I think."

He wondered if she'd even noticed his subject change. Or if she was simply so relieved by it she grabbed on.

They dawdled over dinner, taking a break in the middle so she could call Jason, who didn't sound at all tired despite the hour. Ryder stretched when they finished, then paused, his nape prickling.

Mena saw him freeze, and shadows darkened her eyes. She looked around the room.

He shook his head. "It's okay." *I think.* The prickling didn't continue, and he frowned, scanning the room.

She didn't look like she agreed. Her hand dropped to the side of her leg, where he knew her dagger was strapped.

He caught her other hand and led her out of the restaurant. When they reached the lobby, the feeling returned, magnified, and his gut tightened in anticipation of a fight. "Car," he breathed, keeping his pace steady and his fingers tight on hers.

She nodded, just a tiny bob of her head, her gaze flitting all around.

He hit the button on the keyring to unlock the car doors,

and they both slid in, locking the doors behind them. He started the car fast and backed out of the parking spot.

As he reached the exit from the lot to the main road, he saw a big, burly guy rush from the front door of the hotel, then run to a car several spots from where they'd parked.

Ryder floored it and whipped into the light nighttime traffic. That would make it a challenge to lose this guy.

"How do they keep doing this?" Mena asked, and in the light from the dashboard, he could see her clenched fists on her knees.

"Just lucky this time, I think." He patted her hand, watching the rearview mirror. The other car was out of the lot now and gaining on them. "Unlucky for us, though."

He pressed harder on the accelerator, his gaze scanning the signs for the highway. Making his choice, he slowed only a little, then turned onto the eastbound ramp and sped up again. There was more traffic on the highway, and he was pretty sure with his old intelligence job, he had more evasive driving experience than the Harvesters.

He hoped so, anyway.

The other car managed to stay in his rearview mirror for nearly an hour, until Ryder took a last minute exit onto another interstate, blending into even heavier traffic, then exiting to go in the opposite direction almost immediately.

That took care of their tail.

His pulse pounded steadily, if a little too quickly, but Mena was holding onto the door as if her life depended on it.

He eased into the westbound traffic and patted her knee. "We need a new place to crash tonight."

She let her breath out. "Okay."

"It's okay, baby. He's gone."

She fished her laptop out of the bag at her feet.

Ryder had to wonder, though, *how* the Harvesters kept getting so lucky. There couldn't be enough of them to cover every interstate in the country, hoping they'd get lucky at a motel or hotel off of a highway. And since he'd already changed cars twice, it wasn't as if they could track them that way.

He frowned, tapping his fingers on the steering wheel.

"How about Nashville?" she asked after a few minutes.

"Too big, remember? Or not big enough now." He forced a laugh. "Find something further west, something smaller, and off the interstate."

She went back to work. "Okay, Columbia. It's southwest of Nashville."

"All right."

Her fingers clicked over the keys as she searched. "Do you want me to take a turn again? You've been driving since mid-afternoon." She closed her laptop and put it away.

He shook his head. "I'll take this shift, baby. Just in case." He didn't need to say in case what.

Mena didn't reply, but her fingers tapped on her knees, soundlessly. She was far more alert than when they'd stopped to check in at the last hotel.

Ryder kept his attention on the road ahead and on the mirror for traffic behind them. It was unlikely the Harvester would find them again tonight. Not in the dark. Especially not if the guy was working alone in this area.

But he didn't really know what he was up against, and the uncertainty made him more than a little nervous.

Aristotle noted the rage-induced shaking of his hand in his lap. They had lost her again. A chance sighting, and Georgios had lost her.

Elek's throat-clearing interrupted the angry flow of his thoughts. "I am sorry, Great-uncle," his nephew began. "I have chosen badly. So badly."

The older man made a dismissive sound and linked his fingers beneath his desk. "It is not your fault. I have clearly been remiss in arranging training for our family. The fault lies with me."

Elek frowned. "But I--"

Aristotle held up one hand, and his nephew closed his mouth. "We will make immediate arrangements for further training for some of your cousins. I need you to find options for intelligence training, something like this man would have had after he left the military." He reached for his laptop. "I will see who we know who may be of assistance. You make a list of appropriate candidates in the meantime."

Elek understood it was a dismissal and rose, murmuring, "As you wish. Thank you, Uncle Ari. I will work harder."

Aristotle watched him go. He ought to have started training Elek sooner. Instead, he'd foolishly believed he could continue to manage everything himself. As if he would be around forever.

So certain he would be there to see the Medusa killed.

How arrogant.

Rather than dwell on his own mistakes, he turned his mind back to the current problem.

It had been eight years. Eight long years of training and hunting. By now he should have great-nephews who were equal in skill to those he'd lost in the battle for the last Medusa.

Judging by the performance of his nephews in the past

few weeks, that was not the case. Much as he'd hated how far Stavros pushed the boundaries, hated his unnecessary viciousness, he needed one of his nephews now to step up and be brutal, be as determined as Stavros had been to kill the monster. But Kallan had killed his cousin when he'd fallen for the last Medusa.

Aristotle struggled to his feet and paced the length of his study. So far, none of the current generation of Tassos hunters seemed equal to the task.

He glared out his window at the darkness.

The longer they failed at this duty, the angrier the Goddess would become. And the more likely someone in the Medusa's family would discover his family's connection to theirs.

He could *not* allow that to happen.

He made his way to the desk and rested both hands on the edge. Somehow he had to ensure they didn't fail again.

Philomena bounced the pen off the notepad beside the phone in their room while Ryder brushed his teeth. She didn't have quite the same urgency knotting her belly as last night, but nervous butterflies still circled. Even after Ryder had physically exhausted her, she'd lain awake into the wee hours of the morning, staring up at the darkness. Wondering when the next Harvester would cross their path.

Worse, though, was Andi's email from several days ago. Her cousin had been adamant about the cause of the goblet's color-change. Philomena started shaking every time she thought about being in love with Ryder. One of them was going to be hurt badly when this ended.

The only thing in Andi's email that didn't make her quake was the mention of old journals from previous Medusas their Great-aunt Lydia had been attempting to track down for several years. They should prove to be interesting reading. But she had more important things to worry about now than journals she hadn't yet seen.

"We probably shouldn't go to New Orleans now," she said when Ryder came out of the bathroom, finger-combing his damp hair.

His dark eyes narrowed. "Why not?"

"They know where we were last week, roughly, which means they know the direction we were heading last night, and it's a fair guess to think you could get lost in New Orleans." She'd made up her mind before she'd finally slept several hours ago. "I don't think it's safe for us now."

He inhaled slowly, his hands settling on his hips. "Is this what kept you awake last night?"

She lifted one shoulder a little.

"Are you sure?"

She nodded.

He tilted his head to one side, still studying her. "All right. Then we need a new destination."

"Either west or east, but not directly south."

A faint smile tugged up one corner of his mouth. "Like where?"

"Texas or Florida, I'm thinking."

"It's spring break time, isn't it?" She could almost see the wheels turning in his head when his gaze shifted away from her, fingers tapping on one hip.

Her gaze followed the movement of his fingers for a moment. "I think it might be."

"Florida then."

That made her feel a bit better. A very tiny bit. Plus

Florida kept them closer to home, even though home wasn't safe.

"All right, baby. Are you ready?"

She rose and gathered her coat. "Yes."

"You can navigate for a while, maybe take a nap, since I know you got less sleep than I did," he said, catching her hand when she reached for her suitcase. He drifted a kiss on her lips, holding her gaze. "No arguments."

Philomena nodded slowly. Arguing with him would do no good. Arguing with him over anything seldom did her any good. The man was simply too bossy. She picked up the suitcase.

"Maybe we can make a short stop to see Jason and Aggie on our way."

She sucked in a quick breath, startled. "Really?"

He grinned at her. "We'll be heading sort of in that direction anyway, so it's just a little out of the way." It was his turn to shrug.

She dropped her suitcase onto the bed and threw her arms around him.

His hands settled at her hips, and she felt his smile against the side of her face.

Excitement quickened her heartbeat now. "Thank you, Ryder."

He kissed the top of her ear. "But we should hit the road."

She released him, planting a hard kiss on his mouth before she stepped back, smiling.

"So," he said, after they'd settled into the car, "we need to plot a route from here to Hammondville, Alabama. Should take us a few hours."

She started her laptop and found them a fairly direct route while he called Danny to tell him of their new plan.

The thought of seeing Jason and her mother made her eyes sting with happy tears.

Ryder caught her hand a long time later, linking their fingers on the seat between them. "Soon, baby."

She smiled at him through her tears and squeezed his fingers. "I know."

The thought that she could see her family pushed out any remaining worry over running into Harvesters.

CHAPTER ELEVEN

Ryder had barely stopped the car before Mena was out, running across the brownish winter lawn. She scooped up the little boy who'd raced toward her from the rustic cabin. Ryder pulled the key from the ignition and got out, stretching. Watching her. Her black curls were loose, so the cool breeze made them stream out behind her like ribbons as she spun a giggling Jason in a circle.

His son's arms wrapped tight around her neck, and even from this distance, Ryder heard him chattering away. He shut the car door and started toward them. He wanted homecomings like this for the rest of his life--minus the hunters trying to kill her.

Danny stood on the porch, and Aggie in the open doorway behind him. His friend looked alert, but not overly concerned, his shoulders relaxed as he slid his hands into his jeans pockets. Aggie, however, had worry lines fanning out from her eyes and wrinkling her forehead.

Before he had time to think too hard about possible causes, he reached Mena and patted Jason on the back.

"Daddy!" His son released Mena and leaped at him.

Ryder caught the boy and gave him a squeeze. "Hey, buddy. It doesn't look like you're having any fun on your adventure." Gods, he'd missed Jason. He kissed his son's forehead.

"Ha! I'm havin' more fun than I ever had in my whole, whole life!" His son pecked a kiss onto Ryder's cheek. "Didja know there's horses here, too? I been ridin' again."

He watched Mena skirt Danny to get to her mother, who gave her a hug nearly as tight as Jason's. He turned his attention back to his son. "Again?"

"Yeah. Will you ride with me?"

"Not this time, Jase. This is a quick stop for us." He strode up the gravel path, hefting his son to one side. "Danny."

His friend nodded. "I have some things for you to take a look at when things calm down some."

"Anything urgent?"

Danny shook his head. "Nah. But Carys shipped us paperwork to set up trusts for your girl and her mother." His gaze shifted to Mena. "She looks tired."

"So does Aggie."

The other man huffed out a breath. "She's worried about everyone. Had an email from one of the cousins that Desi was going to visit."

This was the second time he'd heard that now, which meant Desi might really be heading toward her mother's. Which could be a very bad thing for her.

"She leave a number with anyone where she could be reached?" His son wriggled, and Ryder let Jason slide to his feet, patting him on the head before the boy darted inside.

"What do you think?"

Ryder laughed shortly. Planning never had been Desi's strong suit. He shifted his gaze to Mena and Aggie, who were both wiping tears from their faces. He could worry about Desi later. "Let's move this reunion indoors," he said to Danny, who stepped with him toward the women.

Aggie had been cooking. And baking. Ryder smelled the cookies before they crossed the threshold.

"Did you eat lunch?" she asked when he walked into the little house.

He laughed. "Are you kidding? Once she knew where we were heading, this one wouldn't even let me make a pit stop." He loved the color that washed over Mena's face at his teasing.

Her mother tsked, moving away. "Philomena, honestly. You'd think it had been a year since you were away. Give the man a break."

He tugged lightly on one of Mena's curls, and she smiled at him, a gentle curve of her lips that made his heart swell with affection.

He settled onto a cushy leather sofa with Jason. His son brought out some drawings of the horse he'd ridden. Half of Ryder's attention, though, remained on the two women in the kitchen, making sandwiches and preparing plates of snacks while they spoke quietly.

His friend lounged in a nearby chair, one foot resting on his knee. "Had an email from Joel earlier, too," Danny said after a few moments, once Jason's chatter paused. "Since you've been driving, you won't have seen it. You'll want to."

Ryder frowned, but Aggie reached him with a plate then, shooing Jason off his lap. "Thanks, Aggie," he murmured, shooting her a quick smile.

"Thank *you*," she whispered back, smiling as she patted his shoulder.

He sighed as she moved away, handing a plate to Danny before she returned to the kitchenette for more plates.

Mena set several plates of goodies onto the blanket chest in front of him that served as a coffee table, then sat beside him, letting out a long breath.

He patted her knee, then held out his plate. "You didn't eat either."

Her mother handed her a plate. "She will. Eat yours, Ryder." The older woman sat on the sofa across from them.

He relaxed as his son chattered from the floor while he colored another horse picture. Mena spoke quietly with her mother, evading a few questions about their trip so far and asking some of her own. When Ryder had finished his sandwich and several cookies, Danny cocked his head toward the kitchen. Ryder nodded once and pushed to his feet. He tousled Mena's curls when she shot him a questioning look, then walked to the breakfast bar.

His friend had his laptop open by the time he got there, and turned it so the screen faced Ryder. Joel's email.

"Same men returned to the house in Virginia." Ryder paused in his reading. "So Ari is still there. Or is back there. Hm."

"Overheard complaints regarding time demands being made of them, one said he was going home to wife and kids no matter what after this follow-up meeting. Gripes about the cousin Elek who Ari is grooming."

He scanned the rest of the email, which Joel had copied to him. So they weren't all happy. He wondered if he could use that to his advantage somehow. Probably not. He doubted they were all family men. The man he'd killed at Aggie's hadn't worn a wedding band and had nothing in his wallet to indicate he had anyone waiting for him if and when he'd completed his task.

"I figured you hadn't seen it yet, but it's not very useful,"

Danny said, leaned on one of the stools, elbow on the counter.

"Maybe not, but still good info to have."

His friend produced a large special delivery envelope next, and Ryder pulled out paperwork from the attorney he'd had Carys contact. A set for Aggie and a set for Mena.

She'd fight him on this, he figured. But she'd sign them, because it would keep Jason safe.

He smiled grimly and stuffed the pages back into the envelope. That could wait till later.

PHILOMENA KNEW THE TIME WAS COMING WHEN SHE had to say goodbye to her mother and Jason again. The afternoon rushed by, and now they all sat with supper plates balanced on their laps, or, in Jason's case, at the breakfast bar. The knot in her belly had returned, making the meal on her plate quite unappetizing.

Ryder rubbed one hand up the middle of her back, his touch reassuring, but not enough to erase the fear.

She played with her food, nibbling at the mashed potatoes, but mostly just pushing everything around on the plate.

"You'd better eat more," he said quietly, leaning nearer.

"I'm not very hungry." Still, she lifted another piece of fish to her mouth, forcing herself to chew, then swallow it, and hoped her stomach would keep it. She forced a smile for her mother, too, though her mom would know it was insincere.

Ryder and Danny spoke casually of things like basketball and preseason baseball. She watched Jason, who played with his dinner, too, though he ate more than she did, taking breaks to spin around on his stool, grinning at her when she caught his eye. Her mother ate slowly, her gaze more observant than Philomena would have liked when it landed on her and Ryder.

"Ladies," Ryder said after everyone had finished, "you'll remember we talked about setting up a trust for future safety, right?"

Philomena tightened her grip on her fork, shifting her gaze to the blazing fireplace. Her stomach flipped over.

"We had Carys get our attorney to prepare the paperwork for you. All it needs are your signatures." He set one hand on her knee, but she didn't look at him, her jaw tightening, along with her spine.

Her mother sat forward. "Give it to me. If it will keep Jason safe, I'll sign it. Then I can sell the house and buy something else. Somewhere safe."

Philomena bit her lower lip. Trust her mother to push the guilt button right away.

Danny whipped out a large messenger envelope and pulled a handful of papers from it.

Her mother quickly scanned, then signed the pages.

Ryder took another set and put them into Philomena's lap. "Mena."

She glared at him. "That's my home," she said, keeping her voice low. She knew she was being stupid. As long as the Harvesters were after her...

"It _was_ your home," he countered, his dark gaze steady on her face. "It's no longer safe."

She swallowed around a lump in her throat. Signing this paper was too final. Selling her house would mean she could really never go back. _Ever._

"Are you going to make me play the guilt card, too?" he teased.

"Don't you dare." She scowled at him. He didn't need to remind her that her family was in danger because of the curse she carried. She'd do anything to keep them safe, out of the Harvester's reach. "Give me a damn pen." She yanked the papers from his grip, her vision blurring when he held out the pen, too.

His big hand settled on her back when she took the pen with shaking fingers. "Breathe, baby," he murmured, his warm breath stirring the hair at her temple.

She sucked in a quick breath, blinking hard to make the tears go away. At least enough for her to see the papers she was about to sign.

"Now what?" she managed after scrawling her signature several times and handing the pages to him.

Danny cleared his throat, leaning his elbows on his knees. "These get sent back to Carys, who'll get them to the attorney who finalizes everything. When you're ready, the houses can be sold via the attorney, the money deposited into a bank account set up for your trust, and you can buy your next home without anyone knowing who's doing the buying."

Philomena blinked away more stinging tears, turning her gaze to the orange flames in the fireplace. "I suppose you have a realtor ready, too, don't you?"

Ryder sighed. "I believe in being prepared, Mena."

Of course. She pushed to her feet and walked to the window, looking out at the dusky sky. She didn't want to cry in front of Jason. She'd managed not to do much crying in all the time she'd had him, but his father was making it a real challenge right now.

Papers shushed behind her, and then she heard heavy footsteps crossing the room away from her. Danny, putting the paperwork away. Then quieter footsteps coming toward her. Too light to be Ryder. *Mom.* She shut her eyes, feeling one of those hot tears slide down her face.

"Philomena, dear." Her mother's hand settled in the center of her back. "I know it's hard, but it must be done."

She took in an unsteady breath. "I'm so sorry, Mom." She couldn't even look at her mother.

Aggie sighed softly and slid her hand to Philomena's shoulder. "It isn't your fault, my girl." She kissed Philomena's cheek.

But she couldn't help thinking it was.

If she'd moved away when the curse chose her, away from her mother, the danger would be following only her now.

If she'd moved away then, she wouldn't have had Jason for the last six years.

A sob lodged in her chest, and she tried desperately to swallow it down, but it wouldn't be budged.

A heavier arm landed on her shoulders from the other side, and her mother's hand fell away.

She turned into Ryder's chest, letting him gather her close. She gripped his shirt, the cotton bunched tight in her fists, while she pressed her face nearer.

"It's all right, baby," he whispered.

The sob grew bigger. She wasn't going to be able to keep it in much longer.

As if he understood, Ryder guided her out of the cabin, away from the little house. Far enough away for her to release the sobs crowding now in her throat. He held on while she cried, anchoring her.

Her furious grief and helplessness passed quickly, leaving her drained. She shivered and felt goosebumps on his arms, too. "You didn't even put on your coat," she managed raggedly, wiping one wet cheek with the back of her hand, her gaze taking in the giant wet spot in the center of his chest.

"It wasn't important."

She shut her eyes, heart racing at his simple declaration and all it meant. She was in *so* much trouble, trouble that had nothing to do with the men hunting her. She inhaled deeply, steeling herself before she swiped her hand over her other cheek, then looked up at him. "How much of a mess am I?"

He cocked his head to one side, his dark gaze sliding over her face. "I guess that depends on how many times Jason has seen you cry."

"Pretty bad, huh?" She took another deep breath and let it out. "Well, I suppose it can't be helped." She stretched to kiss his cheek. "Thank you, Ryder."

They walked back to the house hand in hand. She headed straight to the bathroom and attempted to repair some of the damage, rubbing cold water on her puffy eyes and red nose. It didn't help much, but she felt a little better when she'd finished.

Jason didn't even notice when she returned to the living room. He was too busy demonstrating his horse-riding skills to his father. She leaned against the doorway and studied them, the beautiful boy she'd spent the last six years raising, and the sexy, dangerous father she'd spent the last six years avoiding. They looked so much alike, with their dark eyes and the dimples when they smiled.

She realized Ryder was watching her now, and she flushed a little at his thorough perusal.

"Hey, buddy," he said when Jason finally paused for breath. "Isn't it bedtime?"

"Aw, Daddy."

Philomena smiled behind her hand.

"Yep. Plus Aunt Mena and I have to get rolling." He scooped his son into his arms. "So get your pj's on, and then we can tuck you in before we go."

They passed her on their way into the hall, Ryder's arm brushing hers as they went.

Philomena shifted her gaze to the fireplace, not wanting to think about leaving Jason so soon.

"Philomena, have you heard from your sister?"

She focused on her mother, who was cleaning up the living room. "No. But I heard she was heading toward home."

"I emailed your cousins Electra and Thalia to tell her that the house isn't safe, but I don't know if Desi will get the message." Aggie frowned, concern lining her brow.

"I'll email Electra when I get settled tonight. Let her know it's vitally important that Desi knows not to go there." Philomena rubbed one hand over her forehead, tension knotting behind her eyes. If anything happened to her sister, that blame could be laid at her feet, too.

"I'll call Aunt Lydia later, too, and see if she's heard anything we haven't. She might know where Desi is."

Philomena tried to remember where her sister had been the last time she'd heard from her. California? New Mexico? She wasn't sure. It had been a year ago. Well over a year, now that she thought about it.

Ryder returned with a pajama-clad Jason riding piggyback and giggling.

She smiled at the sight, pushing her wayward sister from her mind for now. "Wow, look at you. All brushed?"

"Yep." Jason looked at her. "I know a secret." He grinned, and her heart squeezed.

"Really?" She lifted one eyebrow and followed them to the sofa, where Ryder sat to let his son get off.

"Yup." He continued to grin at her.

"Huh." She glanced from him to Ryder, who wore an identical grin.

"But I can't tell you."

Her gaze got caught on Ryder's, which danced with mischief. "Well, that's what a secret is, something only two people know and can't tell anyone else." Her heart beat faster at the look in Ryder's eyes.

"You gonna tuck me in, Aunt Phila?"

She dragged her gaze away from Ryder's, back to Jason. "You bet, buddy." She bent to scoop him off the sofa. "Kiss Grandma goodnight." She moved to the other sofa, where her mother had taken out her crocheting needle and yarn.

"Night, Gramma." Jason leaned down to plant a smacking kiss on her cheek.

"Good night, Jason. Sleep well."

Philomena carried him back the hallway to the room he was sharing with her mother, and plopped him onto the bed he said was his. She pulled the blankets down so he could scoot in, then tugged them to his chin when he finally lay down. She brushed his dark hair away from his forehead. "You're going to keep being a good boy for Grandma and Danny, right?"

His mouth twisted. "You know I'm always a good boy."

She smiled. "Yes, you are." She kissed his forehead.

"I hope you have the best dreams," he said.

Philomena shut her eyes against the stinging. "I hope you have even better dreams, buddy."

"No, you have the bestest." He sat up and gave her a tight, squeezing hug.

She squeezed him back, swallowing hard around the lump in her throat. "You have the bestest, bestest dreams ever, Jason." His little heart beat steadily against her chest, making *her* heart ache. She'd do whatever she had to to keep him safe. Easing her grip on him, she kissed his cheek. "I love you, sweetie. Sleep well."

When she got to her feet, Ryder was there to take his turn kissing his son goodnight. She moved to the doorway, concentrating on breathing steadily and dislodging the lump in her throat.

Ryder joined her here a moment later, catching her hand and guiding her back out to the living area. "It's time to go."

Worry lined her mother's forehead. "Do you have to? At this hour?"

He nodded. "The more distance between us, the better."

Philomena wondered if Danny had shared any of their Harvester run-ins with her mother, or if this was just plain old Mom worry for their safety.

Aggie nodded slowly. "If you think it's best." She got to her feet and hugged Philomena tight, making her tear up again. "I packed some cookies for you. And a couple sandwiches. I didn't know how long you'd drive tonight."

Philomena squeezed her back, refusing to let the tears fall. When she stepped away, Ryder hugged her mother, too, murmuring something she couldn't hear. She lifted her coat to distract herself from the goodbyes, sliding her arms into the sleeves.

Ryder waited, food packages in hand when she'd finished buttoning, and caught her elbow to guide her to the car.

It was cold outside now, and a million stars lit the sky overhead. She looked up at them for a moment, wishing her life hadn't been turned upside-down, before getting into her seat. She took the foil packets from him, then watched him walk around to get into the driver's seat.

"Thank you," she said when he put the key into the ignition. "For bringing me here to see them."

"We weren't too far." He shot her a quick smile and pulled out of the driveway.

She didn't argue, just shut her eyes.

"We need to find a place to stay tonight, baby, if you would do a quick search."

She nodded, twisting to put the food in the back seat, then reached for her laptop.

"Maybe across the state line into Georgia," he said as he drove, watching the road signs ahead.

"Okay." She pulled up the search and scanned for something. "How about Rome?"

"I've always wanted to see Rome," he teased.

She smiled reluctantly and found them a place.

"We'll figure out our next destination tomorrow. After we've had some rest."

Philomena nodded, then opened her email program. Nothing new. But she shot off a note to her cousin, asking her to pass along the message to Desi if she could that she absolutely could *not* go to Aggie's. And another to her sister to warn her the Harvesters had found them and the house wasn't safe.

Just thinking about it made her stomach tighten with worry.

For once, it would be nice not to have to worry about Desi doing something she shouldn't.

Philomena shook her head. Unlikely.

～

Ryder felt better when they got underway in the morning. He'd been cautious, watching the rearview mirror all the way from Alabama into Georgia last night. Even after they'd checked into the motel, it had taken hours to sleep, despite spending an hour or so making love to Mena. His brain wouldn't shut off.

Today, though, confidence replaced the tension. Sharing his plans for the future with Jason last night had been impulsive. Telling his son he intended to marry Mena and make her officially Jason's mom had made his son very happy, in turn making Ryder even happier. This morning, they'd had a leisurely breakfast at the motel restaurant, planning their route into Florida as they ate. He'd also had Carys arrange for him to get a new rental car in Atlanta. That would be their first stop. Then they could get on the highway and drive south.

It was a good plan.

The car swap at the airport in Atlanta went smoothly. Mena insisted on driving part of the distance, so he let her get behind the wheel when they left with the new car.

The drive out of Atlanta was slow, the highway congested, and he kept an eye on the other cars and their occupants. No prickly feeling at his nape.

After lunch, he took over the driving. There were no new emails, though he knew Danny was moving his little band to a different spot today, as well as getting the trust paperwork expressed back to Carys.

Ryder relaxed a bit more when they got onto the smaller highway to head toward Tallahassee. Less traffic made for easier car watching.

Mena worked on the website, making the last tweaks she'd said she wanted to make.

"Are you going to show me this website one of these days?"

Her lips curved upward, but her gaze was unfocused when she met his. "Eventually. I keep finding little things that aren't quite right."

"Perfectionist," he teased.

She shook her head, her attention on her work.

"Hey, there's a rest area a few miles away. How about if we get out and stretch our legs? Get a fresh soda. Something to snack on."

"Okay."

From the absent tone of her reply, he knew she wasn't paying full attention to him.

That was all right. He'd have her full attention in a few hours when they got checked into their next hotel, and he intended to hold her attention for a couple of hours, at least. He grinned to himself as he guided the car along the highway.

PHILOMENA CAUGHT HERSELF HUMMING AS SHE finished the coding and stopped, typing one last command into the system. "There." She smiled over at Ryder. "Done."

"For real this time?"

"Yes, for real." She rolled her eyes. "You can take a peek at it when we stop for the night." She shifted her shoulders, feeling a twinge. Working in a moving car wasn't something she'd done before, and it wasn't comfortable.

"Then we can share with Joel and Danny, right?"

"Mm-hm." She powered down the laptop and put it away, still trying to stretch her shoulders.

"Need a massage?" He waggled his eyebrows at her.

"Has anyone ever told you you've got a one-track mind?" She felt the blush creeping up her cheeks.

"Never before." His grin turned wicked. "I blame you."

Philomena shook her head, looking out the window when the car decelerated. The rest area. She did need to stretch.

When he parked the car, she got out slowly, leaning to first one side, then the other to stretch her back. She shot a quick smile at him when Ryder's hands landed on her shoulders, his thumbs digging into the tight muscles there. "Oh, that's nice." She shut her eyes, letting him work on the ache there until it eased a bit. "Thank you."

He kissed her cheek lightly. "No problem. Shall we?"

She shut her car door. They'd parked nearly at the end of the available parking spaces, away from other vehicles, so they had a bit of a walk to the building housing the restrooms, refreshments, and other travel conveniences. The trek was nice. It was far warmer in Georgia this time of year than it would be at home in Pennsylvania.

Philomena swung their joined hands as they walked, seeing Ryder's smile from the corner of her eye. They strolled in the front door, and she glanced around. To one side, there were fast food counters and a newsstand. To the other, a convenience shop with more food and drink choices, as well as other things travelers might need. The restrooms were on the opposite side, flanking a door that led outside, and through which she saw an overgrown field with scrubby bushes throughout leading to a tree line farther away.

"Pit stop," she said, nodding toward the restrooms.

Ryder nodded, and they walked in that direction, parting to go into the separate bathrooms.

Philomena waited in a long line for her turn, then found

herself humming again as she washed her hands. Her reflection showed pink cheeks and a faint smile curving her lips. She averted her gaze, not wanting to think too much about the source of her current contentment. She could blame it on finishing the website at last, but that would be a lie, and she knew it. Perhaps she could just enjoy it.

She walked out of the ladies' room and looked around for Ryder. Somehow, she doubted he'd had to wait. She found him in line at the convenience store at the other end of the large room, two soda bottles and some snacks in his hands.

Still smiling, she started to cross the building, weaving between a woman with a toddler and a trio of teenage girls.

"Excuse me." A big, dark hand landed on her arm.

Her heart pounded harder. Her gaze slid up over the scythe pendant at the man's throat before meeting glittering black eyes.

"You will come with me, Medusa," the man said quietly. "I have a gun in my pocket, aimed at you."

Something *was* in his jacket pocket, she realized, and she didn't think it was just his other hand.

She was going to die.

She shot a glance at Ryder's broad shoulders as the Harvester forced her to the back door, willing Ryder to look her way. He'd been so good about sensing when trouble had found them the last two times.

The man shoved her through the door.

She'd never see Jason or Ryder or her mother. When the Harvester dragged her at his side, she stumbled into the long grass.

Gods, I don't want to die, she thought, her heart pounding up into her throat and cutting off her air.

The man didn't even look around to see if they were

being watched. No one else was visible on this side of the building, not even a dog-walking traveler.

She wanted to shut her eyes and give in to the panic, but she couldn't. She stumbled again, then forced herself to her feet. He would not drag her through these weeds to her death.

Philomena clenched her free hand at her side, and sucked in a quick breath as she brushed her leg. Her dagger. Holy Gods, she'd forgotten it in her panic.

She shot the Harvester a sidelong glance, but his attention focused on the tree line not so far ahead now.

If he dragged her in there, she was a dead woman.

The next time her boot caught on a clump of long grass, she stumbled deliberately, tumbling down into the damp grass. She fell so her right hand was under the hem of her skirt, on the hilt of her dagger.

"Get on your feet," he growled, reaching for her arm once more.

She whipped the dagger up at the same time he bent nearer, forcing the sharp point deep, high under his ribs.

His dark eyes rounded in shock, probably to match her own. He jerked to one side, and the dagger sliced him even further. A horrible gurgling sound came from his chest. She yanked her hand backward, the blade catching a moment before tearing free. He tumbled to the ground beside her, and the gurgling stopped even though the blood pouring from his wound did not. His eyes stared sightlessly at her.

CHAPTER TWELVE

R yder hit the door and started running. He saw Mena's back as the Harvester dragged her into the scrubby field behind the building. If the guy got her to the trees, he'd kill her. When she went down in the long grass, his heart stopped.

After everything, he was going to lose her, here in this dirty field in The-Middle-of-Nowhere, Georgia.

Hell, no!

Then he saw the glint of her dagger when she thrust her hand up at the same time the Harvester bent over to grab her again. Dark blood spurted from the wound.

His heart started beating again, much too quickly. He was still running, he realized, watching the Harvester lean to one side, tearing his flesh open wider on her blade. Then the man fell to the ground in front of her. No way could he live with that amount of blood loss.

Mena leaned the other way in the grass and vomited, and as Ryder neared, he heard her crying.

Oh Gods, he thought, stumbling to his knees at her side,

giving the Harvester a quick glance to be certain he wasn't breathing. No. *Good.* "Baby, are you hurt? Gods, I'm so sorry." Pulse pounding too loud in his head, he wrapped his arms around her when her stomach was empty. He rocked her back and forth, gingerly feeling for injuries. His entire body shook, almost as much as she was trembling. He held onto her for a long time, trying not to think of seeing her fall and believing he was too late.

Instead, he focused on what he needed to do now.

When she took in a long, shaky breath, he caught her chin, tipping her face toward his.

Her cheeks were chalky white and streaked with tears, her green eyes red-rimmed and wide with horror.

"I need you to focus for a little bit, baby," he said.

She stared up at him, and he hoped she wasn't completely in shock. Not yet.

"I've got to get you out of here. But first we have to wash off." He didn't look at her bloody wrist and sleeve, not wanting to draw her attention there. "I want you to close your eyes now, though. Just for a minute. Keep them closed for me, baby."

He waited until she'd obeyed him, shivers wracking her body, then pushed to his feet. He took a quick glance around to make sure no one could see them. Assured the coast was clear, he caught the Harvester by the ankles and dragged him into the nearby trees. He patted the man down, then took his wallet and the scythe pendant from around his neck. He realized there was a gun in the guy's jacket pocket and left it there. Hopefully when he was found, they'd just think he was up to no good, which was true. Ryder didn't have the time right now to dispose of the body more securely. He had a bigger priority.

Back at her side, he took off his jacket and draped it

around Mena. He wiped her dagger in the grass before sliding it into its sheath, then helped her to her feet, where she swayed. "You can open your eyes now, baby." He cupped her face with one hand.

Her wet lashes lifted, and she stared at him.

"I need you to keep your hand inside my coat for now, okay? We're going inside and get you cleaned up." Adrenaline still zipped through his veins, though he tried to tamp it down.

She nodded slowly.

Definitely in shock.

Ryder kissed her forehead lightly. "Okay. Ready?"

Another slow nod.

He guided her across the field, his heart pounding too fast. If anyone saw the blood, they'd be caught. He hoped one of the family restrooms designed for parents with small kids was empty.

It was. He sent a silent thanks skyward for that.

Once he had her inside, he took his coat off her shoulders, then unbuttoned her jacket, taking it off, too, and guided her to the sink.

When she saw the blood, tears welled in her eyes, and she shook harder.

"Shh. It's all right now, baby," he murmured, soaping up her bloody hand and his. "It's all right. You're safe." The water sluicing off their joined hands was rusty with the Harvester's blood. He noticed several tiny flecks of blood on her face and touched his fingers there to rinse them away. "We're going to get in the car and hit the highway in just a minute." He shut the water off, reaching blindly for a couple paper towels to dry their hands, then to wipe any faint splashes from the sink.

"I'm going to be sick." She turned away from him and dropped to her knees in front of the toilet.

He held her hair away from her face while she heaved up the last of her stomach's contents. Then he got her back to the sink to rinse while she cried harder.

Someone knocked at the door.

"Just a second," he called, banking his impatience with whoever stood outside the door. "My wife is sick."

Some muffled comment reached his ears, but he ignored it.

"Baby," he murmured into her hair, "we've got to get out of here. I need you to focus for me."

Her breathing hitched, but she turned her wet face to his again. Tears still streaked her cheeks, and he thumbed them away.

"I just need you to make it to the car, honey. Do you think you can do that?"

She sucked in a ragged breath and nodded, struggling to stop crying.

He used a damp paper towel to wipe her cheeks dry. Anyone who looked at her would hopefully just see a sick woman with pasty cheeks.

"All right." He wrapped her coat inside his and put the bundle over his arm. "I'll help you, Mena." He wrapped his other arm around her shoulders and steered her toward the door. "Breathe."

A harried-looking woman stood there with a squirming youngster. They stepped away when Ryder guided Mena out of the small room, as if to avoid their germs. *Good.*

When they got to the car, Mena sank into her seat, eyes shutting as more tears slipped down her face.

He fastened her seatbelt and hurried to his own seat.

They needed to get the hell out of here. He'd already fucked up enough for today.

He drove out of the rest area at a sedate speed, but once they got into traffic on the highway, he pressed harder on the accelerator, as much as he dared without getting them pulled over. No need to wave a giant flag for the police to notice them at all. "It's all right now, Mena. You're safe." Noting the goosebumps on her arm below her sleeve, he cranked the heat in the car. Definitely in shock.

He cursed himself for not waiting outside the ladies' room. He'd thought about it when he emerged from the men's room, but figured he had time to get them drinks and snacks before she got through the line bound to be in the women's restroom. This was all his fault.

After about an hour, he started searching for hotel signs. Mena shivered in her seat, arms wrapped around her middle, and tears fell periodically. After another half hour, he found a motel where it looked like they might be able to park in front of the room. He pulled in directly outside the office with its giant picture window.

"I'll be right back, baby." After she dipped her chin once, he got out and locked the door. Checking in took only a few minutes, but it felt like an eternity. He kept peering out the office window to be sure she remained where he'd left her.

He moved the car to the slot directly outside their door, which was at the far end of one wing of the hotel. Hopefully away from any other guests.

He grabbed her suitcase and hustled her inside, feeling the wracking shudders still shaking her. "Come on. Get undressed. You need a hot shower, honey." He helped her, then got her under the water.

She opened her eyes, lashes spiky and wet. "I'm so sorry, Ryder." The steam started to rise around her.

His heart was breaking. "Baby, you have nothing to apologize for. This is all my fault." He cleared his throat. "You get warm. I'm going to bring in the rest of our stuff. I'll be back in a few minutes, okay?"

She nodded, then turned her face up to the hot spray.

He watched her for a moment, finally sliding the shower door shut before he left the little room. He went out for the rest of their things, keeping her coat bundled inside his as he grabbed his bag and her laptop, then shoved the car door closed.

He thumbed on his phone. "Danny, we have a problem," he said when his friend answered the phone. "Can you talk?"

"Yeah, let me step outside."

Ryder went inside, kicked the door shut and threw the deadbolt. "A Harvester grabbed Mena when we hit a rest stop earlier. She had to kill him." He dropped their things onto one of the beds.

"Jesus." Danny's breath rushed out. "How did this happen?"

"My responsibility. I thought I had time while she was in line in the restroom to grab drinks. I was a fucking idiot." He banged his forehead against the wall beside the door.

His friend sighed. "Okay, chill, man. Quit beating yourself up. Nothing you can do about it now. Where's the body?"

Ryder told him what he'd done. "Not my best work. I just wanted to get her the hell out of there."

"She's your first priority." Danny hummed, something he did when he was thinking. It had been a real bitch to make him stop when they were on a mission where total silence was required. "Okay, I know someone in the area who can finish the disposal, unless you want to just leave him there."

"If we leave him there, he's bound to be found soon. I'm fairly certain people walk their dogs in that field. The smell is going to attract them, the blood in the field." He opened his eyes. "I fucked up, Danny. Bad."

"You mean you're not perfect? Wow, alert the media." Danny laughed. "Get over yourself, Ryder. None of us is perfect. It's just too bad your big mistake had to involve Philomena. So I'll call in the disposal crew and deal with him. You just get her taken care of."

"Don't say anything to Aggie, okay?"

"Christ, no. Why would I do that?" His friend sounded highly offended. Or, more likely, alarmed he might have to comfort an upset woman.

Ryder smiled a little at the thought. "All right. I've got to go. Can you call Carys and tell her we're going to want a different car, too? We're close enough to Pensacola to get there tomorrow to get a new rental. No, wait, maybe the day after." He thought about it for a second. "The day after tomorrow. I think we'll hang here another night, just to make sure Mena's okay." They were too close to the rest area for his liking, but Mena's well-being was more impor- tant than putting more distance between them and the scene of the crime, so to speak.

"All right. I'll have her shoot you an email with the details then. Man, relax, okay. I know you're down there blaming this whole thing on yourself, but it's not all on you. Those Harvesters are persistent. They're going to take any opportunity they can to get at her. You just blinked at the wrong time. She's safe now, so move the hell on."

Ryder knew that. He did. But it felt bad. *Big.* How could he have failed so completely?

"Ryder? You listening to me?"

"Yeah." He cleared his throat. "I've got to go. She's in shock. I've got her in the shower to warm up." He dropped their coats onto the floor. They'd be trash, but he couldn't leave them in the hotel trash. He should find a place to burn them.

"Go. I'll email you later." Danny disconnected, and Ryder did the same, dropping the phone onto the bed with his bag.

The water still ran in the shower, the little room's exhaust fan inadequate to the task of handling the volume of steam from the bathtub.

Peering through the mist, he found her sitting on the bottom of the tub, head on her knees. He wrestled with the laces on his boots, then shucked his clothing, stepping into the shower behind her.

"Hey," he said softly, squatting to rub his hand along her arm. "Are you warmer?"

She nodded, not lifting her head.

"Come on up here with me." He set one hand at her waist and used the other to catch her elbow, drawing her to her feet. Unable to hide her tears now, she turned her face into the spray.

Ryder clenched his jaw against the pain in his chest. "I'm so sorry, Mena." He slid one hand up the middle of her back, under her wet hair. "I should never have left you. Not even for a second."

She turned into him, lifting one hand to cover his mouth. "Not your fault," she choked out.

He scooped her hair away from her face, his heart aching at her swollen eyes and red nose. "How can you say that? If I'd been waiting there when you came out, he couldn't have grabbed you."

Mena shook her head. "I didn't run, I didn't yell. I should have."

"Oh, Gods." He gathered her into his arms. "This is *not* your fault." His own guilt jabbed at his guts.

"I was so afraid I wasn't going to see you again. Or Jason, or Mom." A sob broke. "Gods, I was so afraid I'd never see you." She sagged against him, giving in to the tears.

Somewhere deep inside him, a little voice was cheering at her admission, that she'd fear the same thing he had. But the voice putting the blame squarely on his shoulders for this was louder.

"I didn't want to kill him. I didn't mean to," she managed. "I just wanted to get away. I don't even kill the spiders when they get in the house."

"Oh, baby." He held her tighter. "You're killing me. I hate to see you cry." He shut his eyes and held her as tight as he could without cutting off her air. "It's okay. You're safe now, I promise."

The loud voice in his head reminded him he'd promised before to keep her safe, and look what had happened.

He ignored it and concentrated instead on her, her subsiding shivers, her slowing tears. She sniffled, taking in a shuddering breath and releasing it slowly.

"Someone should call the police," she said, her voice rough from crying.

He shook his head. "And tell them what? 'This guy tried to kill the Medusa, so she had to kill him instead? I doubt that'll go over well." He forced a smile. "Danny's taking care of it."

She frowned. "What is he doing?"

Ryder shook his head. "You don't need to know details. You just need to feel better."

"What if he has a family?" Her voice broke.

He gaped at her. "This man was trying to kill you, Mena."

"But if he never comes home, his family won't know what happened to him."

A laugh bubbled up from the center of his chest, and he didn't try to quell it.

She glared at him, her eyes still shiny, then shoved him away.

He caught her upper arms, lightly, chuckling. "Hey, if you want me to find out, I can."

She nodded.

"Gods, I love you." He bent to put a soft kiss on her mouth. "You are going to keep me on my toes for the rest of my life, aren't you?"

Her eyes widened, and he realized what had just come out of his mouth. He'd been trying not to go there again.

Too late to take it back now.

Instead, he let his gaze drift to the dark bruise on her forearm. "Did he do that?" He caught her wrist, gently lifting her arm so he could see the bruise encircled most of her arm. "Of course he did." His urge to laugh was gone now.

Mena stared at her arm, too. "He had a gun in his pocket," she whispered.

"I know." Ryder cupped her chin with one hand, waiting until she met his gaze. "Baby, it was you or him. I'd rather it be him."

She nodded slowly, but he could see the fear and horror lingering in her eyes.

"Come on. You're warm enough now. I think a nap will

help." He shut off the water and guided her out of the tub, wrapping her in one of the towels after he rubbed her dry. His hand slowed and pulse sped up when he got a glimpse of her tattoo, though--*whoa!* Mentioning *that* now didn't seem to be a good idea. He snagged another towel to wrap around his waist.

In the other room, he yanked the covers back on the bed not holding their things. "In you go."

She undid the towel from around her torso and sat, using it to dry her hair a bit more instead of reclining. "Only if you lie down with me."

He'd do anything she wanted, as long as she was safe.

Philomena lay in bed hours later, staring at the ceiling. She'd only slept a little. Even with the curtains drawn and all the lights off, there was too much daylight in the room. And she wasn't tired, just emotionally drained.

Plus every time she closed her eyes, she saw the look in the Harvester's eyes when she'd stabbed him.

Shocked.

She was still shocked she'd done it.

True, she hadn't intended to kill him. But he'd bent over at just the wrong time. And he *had* planned to kill her.

Her mind went in the same circles the entire time she lay there beside Ryder, who didn't sleep at all.

But he didn't try to distract her from her thoughts, for which she was grateful. She needed to deal with this.

Finally, he rolled onto his side, lifting one hand to touch her cheek. She turned her face toward him.

"The first time I killed someone in the military, I puked my guts out for an hour," he said softly. "Sure, I knew in my head the guy had a bomb strapped around his waist and he was coming for my patrol. But I was still sick over it. I was just a kid. He was even younger." His fingers slid along her cheekbone. "I can see his face in my head, if I think about it." His dark eyes searched hers. "But I'd do it all over, because it was him or me. I had no choice. Neither did you."

Her eyes stung at his words, and she rolled into him, letting him hold her against his heart, which beat steadily under her hand. "I know that in my head. I do, Ryder," she whispered. "But I can't stop thinking about it."

He kissed her forehead. "I know." He took a deep breath. "We need to get dressed and go get some supper." He ignored the way she shook her head. "Then we're going to come back here, and I'm going to distract you from all thoughts of today for as long as I possibly can." He kissed her lightly. "Come on." He shoved the blankets off and sat up, pulling her along.

Philomena unzipped her suitcase and pulled out clean clothes, dressing slowly. To keep herself distracted, she watched Ryder do the same. When she reached for her dagger, though, to put it into her boot, she realized the dagger needed cleaning.

"I'll do it." He was only half-dressed, but he took her leg sheath into the bathroom, closing the door firmly.

She inhaled unsteadily and reached for the television remote. Another distraction. She watched the weather forecast for several minutes, then changed the channel, and again, pressing the 'channel up' button on the remote. A local newscast was on, and the perky blonde behind the desk smiled while she talked about a bus driver strike in a nearby school district.

But she didn't see anything about the Harvester's body being found.

Which meant no one had discovered him. Yet.

Ryder came out of the bathroom with her dagger. "I'll have to give it a more thorough cleaning later, but it's good for now." He tucked it into her boot, then straightened, frowning. "Why are you watching the news?"

She shrugged. "Just surfing."

He turned the television off, sighing. "All right." He went to his coat and pulled a wallet from his pocket.

Philomena gaped at him as he pawed through it, watching him discard a driver's license, credit cards on the bed. "Where did you get that?"

"When I moved him." He shook his head. "Nothing here indicates a family, but we'll make sure." He booted up his laptop and fired off an email to Danny and copied Carys. Even if she'd left for the day, she'd deal with this. "There." He met her gaze, his eyes crinkling a little at the corners. "Do you feel better now?"

She didn't know what to think. Ryder would've killed the man himself if he'd been able, but to humor her, he was having his office find out if the Harvester had a family.

She swallowed around a new lump in her throat. "You're a very nice man, Ryder Ware," she said softly.

He bent to kiss her. "I know. A real saint." He grinned and stepped back. "I need a shirt, or we'll never get served."

Philomena ignored the way her heart raced as he pulled on a clean shirt, then turned to her suitcase and pulled out a cardigan.

"You're going to need a new jacket." His expression was more somber now.

She swallowed. Didn't want to think about that. "Are you ready?"

Ryder nodded and held out his hand to her.

She went, sliding her fingers into his. She badly needed

a distraction, and not just from the day's events, but from the way her emotions were tangled up over him.

RYDER DEVOURED HIS BURGER AND FRIES, AND HALF the fries on the extra plate he'd ordered while Mena picked at her salad and took tiny sips of her soup. He made a mental note to stop and buy some sodas and snack food to take back to their room with them in case she decided she was hungry later. He didn't tell her she should eat, though he wanted to. When she'd been sick earlier, he was pretty sure she'd lost not only her lunch but her breakfast, too.

But he remembered how he'd felt after his first, too. Food hadn't been on his mind either.

Still watching Mena, he ordered a slice of cherry pie when the waitress returned to check on them.

She stared into her salad, occasionally spearing a vegetable on her fork, or lifting her cup of chicken corn chowder to take another sip.

He wondered when she'd realize the cup in her tattoo had changed colors again.

He thanked the waitress when she returned with his dessert, hiding a smile. He'd realized the goblet was no longer silver when he'd been drying her off after the shower. It was pink now, a pale, pale pink in the midst of all the vivid flowers and the shiny green snake.

It probably wouldn't be today. Maybe not even tomorrow, unless he pointed it out.

He grinned into his pie and whipped cream.

"That's a scary smile," Mena said.

He met her gaze and let his grin widen. "I don't know what you're talking about."

A tiny smile touched her lips, almost reaching her eyes. "I don't want to know."

"Okay." He scooped up a big bite of pie and stuffed it into his mouth.

She shook her head and dropped her fork into her salad bowl, the smile a little bigger now, though she was still too pale.

He'd take care of that later, too.

Savoring the pie, he ate every bite, though he did offer the last one to Mena, who shook her head, wrinkling her nose.

"What's your favorite dessert?" he asked, setting his empty plate aside and resting his forearms on the edge of the table.

She gave him a quizzical look, a tiny frown line appearing between her brows. "My favorite dessert?" When he nodded, she shifted her gaze to his shoulder, thinking. "Hm, fresh fruit with homemade ice cream on top," she said after a moment, meeting his gaze. "There's a farm market near home, and in the summer, we buy whatever they picked that day, then go home and make ice cream to go with it for dessert." Her smile was faraway.

Ryder's heart squeezed. They'd have to find a place to live where they could do the same thing. After all this was over and he finally persuaded her they should be together forever.

Philomena smiled at Jason's chatter when they got back to the motel. She sat on the foot of the bed, cross-legged. "You did not," she said, teasing him.

"I did, too. Ask Gramma. She was there. Danny said I'm a good fisherman."

"How big was this fish again?" She smiled again when Ryder winked at her from his spot at the table, where he'd dug out his kit and was polishing her dagger, resharpening the blade.

"Huge. At least six inches long."

"Wow, that's enormous." She shut her eyes and concentrated on her nephew, rather than the rasping sounds of dagger against whetstone.

"I know. I wish you coulda seen it. But it tasted real good."

She laughed. "I'll have some the next time, I guess."

"Yeah, I guess. You wanna talk to Gramma? She's waitin' here."

"Okay. I love you, buddy. Be good, okay?"

"Love you, too, Aunt Phila. Bye!"

She blinked against the stinging in her eyes.

"Hello, Philomena."

"Hi, Mom. So how big was this fish?"

Her mother laughed. "For a six-year-old, pretty big. I'll email you the pictures later, so you can see him."

"Oh, thank you." Her voice caught, and she cleared her throat.

"What's wrong, Philomena?"

She swallowed hard. "I just miss you guys." She couldn't tell her mother about her afternoon. Aggie was strong, but Philomena wasn't sure her mother was strong enough to deal with *that*. "I'm so glad we got to see you."

Her mother sighed, but let the subject drop, shifting the conversation to other things.

Philomena was pacing the room by the time she hung up, the Harvester's face behind her eyes again. Ryder's hand flashed out and caught the back of her shirt, dragging her into his lap.

"Hey." He nuzzled the side of her neck. "You all right?"

She shook her head, but when she would have pushed to her feet, he wrapped his arm around her waist and held on.

"Then it must be time for the distraction I promised you earlier." He nipped at her earlobe, startling her and sending a rush of warmth sliding along her veins.

She inhaled shakily. "I'm not sure that's going to...oh!"

His big hand slid under her shirt to catch her breast, stroking the tip until it hardened against his fingers. "Really?" He pinched the taut peak, and all her nerve endings came to life. "I'll have to try harder." He shifted his hand to her other breast, and when he stopped for a moment, she was panting.

"Ryder?"

"Hm?" He licked the tender spot beneath her ear while he gently squeezed her swollen breasts.

She shut her eyes, leaning against his shoulder.

"How's that distraction working for you?" he teased, dragging his open mouth along her jaw.

"So far, so good."

He laughed, then pushed to his feet and turned her in his arms so he could capture her mouth.

She gave herself up to him, letting him strip her clothing off amid gentle strokes of his hard fingers over her pliant flesh. Accepted demanding kisses that obliterated any other thoughts from her mind.

Fire raced through her when he finally stretched out over her, flesh to flesh. He'd already stroked her to climax twice, and his hard flesh burned against her belly now.

"Please, Ryder," she whispered into his mouth.

"Since you asked so nicely," he growled, lifting his hips away so he could wedge the tip of his cock into her wet sheath, the blunt head stretching her, then sliding deep.

She gasped when he settled fully inside her.

He grinned. "Better?"

She nodded, her breath coming too fast.

He nudged the tip of her nose with his, then kissed her again, lazily this time. As his hips began to move, sliding slowly backward, then pushing deep, over and over, never faster, until she wanted to scream with the pleasure.

Finally, he pressed one finger over her clit, just hard enough to push her over the edge.

Then he did it again.

When Ryder finally let go, Philomena had lost count of her climaxes. He'd turned her brain to dust, so all it was capable of doing was maintaining basic life functions, such as breathing and pumping blood, and both of those much too quickly.

She felt sweat dampening her hair beneath her, the moisture between their bodies, the wetness on his spine when she dragged her fingers along his strong back.

He kissed her once more, lightly this time. "How was that? For a starter?"

She laughed breathlessly, then moaned when he sucked on her collarbone. "A starter? Are you kidding?"

"Give me a couple minutes," he murmured against her throat.

Philomena smiled up at the ceiling.

Ryder's mouth slid lower, finding her breast, its tight tip.

She sucked in a quick breath at the renewed sensation rushing to her womb, making her inner muscles clench hard.

"Yep," he teased. "Just a starter."

She shut her eyes and gave in. The man was determined. And sexy as hell.

Not to mention occupying a large space in her heart.

Her eyes flew open at that thought, her fingers tightening on his shoulders.

Oh Gods, she couldn't.

She was afraid she had.

CHAPTER THIRTEEN

R yder woke in the wee hours when Mena shifted beside him, whimpering. He knew he couldn't distract her forever. He rolled onto his side, curving his body around hers. "Mena." He brushed one hand down her arm. "It's just a dream, baby."

She jerked against his hold, a faint moan passing her lips.

"Wake up, honey." He gave her a gentle shake.

She came awake on a sharp cry, jolting upright.

"Come here." He sat up and pulled her into his arms.

She panted against his skin, and hot tears dripped onto his collarbone.

"Easy, honey. It's just a bad dream." He held her tight while she shivered.

Her fingers dug into his arms.

"I've got you. He can't hurt you anymore." He pressed his lips to her hair. He'd make sure none of the rest of those fuckers hurt her either.

When her breathing steadied, he tipped her chin up and kissed her, lightly.

"Would you hold me a while?" she asked.

"Anytime you want." He rolled onto his back, drawing her with him so she sprawled on top of him, then adjusted the blankets to cover her fully. "Better?"

"Yes, thank you." She took a deep breath and released it in a rush. "How long will I have nightmares?"

He shrugged. "Can't say for sure." His had lasted for six months. He didn't want that for her.

He heard her swallow. "I don't suppose I can talk to a therapist about this, can I?"

He smiled into the darkness. "Maybe. There might be one somewhere in your family. And if not, I'm sure I can find one with a lot of discretion." He stroked her head, twining his fingers in her unruly curls.

"Who did you talk to?"

His smile faded. "There are people to talk to." He'd gone to his required sessions, however, and nothing further. He couldn't see the point in continuing to remind himself of it when all he wanted to do was forget.

Mena sighed softly. "Maybe you should get someone on staff for your people. Just in case."

He hummed his agreement, but he didn't point out that nearly everyone who worked for and with him had already had the same experience in whatever military or intelligence branch they'd worked. Instead, he stroked down her warm back, following the curve of her hips to cup her bottom.

She made a startled sound, then let him shift her so she straddled his hips, his thickening erection sliding along her damp folds.

"You feel so good, Mena," he murmured, dragging his fingers between her thighs, finding her clit, then pressing into her body, feeling another rush of moisture ease his way. "Always so good around me."

As a distraction from her frightening afternoon, sex seemed to work. Her body flashed hot, her nipples tightening against his chest, her pussy slippery around his fingers. He stroked into her until her breathing grew shallow and her hips rocked into his palm.

"Just like that." He eased his fingers from her body and replaced them with his cock, forcing the tip into her clutching sheath. "Relax, baby. Let me in."

She whimpered, shifting her hips toward his so he slid in several more inches.

And later, when she wept again, he was sure it had nothing to do with the events of the afternoon, and everything to do with the emotions and pleasure rushing through her quaking body.

She clung to him, arms and legs wrapped around him, and he kissed away the tears that slid back her temples and down her cheeks. "It's all right, love," he whispered, feeling a lump in his own throat.

He'd nearly lost her yesterday.

It wouldn't happen again.

~

"WHAT DO YOU MEAN ALASTOR IS DEAD?" ELEK leaned forward.

Argos rubbed the bridge of his nose. "I mean an unmarked envelope arrived earlier via messenger. There was a typewritten note with the location of his body and a photocopy of his driver's license."

Ari sat back in his seat. "Goddess," he breathed, reaching for the pill bottle in front of him.

Elek's pulsebeat nearly drowned out the rattle of the medication. "We need to--"

Argos held up one hand. "I knew you'd say that, so I called Petr and Damo. They are bringing his body now."

"How did he die?" Elek asked, a little afraid to hear the answer.

"Gutted." Argos looked faintly ill. "But not where he was found."

"Thank you, Argos," Ari said, waving his hand dismissively.

Elek rose as his cousin left the room. "How did this happen? He never even said he'd found her."

"Perhaps just by chance," Ari said, sitting back and settling his gaze on Elek. "I do wonder, however, about *why* they let us know where to find him. We'll have to go to his wife to tell her he's gone."

Elek didn't care about the why, just the how.

Ari frowned at him. "What are you thinking?"

"I need to know how he found her, and how she got away."

"Unless he made notes we can recover, we probably won't know the answer to your first question, and I believe the manner of his death answers the second."

Elek frowned and began to pace.

Stabbing meant up close. Nestor had been shot, which had not been point-blank range. He had been killed by Ware for certain. Stabbing...

His pace slowed. The stabbing was likely the Medusa. He wanted more information. Where had Alastor found her? Was that where she'd killed him? And why lead them to his body? Why not just leave him to rot?

"She did this," he muttered.

"Probably," Ari agreed. "In her attempt to escape, I imagine. One more reason to kill her."

Elek stopped pacing and dropped into the chair opposite his great-uncle. "Vicious. The method is vicious."

Ari nodded, steepling his fingers in front of him. "I expect nothing less from the monster."

Elek set his own hands flat on the desk and studied them. He had learned many ways to use them to kill a person, as had his uncles and cousins. Alastor would only have ignored those skills if he felt confident enough with another mode. His own blade. A gun. "We need to know if any weapons were found on his body," he said, lifting his gaze to the older man's face. "And we need Argos to pull any useful information from his computer and phone. Then we'll get a better idea if this was intentional or accidental when he found her."

"You take care of that while I call his wife."

Elek left his great-uncle to his onerous task and headed for Argos's computer cave at the opposite end of the house.

Philomena felt better by suppertime. Ryder had dragged her out for breakfast, then back into bed. They'd gone out for lunch at a Mexican place down the road, and she'd eaten a little. He'd exhausted her early in the afternoon, until she'd finally taken a nap. By dinner, she was starved.

Ryder grinned at her over his menu. They were in a Chinese restaurant several doors away from the hotel, and everything smelled delicious.

"So, what's our game plan for tomorrow?" she asked after the waitress took their orders.

His grin faded only slightly. "We're going into Pensacola to swap cars, then we'll mosey along the coast. Blend in with the spring-breakers. Relax on the beach, maybe." His dark eyes promised more.

Philomena took a sip of her water to distract herself. "Any particular destination in mind?"

He shook his head. "Not yet. Why? Do you have ideas?"

She considered that for a moment. "I don't think so. Not Miami, though."

He shook his head, his smile fading. "No. Too big, I think."

Just what she'd thought. Although they hadn't done so well in the small towns either. She played with her straw for a moment, debating with herself. "How long do you think we can do this?" Her heart beat faster.

His mouth set in a flat line now. "You mean traveling?"

She shrugged. "That, too."

His shoulders tensed as he leaned on the table. "The traveling won't be indefinite."

She was afraid to ask about everything else. No, she thought, that wasn't quite the truth. She knew what his answer would be if she asked about everything else. It was her own response she wasn't sure of. Or not ready to share, at least.

He touched her hand, his dark eyes intent when she lifted her gaze to his face. "Mena, you know how I feel about you. I have a lot of patience, so don't think I'm going anywhere, even after we settle this with the Harvesters."

She swallowed, hard, unable to pull her gaze away. Until the waitress returned with fried strips of dough and dipping sauces to tide them over until their meals were ready.

Ryder sighed and sat back in his seat, but he left his hand over hers on the table.

The warmth of him felt so much better than it should, she mused, studying his long fingers.

Philomena closed her eyes for a couple of seconds, then turned her hand under his so their palms were touching. His fingers clenched on her wrist for a second, and she smiled at him, faintly. He stroked one finger over the pulse in her wrist, and a burst of heat shot up her arm.

His grin returned, slowly spreading over his face, and she relaxed a little.

She wasn't ready to go back to a reality without him.

She just wasn't sure she could do forever. Even without this curse hanging over her. Forever required a lot of trust, and she hadn't known many trustworthy men. She wasn't sure she could trust her own judgement now.

Ryder didn't press her when they returned to the motel, instead turning on the television to look at the weather while he started his computer. She took the opportunity to do the same. In case there was anything important waiting, like a new client query, or something from one of her cousins.

When she saw the size of Andi's email, Philomena frowned. What on earth had she sent?

Ryder glanced up from his laptop. "I got something from Kallan."

"One from Andrea here." She clicked on the line to open the message. Attachments, plural. Her frown deepened.

"Philomena, We've hit the Mother-lode, so to speak.

Aunt Lydia has sent us journals from previous Medusas. Oh, my Gods, you should see some of these--*so old!* I've just started scanning some of the more recent ones into the computer and have attached them for you to look at. Kallan thinks we're overdue for a private, family website, where we'd all have access to this stuff. Any thoughts on designs?"

Philomena blinked. Journals. Those would have been helpful years ago. Then she frowned. Uploaded to a website for the whole family. Why hadn't anyone thought of that before? She smiled, dropping her gaze to her screen.

"It's going to take a really long time to scan all of these to digital files, but I was thinking of farming some out among the cousins to get it done faster. Just think of it, Philomena, generations of Medusas to help when there's a change. I wish I'd had these when I got the curse."

Of course she did.

"Or that Aunt Lydia had tracked them down faster. It might not have made me trust in Kallan or my feelings any faster, but knowing Obelia fell in love a hundred and twenty years ago while she was the Medusa, thus passing the curse on to someone else, would have given me a little hope early on, or a morale boost later.

"Anyway, have fun reading. I'm going to keep scanning. I'll let you know if I see anything juicy. Love, A."

"Did you get homework, too?" Ryder asked, leaning back in his seat.

"I got extra, because I need to think about designing a website." She set her laptop aside.

"These journals...this is kind of huge." His intent gaze landed on her face.

Philomena nodded. "Actual accounts instead of hearsay, changed by generations of telling. It's huge." She thought about Andi dealing with her feelings for Kallan, with no idea what she could expect or hope for. No wonder it had taken her so long to trust their love.

Philomena swallowed, her gaze sliding to her laptop while guilt bubbled in her stomach. Ryder had been open and up-front with her from the start. She knew she wanted him, trusted him to protect her. She took a slow breath and reached over to close the email program on her computer.

Ryder pushed to his feet, startling her, and did a slow stretch, arms over his head, his gaze still fixed on her.

Her pulse did a little happy dance.

He smiled as he lowered his arms. "I think it's time for some sleep."

She laughed. "Sleep? With that look on your face?"

He winked at her. "Eventually."

She closed her laptop and took a slow breath. "Another distraction?"

He shook his head. "Just because I want you," he said softly.

Philomena stretched one hand out to brush his stubbled jaw, his skin warm beneath her fingers. "Then you should have me," she whispered back, her heart tripping at the way his eyes sparked in response to her words.

No matter what he said, this really was a good distraction, even though it wasn't necessarily his intention.

Ryder drummed his fingers on the steering wheel of the new car the next day. Mena sat quietly in the passenger seat, watching out her window. They were near the shore, near enough to smell the crisp, salty air, and every once in a while, there was a big enough gap between buildings so they caught glimpses of the water.

He smiled, watching her crane her neck at the next open space. "We should find a spot right on the beach."

She turned to look at him. "Probably not with the spring break people."

He'd forgotten about the timing. "Damn."

She smiled and shifted her gaze back to her window.

He <u>was</u> going to find them a beachfront place. And when the college kids returned to school, they'd have the beach to themselves. All kinds of wicked ideas floated through his head, making him smile.

"When you grin like that, I know dangerous things are on your mind," Mena said mildly.

"Good. Then you're forewarned," he growled, reaching over to give her thigh a squeeze.

She sucked in a quick breath, then set one of her hands over his. "Eyes on the road, Ryder."

He laughed, but left his hand where it was.

He found them a beachfront place, a grand old hotel near the end of the beach in one of the many tiny towns dotting the Gulf Coast side of Florida. There weren't even any college kids clogging the lobby when they checked in. He took that as a good sign.

Their room looked out over the shore, and from the hotel, they simply had to cross the wooden walkway to reach the sand. It would be a beautiful spot to watch the sunset later, he mused, giving Mena's shoulders a squeeze as they stood on the balcony outside their room, breathing in the sea air.

She leaned into his side and wrapped her arm around his waist. "This is nice." Her tone was wistful, her green eyes misty.

He knew she still didn't think this was forever.

He was going to change her mind, if it was the last thing he ever did.

He hoped it *wasn't* the last thing he did.

Sighing, he released her and went inside to get the bags off the four-poster bed. He set his laptop on the round table near the balcony and booted it up.

Mena leaned against the railing, her arms stretched out to either side of her. "Working?"

"Just need to check in." He admired the view for a moment, though, while the computer came to life. She'd discarded her cardigan earlier, and now wore only a thin cotton t-shirt over her skirt. He could see the lace of her bra through the shirt, and it made him want to tug the shirt off so he could get a better look.

Instead, he dragged his gaze away from her knowing smile and sat in one of the chairs beside the table.

A handful of new emails.

Mena came in and pulled her cell from her purse.

He watched her sit on the foot of the bed as she dialed her mother, admiring her long legs. None of her wool skirts were suitable for Florida. They'd have to do a little more shopping.

He could hardly wait to get to the swimsuits.

"Wipe that evil grin off your face," she chided him with her own smile, dropping back to lie flat on the bed. "Hi, Mom. How are you?"

Ryder made no attempt to clear the grin from his face as he opened the first email, from Carys. The trusts were good to go, so they could get paperwork started with a real estate agent to sell the houses. That wasn't going to be a fun conversation, he mused.

"What?" Mena shot to her feet, smile gone, her curls

bouncing behind her as she strode to the other end of the room.

He frowned, glancing at the subject lines of the rest of his emails before he opened Danny's. Then shut his eyes. *Damn.*

"Is she all right?" She shot him a glare as she whipped around to pace out to the balcony.

He watched her. This might be ugly.

"Uh-huh." Another glare on her way back inside.

He resigned himself to an argument, sprawling in his seat to finish reading the email.

"Oh, my Gods." She huffed out a loud breath as she stalked outside again where she stopped dead. "A baby?"

Ryder winced. *Damn, Desi.* He shut the email program and closed the laptop, folding his hands over his middle to watch her pace, her free hand clenched into a fist at her side. Yeah, this would be ugly.

Mena finally clicked off the phone and tossed it blindly onto the bed. "Did you know about this? About Desi and the Harvester at Mom's?" Her words could have chipped rocks, they were so hard and sharp.

"Just found out after you." He indicated the computer.

"We have to go back." Her mouth tightened into a flat line.

"No."

Her green eyes widened at his mild refusal, then narrowed, spitting fire. "My sister had a run-in at Mom's with a Harvester while she had *a baby* in tow. These people won't stop, Ryder. If I go home, I can deal with them. My family can be safe. I don't care about me."

He shot to his own feet, not feeling at all bad about towering over her. "I care about you. You are not going anywhere near your mother's house, Mena. If your sister isn't responsible enough or smart enough to listen when people tell her to stay the hell away, that is her own fault, not yours. My *mission* is to keep you safe, dammit, not to deliver you to the Harvesters."

She glared harder at him. "I don't want to be your 'mission', Ryder. I am falling in *love* with you, dammit, and I want my family safe, including you and my irresponsible sister. If that means I have to go back and stand in their way, then I'm going."

His heart stopped beating for a second, then bounced off his ribs, back and forth, hard and fast, with no regular rhythm. He felt the smile breaking over his face, as her cheeks went white, her eyes rounding in shock, lips dropping open for a second before closing firmly. "Say it again," he said slowly, reaching to catch her upper arms and steady her when she swayed a little.

Her lips parted, but nothing came out for a moment. "Oh Gods," she whispered finally, shutting her eyes for a second.

"Tell me, Mena." She *had* to say it again.

She met his gaze, hers swimming with sudden tears. "I said I'm falling in love with you." Her voice broke.

He yanked her close and covered her mouth with his, triumph rushing through him, along with a huge swell of emotion in his chest. Her fingers dug into his shoulders, and she lifted into his kiss, making him gentle it when he would have ravaged her mouth in his victory.

She loved him.

He lifted his head before he wanted to, his body humming with excitement, and thumbed away the tears on her cheek. "*This* is why I'm not taking you back to the Harvesters, baby," he whispered. "I won't let them have you. You are mine."

A shaky smile touched her lips. "Ryder,…"

He kissed her softly. "It's all right, honey." He knew the emotion was overwhelming. His own was almost choking him at the moment.

He might not be able to express himself verbally right now, but he could show her.

And he did. With tender touches that had her lifting from the rumpled bed to seat him deep inside her. With kisses that turned *his* brain into mush and had her fingers digging into his nape to keep him near. With slow, teasing strokes of his body into hers that made her quiver in anticipation until neither could resist the pull any longer.

Ryder lay sprawled over her later, knowing the grin curving his lips was the same one she'd called dangerous earlier. He didn't care. He just wanted her to keep telling him.

Mena stretched up to kiss his chin, shifting slightly beneath him.

He rolled to his side, keeping her in his arms. "Did I crush you?"

She shook her head, a faint smile curving her lips.

He licked the tiny mole beside her mouth.

Her eyes fluttered open.

"Had to."

Her smile widened.

"Say it again."

The smile softened. "I love you." Her green eyes searched his face.

"I love you, too." He brushed her hair away from her face, back over her shoulder. "That is why we're not going anywhere near that house. I want to spend the rest of my life with you, Mena, which can't happen if you sacrifice yourself to the Harvesters."

Her smile vanished. "I know."

"Just so we're in agreement." He kissed the tip of her nose. "Desi's fine, you know."

"I know." She sighed. "She didn't tell us she had another baby."

He winced. "Of course she didn't."

Mena sat up, and he had to release her. "How could she have another baby?"

"Did you happen to get her number from your mom?"

She shook her head.

"It's in the email from Danny. You can call her. Later," he added when she swung her legs over the side of the bed, catching her wrist. "I'm not done with you yet."

She laughed, reluctantly. "Are you trying to distract me?"

"No. I'm trying to make love to the woman I love." He tugged her down beside him. "Is that okay with you?"

Mena cupped his face between her hands. "I guess so."

"Wow, such enthusiasm," he teased, rolling onto his back and pulling her on top of him. "Maybe you should do all the work this time."

She arched one eyebrow at him. "Maybe I will." She reached between their bellies to wrap her fingers around his erection.

Ryder groaned, lifting into her caress.

He wanted at least fifty more years of her.

And he'd do anything to get it.

PHILOMENA SAT ON THE NEW BEACH TOWEL, HER LEGS crossed, and watched the bright waves washing onto the shore. Ryder lay beside her, shirtless, hands behind his head. "You should lie down. The sun feels great on my face."

"I don't need a sunburn that badly." She glanced at him, and her heart beat a little faster. How had she fallen in love with him? She'd tried very hard not to. Maybe she hadn't tried as hard as she should have to avoid falling into bed with him. Hell, she hadn't tried at all to avoid that after the first time. The man was irresistible. She smiled to herself. No one could have told her a month ago she'd be in love with Jason's father. No one could have told her she'd be in love with anyone.

Her gaze slid from his closed eyes to his mouth, then his wide shoulders, strong chest.

He really wasn't her usual type.

She dated guys who weren't so macho. So buff. So *alpha*.

She hated to admit it, but his assessment of her dates had been pretty spot-on. She never had dated anyone who would be a challenge, any man who would present a problem when she told him she no longer wanted to see him. Because she knew she'd never trust any of them to stick around. But Ryder was another story.

She shifted her gaze to the water. There were a few die-hards in the water, college kids on spring break, shivering on their wave boards.

Ryder's hand landed on her back, rubbing a small circle. "Lie down, Mena."

She sighed and did as he asked, and his hand caught hers. "Better?"

"I thought you'd enjoy the beach."

"I do. I just can't stop thinking."

His low chuckle made her pulse quicken. "That brain of yours just won't quit, will it, smart girl?"

She blushed, closing her eyes behind her new sunglasses.

He shifted beside her, and when she opened her eyes, he was on his side, head propped on one hand. Watching her.

"What?"

"How about we make a deal?"

She raised one eyebrow.

"I won't pitch a fit when you call Desi later, and you stop thinking about the Harvesters for a little while."

She didn't correct him. "Why would you pitch a fit when I call Desi?" She frowned, rolling to face him.

"Because she's going to upset you."

Philomena's frown deepened. "That's not fair."

"But true. Remember, I know your sister, too, baby."

She shoved upright, swallowing. "Thanks for reminding me." *That. That* was why she hadn't wanted to get involved with him. She glared at him, reaching for the bag she'd carried down from their room to carry their weapons, sunscreen and room key.

Ryder sat up, too. "I didn't mean that," he growled, catching her wrist. "Desi is manipulative, and she'll make sure she gets you good and upset about her run-in at your mom's. She'll conveniently forget she was warned more than once not to go there. Instead, she'll carp on about how she had her *baby* with her, and how *dangerous* it was." He glowered at her. "She was probably coming to dump her new baby on you."

"That isn't fair," she protested, though a small voice in the back of her head pointed out he was very likely correct.

"Stop it, Mena."

She shut her mouth tight, annoyance coursing through her.

"Your sister will deliberately upset you when you call her, and that isn't fair to *you*. She doesn't know you've had your own run-ins with the Harvesters, and yours were far more dangerous than hers. And she won't care, because that's how she is. Selfish and immature. Gods, why did she have another baby?" He dragged his hands back over his hair, shaking his head.

"I'm actually surprised she hasn't had more," Philomena said before she stopped to think about what she was saying. She covered her mouth for a second.

Ryder shot her a wry grin. "You have a good point there." He leaned over and kissed her briefly. "Are we done arguing?"

She swallowed, considering his words. "I suppose."

"Good. Lie down again. Don't think about anything except the nice warm sun on your face. And what I'm going to do to you when we get into our room."

She lifted one eyebrow. "What are you going to do?"

His grin widened. "You want all the details now, or would you like to be surprised?"

Her heart pounded harder in her ears. "Maybe you should surprise me," she managed.

He leaned in and kissed her, lingering this time. "Okay. Come on."

She set the bag back down and eased back, releasing a long, slow breath.

But she was too aware of Ryder beside her.

And a little voice in her head kept reminding her she couldn't run from the Harvesters forever.

Ryder knew she hadn't relaxed. Part of that was his fault, he admitted to himself. The other part was she just couldn't shut off her busy brain. When they strolled back across the beach to the hotel later, hands linked between them, he studied her face. Her nose and cheeks were pink, despite the sunscreen he'd put on her face earlier. And a tiny frown line marked the space between her eyebrows.

He pretended not to notice when they got into their room and she dropped the bag and towel inside the door. Or when she took her cell phone from its charger and dialed the number he'd given her from Danny's email.

He did not, however, pretend to ignore her conversation with her sister.

"Desi, it's Philomena."

He sat in one of the chairs at the table and propped his feet on the other one, folding his hands over his abdomen and watching her pace the room. *Already.*

"No, I'm not home. I can't go home. I know you were told about the Harvesters. Why did you go there after you were warned not to?" She unclipped her dark curls, and they tumbled down her back as she tossed the barrette onto the dresser.

Ryder cocked his head, watching her skirt flare out behind her as she turned to pace back toward the balcony. When the light hit it just right, he could see her long legs through the flimsy material.

"Of course it wasn't a joke, Desi. None of this is a joke. The Harvesters tracked me down there. We can't go home...No, I'm not with Mom right now." Her mouth pinched tight. "She is somewhere safe, with a friend of Ryder's."

He rolled his eyes, knowing Desi would get herself all wound up now.

"Yes, Ryder's...Yes, I've seen Ryder. I'm with him right now, actually."

He winced when she shot him a glare.

She was silent while her sister talked. For quite a long time. "Desi, I'm not even going to discuss that with you," she said finally. "When did you have another baby?...A year? You had a baby a year ago and didn't tell us?" Her voice raised in anger, and she strode into the room from the balcony again, her curls streaming behind her.

Ryder shut his eyes for a second. Well, that wasn't good.

"You're what?" Mena stopped walking, her shoulders stiff. "To whom?"

He could almost see the tension coiling tighter in her spine.

"Were you planning to tell us about it, or just leave Mom in the dark about that, too?" she asked coolly.

Uh-oh. He set his feet on the floor and leaned forward, poised to move.

"Really?" Her low tone was dangerous now.

Ryder got to his feet slowly, trying to decide how to defuse this.

"When is this wedding?"

His eyes widened. Wedding?

Mena's head moved slowly from side to side, and he took a few steps toward her, trying to get a look at her face. She sighed, and some of the tension left her shoulders. "Desi, as long as I'm the Medusa and the Harvesters are hunting me, I can't come to a wedding with all of you. It isn't safe."

He went to her then, setting his hands on her shoulders, lightly. He was somewhat relieved when she didn't shrug him off and walk away. He used his thumbs to massage away a bit more of the tension knotting her muscles.

"I'd love to see her, Desi," she said softly. "But I can't now." Her head bowed.

Damn Desi. Ryder took one last step so his chest rested against Mena's back, and he slid his hands around her waist to hold her still.

"He's fine. Big."

He narrowed his eyes at the back of Mena's head. Desi was *not* going to take Jason away from her.

"Look, Des, I'll call you in a few days...Okay, bye." She pressed the off button with her thumb and took a deep breath. "Desi's getting married and wants the family there."

"Is she having trouble understanding English these days?" He rested his chin on the top of her head.

"You know she only hears what she wants to hear, Ryder."

"And this baby is a year old?"

She nodded. "A little girl. Her name is Amaryllis."

He heard the longing in her voice and wondered if she realized it was there. "And who's the guy?"

"Levi Something. He's Amaryllis's father." Mena sighed.

So Desi was settling down? He found that hard to believe after the past six years. He rocked Mena slightly from side to side. He'd reserve judgment on Desi for now.

"So is this where you pitch your fit?" she asked.

"Why?"

"Because we agreed you wouldn't pitch a fit after my phone call if I stopped thinking about the Harvesters."

He smiled. "And I know you didn't stop thinking about them. Hm." He kissed the top of her head. "I'm not going to pitch a fit even though I know Desi's upset you."

"Really?"

"No. I'll let this one go."

She turned her head around to look at him, green eyes narrowed. "Why?"

"Because we are going shopping, you and me."

Her eyebrows shot up. "Why?"

"Because you need more than one skirt to wear on the beach. Maybe a bathing suit."

Her expression shifted to skeptical. "You've seen me naked, Ryder, why a bathing suit?"

"Because I want to."

She shook her head. "If we have to."

"Oh, we have to. But not right this minute." He turned her in his arms and fitted her close against him, his body already on alert.

The green of her eyes darkened as she met his gaze.

"No, right this minute, I'm going to see you naked again," he teased, sliding her skirt up her legs and slipping one hand beneath it to her soft hip.

"You might have a problem."

"Yeah, it's called addiction to Mena. And the only cure is more of Mena," he breathed against her mouth.

Her soft laugh made him smile, but only for a second, before he kissed her, intending to melt down her brain so she couldn't think for a while.

ELEK STUDIED THE MAP. THERE REALLY WASN'T A pattern to the encounters. Between the second and third, there was an enormous distance, as well as the time gap. He was more interested, though, in the direction of the confirmed meetings.

From Tennessee to Georgia.

Essentially, they had made most of a very large circle

from their starting point in Pennsylvania. Obviously, they had gone west after the chase in Philadelphia, then south, and now back to the east. If Ware was doing it intentionally, he might rethink since Alabama. If he did, would he go south or west?

And if his circle was purely by chance, then his next move would be equally random.

Elek couldn't believe this man did anything without a plan and several contingency plans in case his first was compromised. His background was too regimented--his military father, his own career...

No, there had to be some plan, even if Elek couldn't see it.

Which meant if he'd been circling intentionally, his back-up plan would be--

Continue and throw them off?

Go a different direction to throw them off? And which direction? They were running out of south, unless they left the country, and he highly doubted they would do that without the rest of the Medusa's immediate family.

Which meant west. But what if it wasn't?

Elek covered his face with both hands and exhaled heavily.

Goddess help him, he had no idea what to do.

He sat straighter, then pushed out of his seat, striding along the hall. "Great-uncle," he said as he entered Ari's office, "I need advice."

The older man looked pleased. "Sit down."

Elek dropped into one of the pair of chairs in front of the desk and explained his thoughts. "But I can't decide which direction to cover."

"Cover both. We have the resources."

Relief oozed along Elek's veins. "Why didn't that occur to me?"

The older man smiled. "You're too close to it. Sometimes you need to step away, sometimes you need a new perspective. Which is why I am here, to help guide you."

Elek exhaled heavily. "I have so much to learn."

Ari's smile gentled. "You are doing beautifully, Elek. I am very proud of everything you have accomplished in so short a time. We are very close to finding this monster, thanks in large part to you. The Goddess will no doubt be pleased as well." He sat back in his chair. "Go notify your cousins in the areas you want to cover, then take the rest of the evening off. Relax, see a movie. Don't think about this for a few hours. That is an order."

Elek swallowed his protests, nodding as he rose. "Thank you, Uncle."

There was no way he could forget about it for the evening, even with a good solution to his immediate dilemma. But it would let him try to think ahead to the next step--once they'd located the monster, they still needed to find and destroy the goblet protecting her family.

Then his family could rid the world of all of the monsters.

PHILOMENA TAPPED HER FINGERS ON THE KEYBOARD OF her laptop the next morning, scanning her email. Nothing new. And nothing especially interesting so far in any of the entries she'd skimmed from Annis's journals. Just Annis's daily notes.

She wasn't quite sure what she was hoping for. Something.

"Time to shop," Ryder announced, setting down his juice and the morning paper the hotel provided for their guests.

She closed her laptop. "Now?"

He nodded. "Before all the partying kids roll out of bed to start over for the day." He winked at her.

She sighed and pushed to her feet. "Fine."

He caught her wrist. "I thought women loved shopping."

"Not this one so much."

He studied her for a moment, his dark eyes thoughtful. "Why not?"

"Clothing is just a necessity, and I need concealment and easy access to my dagger, so my choices are limited." She lifted one shoulder in a shrug. "There are other things I'd rather do. Play with Jason. Read a good book."

"Make love."

Her cheeks warmed. "That, too."

He cleared his throat. "Later. You need clothes. I need shorts."

She let him steer her from the room, noticing the 'do not disturb' sign hung on the outside of their doorknob. She supposed it might be hard to explain to the housekeeping staff the gun and the handful of knives in his bag.

There were lots of little shops within walking distance of the hotel, so they left the car in the hotel lot and moseyed down the street, pausing to peer in windows as they went. Ryder guided her into a big shop a few blocks away, displaying mostly swimwear and beach gear in their front windows. He selected a handful of swimsuits to her one, and, with his hand at her back, pushed her into a fitting room.

Philomena smiled at the closed door, then turned to

undress. She took her dagger off her leg after dropping her skirt to the floor, then sucked in a hard breath.

"What's wrong, baby?"

"Oh, my Gods," she whispered.

Ryder stepped into the tiny room, his dark gaze narrowing on her hip, where she stared in the mirror.

The goblet in her tattoo was no longer the pink it had been the past few days. Ryder had pointed it out in the shower the other morning. Now it was simply the color of her skin beneath all the other vivid shades in the tattoo.

Still there, but fading fast, it seemed.

He traced it with one finger, his expression thoughtful.

She swallowed, then cleared her throat. "What are you thinking?"

He shook his head slowly. "I'm thinking it's going away." His gaze met hers in the mirror. "You may not be stuck with the Harvesters hunting you for much longer."

Hope exploded in her belly, but she quashed it, her gaze dropping to her hip again in the mirror.

"Put the green bikini on first," he said gruffly after a second.

She blinked, dragging her attention back to the present, then looked at the tiny suit he indicated. "Are you serious?" She gave him a wide-eyed look.

The wicked grin that was becoming so familiar curved his mouth. "Absolutely, baby." He kissed her lightly and stepped outside.

The suit was indecent.

Two tiny scraps of material covered a small portion of her breasts, held in place by a hook in the back and two skinny strings she tied behind her neck. The bottom left most of her behind bare. The only redeeming quality she could find was the color made her eyes look even greener.

She could certainly not wear this outside where people would see her.

Ryder's eyes darkened when he reopened the door. "Wow."

"You are such a guy," she said, smiling reluctantly. "It's not decent."

He raised one eyebrow. "All the important parts are covered."

"I disagree." She turned when he moved his finger in a circle.

He groaned behind her, and she glanced at him in the mirror, seeing the dark flush blooming on his cheekbones.

Somehow, she didn't think this shopping trip would last long.

She tried on the other suits, including the one-piece she'd chosen that covered up everything she wanted covered in public.

If his frown was any indication, Ryder hated it. "You're kidding."

She shook her head. "I like this one."

His gaze scanned the black suit from top to bottom, and he shook his head. "It's boring."

"I like it." She folded her arms on her chest.

"You can get it, but you're getting the green one, too."

"I can't wear that outside."

He slanted her a dangerous smile. "Who said anything about outside?"

She laughed as he exited, then redressed in her t-shirt and skirt, fitting her dagger sheath onto her leg once more.

Her carry-on suitcase was going to be very overstuffed by the time they got home.

She paused in tying her sneakers.

Except they weren't going home.

A lump welled in her throat.

She loved being with Ryder, but she couldn't live on the run like this forever.

They'd have to find a way to stop.

She was just afraid they might not find an idea they agreed on. Or that the Harvesters would catch up with her before they came to a consensus.

CHAPTER FOURTEEN

Elek glared at the email on-screen. Tymek and Mikolaus had met up with her mother and nephew last night in North Carolina and let them walk away unscathed, completely untouched, because of the big man in their company.

He had specifically told everyone they would use her family given the opportunity, and they had allowed the trio to walk away.

"Goddess, damn them," he muttered, shoving to his feet. "Idiots."

What was so difficult to comprehend about their instructions?

He punched in a number on his phone and waited.

"Cousin," Mikolaus greeted him.

"Why do you not have the mother and nephew in your possession?"

His cousin was silent for a few seconds. "I wanted to take them," he said finally, "but Tymek cautioned we should wait to see if they met the Medusa."

"Why would they do that?"

"I don't know."

"Do not take advice from Tymek," Elek said, some of his annoyance fading. "Our mission is to kill the Medusa, and we have reached a stage where we must use any means available to us."

"I understand, Elek."

"Then if you get another opportunity, I expect you will use it wisely."

"Thank you. Goddess guide us."

Elek thumbed his phone off and took a deep breath. He needed to consult with Ari--Tymek would have to be dealt with. And someone else must be dispatched to cover his area since he couldn't be trusted to do the job. Elek did not believe Mikolaus would have further problems following simple directions.

ARISTOTLE REPLACED HIS TELEPHONE RECEIVER INTO its cradle and smiled. *Finally.* It seemed they may have gotten a bit of good luck.

Argos had found a car rental reservation from Ware's business to an agency in Florida. Of course, it wasn't in his name, but after their run-in with Gregos in Philadelphia, they wouldn't take a chance on using his name. Just in case. Argos was a smart boy, good with computers.

At last. They were closing in on this one. His pulse quickened in anticipation.

Then Aristotle's gaze dropped to his brother's picture on the corner of the desk. He flipped it face-down. The sight of Iphis's face made his heart strain to pound harder, and he didn't have time for an episode requiring a physician. Not now.

Not when they were so close.

MENA FROWNED AT THE SHORELINE.

He knew wheels were turning in her head, and he wondered in what direction.

She glanced at him over her shoulder. "The Harvesters are accustomed to the hunt, to always chasing."

Ryder had a feeling this wasn't going to go in a direction he'd like. "Yes. It's the nature of this curse, I suppose."

"Why not take the fight to them instead?"

Holy shit. He pushed himself upright on the towel. "Absolutely not."

She twisted to face him, settling on her knees. "There is nothing in the legends or the lore that says we can't meet them head-on."

He tried to get his brain wrapped around this new direction of hers. "Probably because their mission is to kill the Medusa, and going to them simply makes their job easier."

"I'm tired of being prey."

"Are you tired of being alive?" he shot back.

"Do you really want forever?"

Ryder leaned back on one hand, startled, then glared at her. "That isn't fair--"

"It's not fair to Jason to have to live on the run, hiding with my mother and Danny. There's nothing in the lore that says he should have to be uprooted from the life he knows and move around so I don't get killed." Mena held his gaze. "I want the same forever you talked about. I want it. But I can't think about it, not really, when any day, a Harvester might stumble on us and kill me."

He tried to think of an argument that would totally shut her down. He couldn't. But there was no fucking way he was letting her go right to the Harvesters. Not after he'd managed to get her away. Not now that he knew she was falling in love with him, too. "I can keep you safe, Mena," he said instead.

A sad smile curved her mouth, but didn't quite reach her eyes. "You have, more than once, and I'm glad for it. But I can't spend twenty years, or five years, or even another month, living like this. We've been on the run long enough. Nobody should have to live this way. Not you, not my mother, not Jason. Your business can't operate indefinitely without you there." She reached out to touch his hand, and he realized he'd fisted it on the beach towel beside him. "At least think about it, Ryder. We can take the fight to them, surprise them. We can beat them."

He knew she was aware the only way she could beat them was by passing the curse on to another cousin. Or dying, and he had no intention of letting her die.

"Please."

He realized she still waited for an answer. "I'll think about it," he finally managed, twisting his hand beneath hers to catch her wrist. "I've had enough sun."

She nodded, her fingers tightening on his hand. "Thank you."

No fucking way.

Ryder lay awake that night, long after Mena has fallen asleep, snuggled against his chest. He stared into the shadows, aware of the faint line of light sneaking between the closed curtains. Of the occasional drip coming from the bathroom sink. Of the muffled sound of a car door from outside the hotel. Mostly, he was aware of her soft, warm skin along his own, her quiet breathing, the familiar scent of her.

There was no way he could allow her to go rushing off to fight the Harvesters on their own ground. Not after all he'd done to keep her alive.

Yet... He stifled a curse. She'd played the forever card. The one thing he most wanted, and he could have it, if she trusted him and herself enough. If he let her do this on her own terms, there wouldn't be forever, because the Harvesters would kill her.

Fuck.

But she did have a point. No one could be expected to live this way forever. Hell, his guys hadn't signed on as partners or employees to do Medusa protection into eternity.

He stifled a growl.

He'd have to craft a compelling argument to keep her from rushing off to fight the Harvesters on her own.

Or a decent plan to take her there and win this fight.

He scowled toward the curtains and the tiny line of light between them.

Because he wanted forever. He wanted Mena forever, and if he wanted her full trust, he'd have to give a little.

Gods help him if he wound up losing her.

On the other hand, if they succeeded, the curse would move on, and they could have that forever he wanted.

He squeezed his eyes shut.

This would have to be a helluva plan to work in their favor.

❦

Mena didn't say anything to Ryder at all the next day about her suggestion. Not a single word. They lolled in bed till mid-morning, then lounged on the beach half the day. But she knew he was thinking about it. She knew it from the stiff set of his shoulders, from the way his mouth flattened each time they sat silently for more than a few seconds.

He was considering it.

She leaned against him and felt him start, then his arm came around her shoulders. "It's going to be okay," she said.

He grunted, which made her smile.

She settled closer, and he relaxed a little, his breath sighing out softly. "How about we call Jason and find some supper, and then go back to our room, so I can do some exploring?"

"Exploring?" He tipped his head to meet her gaze, one brow lifting.

She winked at him. "Mm-hm."

His eyes darkened. "I see. Well, if you're on a mission, then we should get started." He sat straighter, then pushed to his feet, catching her hand.

Mena let him pull her up, happy to have found a distraction. He'd done so well distracting her after their last run-in with a Harvester, she thought maybe it was time to return the favor.

And it seemed to be working. All through their chats with Jason, all through their meal in the hotel restaurant, his attention was now focused on her. She stroked the back of his wrist when he let his hand sit on the table beside his plate, her fingers gliding along a vein that reached to his knuckles.

Ryder swallowed when she rubbed her forefinger in a small circle at the base of his thumb, and she smiled.

By the time they reached their room, she knew he wasn't thinking about Harvesters anymore. All of the tension in him now was anticipation.

She decided he should anticipate a bit longer. "Why don't you turn on some music?" she said as the door closed behind her.

His gaze narrowed, but he released her hand and made his way to the television, clicking his way through the channels until he found music stations. While he searched for music, she locked and chained the door, then turned to him.

He faced her from across the room, wary.

She smiled and strolled toward him. "I think maybe some dancing. We've never danced together."

He swallowed, and she stretched to kiss his throat. His hands settled on her hips. "No, I guess we haven't."

She slid her hands up his chest and around his neck to link at his nape. "Time to remedy that," she murmured, leaning close.

His arousal pressed into her belly. Plenty of anticipating, and he had no idea she meant to really torture him.

She rubbed her cheek on his chest, relaxing in his arms

as they swayed around the room. For a little while, she could almost believe they were just a normal couple enjoying a mini-vacation. And she needed him to believe it for a while, too. So she nuzzled his throat, nibbling down into the hollow where she flicked out her tongue to taste him.

His fingers tightened on her hips. "Mena?"

"Hm?" She licked him again. Salty, from the sea air. Musky--all Ryder.

"How long are we going to do this?"

She tipped her chin up and smiled at him. "A while."

His dark eyes went nearly black. "That's what I thought."

She stretched on tiptoe to kiss him, lightly. "I want to explore."

He cleared his throat. "I guess you're going to want to take your time."

"Absolutely." She dragged her fingers through his hair, making him shiver. "I think it's overdue, really."

His erection nudged at her belly. "Baby, you know I'm going to get you back later, right?"

She laughed. "You've had your turn, Ryder. Now it's mine, so shut up and enjoy." She nipped at his lower lip and enjoyed the hiss of his sharp inhalation.

She did take her time, unbuttoning his shirt as they danced, kissing her way across his chest, pushing his shirt off, and kissing around to his back.

He set his feet while she worked her way over the muscles there, his breathing rough.

"I really should have done this sooner," she murmured between kisses. Then slid one hand around to his belly, lower, to wrap around his erection.

"Fuck," he muttered, jolting at her caress.

"Oh, we will, but not yet." She smiled as she squeezed, then released him to continue on her way. "Not just yet." She eased away and tugged her own shirt off, then discarded her bra before stepping in to press her breasts to his back. Her tight nipples rubbed along his hard muscles, and his breath caught again. "You feel so good," she whispered, slipping her hands to his belly and stroking upward.

"So do you."

She pressed closer and stretched to kiss one shoulder blade. She really did want forever with this man, but they had to work on it together. Tonight, though...tonight was all about him.

She teased him, tasting, touching. Eventually, she shoved off her skirt and his shorts and got him horizontal so she could really explore. All the hard dips and ridges of his chest and abdomen. His stiff, swollen shaft jutting up.

She licked the damp tip and noted the way his fingers curled into the sheets. When she eased her mouth over the entire head, his eyes squeezed shut, and then she stopped watching, instead focusing on the feel of him beneath her. She could tell by the way his breathing caught and roughened, the way his hips jerked to meet her, when he was getting close, and she simply eased back, instead stroking his strong thighs, his hair-spattered calves. When he relaxed a little, she bent close to suck him into her mouth, loving the salty taste of him.

She lifted her head to admire his erection, then yelped when he yanked her over him.

"I can't. Not anymore, baby. I need to be inside you." He didn't ask, didn't wait for permission, just positioned her exactly where he wanted her and thrust up, deep inside her.

Mena cried out. Her inner muscles clamped hard at the invasion.

"Fuck," he groaned. "I can't wait. So tight, baby."

She let him guide her movements with his hard hands on her hips. Quick, hard strokes of his cock inside her, and she went flying in moments, then heard his guttural curse a second before he pulled her hard against him, his release triggered by hers.

She collapsed onto his chest, her quick breathing painful.

Ryder wrapped his arms around her back, and she realized she was as sweaty as he was when his forearm slid along her spine. He panted underneath her, his body slowly relaxing.

She woke from a light doze when he rolled her onto her side and stretched over to shut off the lamp on the night stand.

"Shh," he whispered. "Close your eyes."

She smiled and kissed his chest, obeying. "I didn't mean to fall asleep."

"Exploring is hard work." The tease in his voice made her smile widen.

"I enjoyed every minute of it."

"Me, too, baby." He kissed the top of her head.

For a few minutes, they were silent, breathing softly, in the dim light from across the room. He stroked from her nape to her hip, slowly. Gently. She listened to his steady heartbeat.

"We have to have a really excellent plan," he said at last.

Mena tipped her head back to look at him. She hadn't expected his brain to still be functional after all the teasing and sensual torture this evening.

He met her gaze, his sober. "And until we have a plan, you're not going anywhere near a Harvester."

She nodded, a lump welling in her throat. It was a huge concession. She knew that. "Go to sleep, Ryder. We have time." She brushed his hair away from his face.

"I know." He gathered her closer and yanked the sheet over them.

She shut her eyes and took a slow breath. One step closer to the end. Hopefully the end of the curse for her and not the end *of her*.

～

Over the next few days, Ryder wished he could take back his promise. Mena didn't try to push him to move faster, just offered ideas or suggestions, or pointed out flaws in their initial plans.

There was simply no good way to do this. He couldn't see how taking Mena toward the Harvesters instead of away was going to let her get rid of this curse. All he could see were endless possibilities for her early death, and he refused to allow that.

He pushed to his feet, looking at the rain outside their balcony doors instead of at the papers spread over the table. He didn't need to look at the papers to know the messy notes and scribbles there were useless.

Mena remained in her seat, silent. Calm.

He scowled at the wet glass. She hadn't argued with him about this since he agreed to her reckless idea. No, she'd been perfectly reasonable, thoughtful. Because she knew he had to agree.

Because he wanted it all.

"Is there any way to know if Ari has stayed in Virginia?" she asked, and he heard papers shuffling.

Of course there was. He'd have one of the guys snoop around and see what he could see at the family compound there, and it would be an easy answer to one question. Too bad there were a thousand more in need of answering. "Yeah, we can find out," he said finally. "And how many more are coming and going."

"Then we'll know if he's still making plans for hunting parties."

Ryder's scowl deepened, but he kept his mouth shut. He slid his forefinger down the window, following on the inside the path of the water outside. Shadowing it as it trickled, weaving from one side to the other. And his frown eased a little. They could shadow some of these Harvesters, as he'd done himself.

He was a fucking idiot.

He turned around and found Mena studying one of the notepads. "We need to find out who's there, who's just checking in briefly. The ones who are there longer are the ones Ari will be making plans for, the ones he trusts to get the job done."

She glanced at him. "That sounds right."

"Of course it is." He winked at her. "So we need to find out how many of them there are. I'll arrange for one of the guys to find out, and then we can shadow a couple of them, see where they're going, what they're doing. Then we have a better idea of Ari's strategy and can figure out our own." Something better. Something that wouldn't get her killed.

"Okay." She sat back in her chair. "And then we go?"

Right back there. "Once we've figured out what we're going to do, yes." He sat again, reaching for his laptop. He shot off an email to Carys and one to Ken, briefly outlining what he needed.

"Don't you have clients who want to meet with you?" she asked.

Ryder shook his head. "Joel is the face man right now. He's capable of dealing with any face-to-face meetings, and probably better at it than Danny or me." He set the computer aside. "And don't think you're getting rid of me. My business is in perfectly fine hands. Just as you will be in a few minutes." He rose and held out one hand.

Her eyebrows lifted. "Really?"

"Let's go. We've been working on this all day, and it's time for a break." He caught her wrist. "You need to get naked."

Mena laughed, but let him pull her from her seat. "You're out of your mind."

"Not yet, but we can work on that, too." He towed her over to the bed and made her sit. "I'll work on getting you naked."

She stopped him when he grabbed the hem of her skirt, setting her hands on his wrists. "We're going to be fine, Ryder," she said softly.

"I know." He pushed her skirt higher, so her legs came into view. "Aren't you pretty?" Higher, and silk panties were visible. "Better." He bent to kiss her, hard, then gave her a little push so she fell onto the unmade bed, laughing. "That's more like it."

Philomena needed to move. Pacing the room wasn't nearly enough movement. Not enough distance. This being in limbo thing really sucked. She resisted the urge to rise and forced her tapping foot to still. Ryder was already aware of her restlessness, and she didn't intend to put him on edge, too. More on edge, she supposed, since he was as keyed up as she was. It had rained for the past two days, keeping them in their room, and now they were waiting to hear from Ken and Joel about the goings-on at Ari's.

In this case, no news was not good news. Though she supposed it was good enough she was alive.

Ryder muttered beside her, and she watched him scribble something else onto his note pad. His laptop chimed quietly, and she refrained from leaning over to look at the screen. It was probably Carys, with more non-news to report.

She pushed to her feet and moved to the window when he slid the computer closer. Even though it was still cloudy, the spring-breakers were out in full force today. The beach below was crammed full of people, bright towels dotting the sand. Even with the glass doors shut, she heard the sound of shouts and bird calls mingling.

"Fuck."

She shut her eyes for a second, then turned around.

He scowled at her. "Only two guys are there with Ari, the rest are all coming and going randomly."

Well, that would put a crimp in his plan to shadow these guys.

"And the two who are there aren't leaving. They're actually staying there, with just brief forays out of the compound. Son of a bitch." He shoved away from the table.

Mena kept her sigh in and went to sit at the foot of the bed, while he paced the room.

He remained silent as he strode around the small space, over and over, and she rested her hands flat on the bed, leaning back a little to watch him. She knew what her plan would be now, but she wondered if he would come to the same conclusion or keep resisting.

Resisting, she thought, her gaze following him to a stop inside the sliding glass doors. He would fight this all the way. She knew that. She knew him well enough to know he wouldn't want to just wing it.

Not Ryder, who planned as much as he could.

Although, she mused, as he pressed his forehead to the glass, he'd allowed them to travel randomly for a little while, but she imagined that suited his plan to throw off any Harvesters who might've stayed on their trail.

"We'll have to go," he said finally, not moving.

She blinked. "What?" She knew he hadn't said what she thought he'd said.

He turned his head to look at her, his expression stark. "We'll have to go. There."

Her heart thudded faster, and she swallowed.

"We'll have to go. Take the fight to them." He shoved off the window. "I don't like it, but I can't see any other way to finish this."

Her heart squeezed at the mix of anger and resignation in his dark eyes. "Then we win," she whispered, pushing to her feet.

He hauled her into his arms and held her tight. So close she heard the hard beating of his heart beneath her ear. So close she could feel the tremors in him. "If we want it all, we have to. We have to win," he rasped against the top of her head.

She shut her eyes and slid her arms around him while she sent a silent plea to the Gods for help. They really had to win, because she did want it all with him. With this man.

The Harvesters would not be the end of her.

THEY DROVE NORTH THE NEXT MORNING, WINDING into Georgia, before reaching South Carolina. He found a hotel when he'd had enough driving for the day, and settled them in for the night. He didn't care if it wasn't dusk yet. They grabbed a quick supper in the adjoining restaurant and retreated to their room.

Mena's green eyes were shadowed and framed by stress lines. She needed some sleep. While she kicked off her shoes and unbuttoned her sweater, he pulled up his email.

One from the office with a large attachment got his attention first.

Ryder watched the attached video, studying the man Joel said seemed to be taking over from Ari. Tall, sturdy, with intelligent eyes. Wary. Elek Tassos would be formidable eventually.

But he hadn't Ari's years of experience in the hunt. And even with the old man's guidance, he would still make mistakes.

Like sending his cousins and uncles home to hunt their own territories instead of focusing their energies into more specific areas. That was a mistake, and Ryder would have to take advantage of it. Somehow.

"He looks a little like Kallan, but younger. Harder. Not nice," Mena said from beside him.

He grunted. He didn't think any of Kallan's cousins were very nice, no matter what the hell they looked like.

"What do you suppose he's trying to plot, holed up there in Ari's big house?"

Ryder shot her a sidelong glance that made her laugh.

"I know *that*." She smiled wider. "I meant...how does he really think he's going to manage this when he doesn't have any more clues about our whereabouts and plans than we do about his?"

He didn't answer, just closing the video and then his email before setting the laptop aside. He dropped onto the bed and stared at the ceiling. "Good question. If Athena isn't helping them, aside from their 'special powers', then they're working blind, too. So he's trying to figure out what we're doing. And, since he doesn't know me, doesn't know you, he's got to guess. Plus he doesn't even know where we are right now, and we have the advantage of knowing exactly where to find him and his great-uncle and their computer geek. Not that knowing does us much good, when they're safe inside those walls."

Mena twisted to look at him, her smile gone, and her eyes shadowed. "But they come out from behind their walls, at least Elek and Ari. As do the rest of the Harvesters who visit there."

"We can't pick them off, one by one. Even if it were possible, there are thousands of them around the world. Unless they were all in one place at one time, and we blew it up, we can't get rid of them all."

"We don't need to get rid of all of them. Just the ones here, the ones who could actually do damage to us."

He tipped his head to study her. "Any who cross our path." He noted her swallow, the faint shadow behind her eyes before she nodded. "That could be a lot, baby."

"Maybe. Maybe not." She frowned a little.

He didn't argue with her. Reminding her now of the one she'd already killed didn't do them any good. Especially when the chances were pretty high she'd have to do it again to stay alive. To have forever.

CHAPTER FIFTEEN

They got a new rental car the next day, then continued north. They took a break around midday once they crossed into North Carolina, stopping for lunch in a small town not far off the interstate. Mena didn't rush him, so he steered her into several little gift shops to kill time. He was in no hurry to deliver her to the Harvesters.

Eventually, they strolled back to the car, where they sat to work out the next leg of their journey. Mena tucked her laptop away, and he felt a prickle at his nape, sending him on alert.

Holy hell. *Him.*

Ryder watched the man stride up the opposite sidewalk to his car. The guy had no idea how close he was to his target. Good thing, or he'd be dead already.

Mena shifted beside him, her gaze on the man as he slid into his seat. "He's the one who chased us in Philly."

"Yes."

Her gaze narrowed. "And shot at us."

"Mm-hm." He stifled a grin. She was getting annoyed all over, just thinking about it. *Good.*

"What do you suppose he's doing here? If Philly is where he lives, where he works, then he's not in his home area."

"No idea." Ryder did wonder, though, if maybe they hadn't been as careful as they should have been. Maybe the guy knew they were watching, knew they were within reach. Thinking it made his gut knot.

There was no way. None. This one's departure from his territory had to be something else. Something Ryder couldn't have guessed. Couldn't have foreseen.

The Harvester started his car and eased away from the curb, and Ryder let him go, before he started their car, too, whipping out into the street and cutting over to the next street at the first corner. Then he waited at the stop sign as the Harvester passed them before he eased into traffic.

"He won't be expecting anyone to follow him," Mena said after a few minutes.

Ryder agreed, though he kept his mouth shut, watching the car ahead slow for another turn.

She slouched lower in her seat. "Are we far enough back to keep following him?"

"For now." He made the turn, grateful for the two cars ahead of him, leaving a sizable distance between them and the Harvester. "But if he stays on this route instead of getting on the highway, we'll run out of cover."

She made a soft sound, leaning closer to the door so she could see the Harvester around the other cars.

Ryder didn't know why he thought they should follow. He wasn't sure what they could learn trailing this one guy. If he was closer to Washington and Ari's home, maybe, because there would likely be others around. But this guy? He was an order-follower, not an order-giver.

But what order was he following? Surely with all the

close calls in recent weeks, he wasn't just taking a break from the hunt.

The car ahead made the turn toward the highway, and Ryder wasn't sure whether to be relieved or not. The highway meant more traffic. And more likelihood the Harvester would notice them tailing him eventually.

Mena sat straighter in her seat when they got onto the ramp. "North. Heading for Virginia? To Ari's?"

"Maybe. But we're still pretty far away, and I have to wonder what he's doing so far south after our meeting in Philly."

"I bet Ari wanted him out of there after he screwed up."

He considered that as he eased into heavier traffic. "Punishment. Which would mean some crap job, no part in the hunt?"

"Possibly. Ari's vindictive enough to do that, even if was the first time a guy screwed up. Kallan told us some things about what happened before they found Andi, and I think he would pull this guy out of the hunt altogether, just to make a point to the others. Kallan said one of his cousins made a mess of something, way before they found Andi, and Ari stuck him in the family museum, archiving arti-facts. Serious punishment to a guy raised as a hunter." She sighed. "And very short-sighted, I think."

Why would anyone do something like that? Ryder had seen fuck-ups during his time in the military, and later with the intelligence agency, but taking a highly trained soldier out of the fight didn't do anyone any good. Not in the long run. Plus it made for a pissed off guy who was much more likely to go off and do what they wanted eventually, prob-ably to leave. Worse, to go do the job he'd been trained to do for an enemy or rival agency.

Stupid.

He couldn't believe Ari was so stupid.

"He's getting off already." She frowned. "Did he see us?"

Ryder had made sure that wasn't the case, so he shook his head. "No, he's going somewhere." Somewhere *not* Ari's. She may be right. He was out of the hunt, at least officially.

Still, Ryder steered the car off the highway, about six cars back now, far enough not to draw attention to them but near enough to see where he was going.

Mena remained silent as they wound along the road, heading into another small town. Until the Harvester pulled into the driveway of a townhouse up ahead. "He lives here," she murmured.

Ryder kept going past the house while the guy unlocked his front door. "Long way from Philly." A dead end. "At least we know there's one less guy hunting you."

She snorted. "Yeah, but if he'd seen me, he would've taken the chance to get back in Ari's good graces."

He steered the car toward the highway. "Okay, back on the road." He admitted to himself he would've enjoyed a run-in with the Harvester, just for a chance to vent some frustration over the gnawing fear in his gut over agreeing to this idea of hers. But he wouldn't admit it to Mena.

PHILOMENA WATCHED HIM DO LAPS AROUND THE SHORT length of the motel room. "You're making me dizzy," she said, reaching out to catch his wrist when he came near enough.

"We're getting too close." Still, he stopped.

"We're nearly a state away." She slid her fingers up his arm. "Come here."

Ryder let her draw him down beside her on the bed, though the disgruntled look didn't ease any. His mouth stayed sulky and tense lines bracketed his eyes.

She leaned into him. "You need to relax."

He frowned harder.

"Wow." She shifted onto her knees and stretched up to kiss his cheek. "Gonna make me work for it, huh?"

Realization dawned in his eyes, and the scowl eased a tiny bit. "Maybe," he said after a few seconds.

"I like a challenge," she murmured, sliding her hand up, past his shoulder to the hair at his nape, a little too long.

He swallowed.

She contained her smile and eased her other hand across his chest, then down to curl her fingers into his belt.

Ryder took a quick, hard breath.

"Hm, where to start?" She leaned in and brushed her lips along his jaw, trailing soft kisses to his throat, to the top of his shirt. "You should lose the shirt." She released his belt to tug at the soft cotton. "Then I can touch better."

He groaned and yanked the shirt off, then tumbled her to the bed beneath him.

"Hey, I was looking forward to a challenge," she laughed.

"I'm easy where you're concerned," he muttered, tugging at her blouse so he could reach her breasts.

She let him take over, enjoying the small respite from the stress. And she smiled to herself when he panted into the side of her neck a long while later. He probably didn't even realize her intention--distracting him from the non-stop tumble of worries and arguments in his head. She tightened her arms around him, her heart thudding quicker again when he returned the embrace.

"Don't think I don't know what you're doing," he growled.

"I don't know what you're talking about."

He gave her ass a squeeze. "Liar." But he didn't move away, nor did the tension return to tighten his shoulders.

Not yet. She knew it was inevitable, but she'd managed to distract him for a little while.

Mission accomplished.

Ryder couldn't help feeling antsy as he steered the car into Virginia. They were too close to the men he'd been trying to protect Mena from. This was the complete opposite of anything he would've planned.

And Mena had been quiet so far this morning. He glanced across at her and frowned at the way her mouth tightened. "Baby?"

"I'm fine," she said.

Shit. That was a lie. He needed to get her someplace they could stay for a few uninterrupted days, and fast.

"Don't you dare."

He glanced over at her. "What?"

"I know what you're thinking. Stop it. We have time. Time enough to get to Ari's."

He didn't argue. It would just waste time. He started watching for signs along the highway.

When he took an exit ramp about half an hour later, she made a disgusted sound.

"Mena--"

"You'd better just be stopping to get gas. We're not too far." She shot him a quick, sidelong scowl.

He'd known last night there was something going on, dammit. And he'd let her distract him without protesting. Because he needed the distraction. "*Fuck.*"

"Maybe later."

He shot her an incredulous glance, startled by the grim smile curving her mouth. Reluctantly, he smiled, too. "Maybe later I'll think about it." He reached over to stroke a wisp of hair from her face. "We need to find someplace, baby," he said, more gently.

"Not yet. Not when we're so near--"

"Pretty soon, we're going to have a lot of people looking over our shoulders, Mena. You can't be out among them when this starts. Think of the innocents."

The curve of her mouth flattened, and she turned to look out the window. "I'm thinking of the not-so-innocents," she muttered.

He scanned for a sign. Anything that indicated a safe place for them for a few days.

Nothing.

He drove vaguely parallel to the highway for a while, searching. A seedy little motel that didn't even look like it should be open for business had a half-lit sign out front reading, "ancy." He drove past, stress knotting at the base of his neck.

She sighed some time later, and he glanced over to see her leaning back in her seat, eyes closed. Her mouth wasn't so pinched now, though both her hands rested on her belly, not lightly, but pressed tight.

Son of a bitch.

He drove faster. He should've stayed on the highway. At least there, he'd see billboards advertising accommodations. Here, he was meandering lost like a damn tourist. He took the next turn in the direction of the highway.

And had to stop himself from jamming his foot on the brake when the same fucking Harvester they'd seen yesterday drove in the opposite direction.

That was too much of a coincidence.

He waited until the rear of the other car disappeared from his rearview mirror, then whipped around to go the other way.

"What?" Mena's hand landed on his knee.

"Our Harvester friend."

Her brows lowered. "Here? Are you sure? Maybe just a cousin who looks like him."

He shook his head. "Definitely the same guy, same car."

She remained silent, but she'd sat up straighter, in spite of the way she kept her hands over her mid-section. When the back of the other car came into view, she blew out a slow breath. "This is a long way from home. Not a coincidence."

"Probably not, but he's too far from Ari's to be rejoining the hunt." *I hope.*

No other cars drove between them, which meant he was taking a chance if the other guy turned off onto another road.

Still...he needed to know what was going on.

Mena set her jaw against the tightening knots in her gut--they weren't just from PMS, but stress as well. How could the same man be here, too, a whole state from where they'd last seen him? Unless he was following them somehow.

She dismissed that as impossible. None of the

Harvesters had any idea which direction they'd headed after their last encounter, though Ari may have called in reinforcements to the region after she'd killed the man in Georgia. Ryder's fingers curled tight around the steering wheel. Too tight. He'd already been worrying about finding someplace to wait out her three days of cursed hell, and now they had bigger concerns.

But they could use her PMS curse to their advantage.

She just had to make him see reason. It had worked for Andi. It could work now, too.

The man in the car ahead didn't seem worried about them behind him. She wondered if he even had any clue they were following. And what she'd be able to do to him in a matter of hours.

The timing sucked.

But because they were so close, maybe she could make Ryder understand this was the way to deal with the Harvesters for them. To get their forever.

Emotional blackmail. She considered that. She'd already done it, to persuade him to head toward the Harvesters instead of continuing to hide.

Her breath caught. How horrible was that? Using the one thing he wanted most to make him do what *she* thought was best? Gods, she was a manipulative bitch.

She'd never considered herself manipulative or bitchy before. Those were Desi's forté, especially where men were concerned.

A lump stuck in her throat. Apparently, she was more like her sister than she knew.

It took her a few seconds to notice the car had stopped. She blinked hard and looked up. They were parked off the road, shaded by a small cluster of trees and tall bushes.

Ryder studied her with a little frown. "Are you all right, baby?"

She nodded once.

"He pulled into a dirt road ahead. I want you to stay here while I check it out."

She opened her mouth to protest, then shut it, thinking of her revelation moments ago. She nodded one more time.

Ryder touched her cheek. "I'll be as fast as I can. Keep the doors locked and if any Harvesters find you, lean on the horn. I'll be right back." He leaned over to brush a kiss on her mouth. "Promise."

Mena caught his face in her hands and kissed him again. "I know," she whispered, hoping he wouldn't hear the choked tone.

He hesitated, and she released him.

"I'll be right here," she said, more firmly.

He got out, and she locked the door behind him, watching his broad shoulders as he eased into the trees. In just a few seconds, he was out of view, and she leaned forward, covering her face with her hands.

"Oh, my Gods," she choked out around the lump. Her eyes burned, and she squeezed them shut.

She needed to tell him when he returned that she'd changed her mind--she'd go wherever he wanted, that she wanted forever, no strings attached.

Pain jabbed at her.

Gods, not now. She couldn't deal with this now, too. She took a slow breath, then another, trying to stave it off a little longer.

The nearby gunshot made her sit straight up, heart pounding wildly.

Ryder hadn't taken his gun.

Oh, Gods!

She twisted in her seat and rummaged through the open duffel bag on the floor behind her until her fingers closed on the gun. She grabbed it, then reached back in for her dagger and leg sheath, fastening the leather around her thigh quickly.

She snagged the car keys and tucked them in her pocket before opening her door. She eased it shut as quietly as she could, then took another steadying breath. She'd be no help to Ryder if she went rushing in and got killed. She forced herself to wait, listening for something.

The gunshot had been close. She heard no voices, no footsteps.

She waited a few seconds longer, then started into the brush where Ryder had disappeared.

RYDER SWALLOWED BACK A CURSE WHEN HE HEARD THE footsteps behind him. They were too light, too careful. She hadn't stayed in the damn car. He knew when the gunshot rang out she'd want to rush in.

He'd still hoped she'd remain in the car.

He glanced back, waiting for her to emerge. The relief on her face made him smile, just briefly, as did the tears making her eyes shiny. Then he saw the weapon she carried. Gods, what was she thinking?

Never mind. He knew what she was thinking. He gestured for her to remain silent, gratified when she did. And unspeakably relieved when she reached him. She crouched at his side and offered the gun.

She shut her eyes tight when he took it, then shot him a questioning look, her head tipping to one side.

He dipped his chin so his mouth was beside her ear.

"Our friend has a friend. Or two." He tucked the gun into the back of his jeans, covering it with his shirttail.

She nodded, and he noticed her hand went to her belly.

"Go back to the car."

She met his gaze for a second, then she looked away and nodded. Just once, but it was enough.

Until the second gunshot rang out, startling her so she stumbled into him.

He caught her before she fell into the brush, but her feet still disturbed leaves and twigs. He winced, and, noticing her pallor, helped her to a more secure position. "Go on, baby," he breathed against her ear.

Fear clouded her eyes now, but she didn't argue.

"I just want to check out what they're doing. Then I'll be back. Promise."

She lifted her chin once in assent, and he released her. He waited until she took a careful step, then another, before he resolutely turned away, trusting she'd do it.

He had some Harvesters to find.

MENA MOVED CAUTIOUSLY, CAREFUL NOT TO SNAP A twig or crunch old leaves. Even if she'd wanted to go faster, she couldn't, panting softly through the stabbing pain in her belly. It was coming too fast. They wouldn't have time to find a safe place.

She stopped and shut her eyes, trying to breathe through the sharp twisting in her gut. It nearly brought her to her knees. *Already.*

"The monster, at last," said a deep, accented voice near her ear as hard fingers wrapped around her upper arm.

Her heart beat quickened, pounding inside her ribs so hard it hurt nearly as much as her belly. *Damn.*

The man's fingers dug into her arm, and he hauled her around in the opposite direction. She stumbled, opening her eyes and trying to focus. The curse hadn't kicked in enough for her to turn him to stone, but her dagger lay against her thigh.

She heard a muffled shout ahead, and her heart jumped into her throat.

"I am not alone." A stranger's voice carried through the trees. "My cousin will find your Medusa. Kill her."

Mena heard a hard thud, and she swallowed, knowing Ryder would fight the other man.

"And I will," the Harvester murmured to her. "It will give me immense pleasure to end you."

"Too bad it doesn't put an end to you as well," she muttered, panting through a sharper cramp. Maybe she'd be able to turn him to stone soon, after all.

"It is unfortunate your protector is occupied. I would like to kill him as well, but Gregos will deal with him. It is too bad we won't have time to make him suffer for killing our cousin." The man continued to pull her into the woods, nearer to the sounds of fighting, not bothering to avoid the fallen leaves or small branches.

That meant there were only the two of them, she realized through the haze of pain. Two against two. This wasn't insurmountable.

She heard Ryder swear when she stumbled again. Close. She smiled at him, trying to let him know it was going to be all right. That they could do this.

And the pain across her abdomen flashed stronger, hot.

She couldn't keep in her gasp, but she managed not to fall to her knees.

"Stop it," the Harvester growled, yanking on her arm. "I will not fall for your ploys. Stand up."

"Piss off," she panted. She needed to curl around a heating pad. And maybe take one of Ryder's magical pain pills.

Or maybe just a little *magick*.

She sank to her knees, feeling the energy of the earth through the thin fabric of her skirt. She couldn't stave off the PMS, but she could protect Ryder.

She ignored the tugging on her arm and visualized drawing up the earth's energy, warm and gentle, before she pushed it toward Ryder. He frowned when the Harvester he was grappling with swung his fist at Ryder and ended up on his ass on the ground several feet away. The man looked stunned, and Ryder took advantage of his distraction to dive in and pummel his opponent.

The man holding her arm muttered something and yanked at her arm again. "Get up, monster."

A vicious cramp made her moan aloud, and she bent forward instinctively, only dimly aware of the additional pain in her arm from the Harvester's grip. "Stupid Goddess," she whispered, her forehead almost to her knees.

"Get *up*, I said!" The man tugged once more, harder.

She fumbled her free hand to the hem of her skirt, pretending she was trying to put it on the ground to push herself to her feet. She moaned again, mostly for show, though the pain in her belly curled tighter. Soon, she'd be able to do some damage to him with her gaze. But she didn't have time to wait. Instead, she found the hilt of her dagger and wrapped her fingers around it. As the Harvester yanked her to her feet, twisting her arm behind her, she tugged the dagger free and swung around.

He shouted, something she couldn't understand, but

warmth splashed over her fingers. His blood. She knew without looking. Behind her, she heard the sounds of Ryder's continuing fight, but she needed to focus on her own battle. This was for her life, dammit. For their future. For forever.

She jabbed the dagger deeper as she looked up into the man's surprised face. Her blade was buried to the hilt in his middle, angled up for maximum damage, as she'd been taught, as all of her cousins had been taught.

He shook his head, as if denying the inevitable outcome, but he staggered back. She followed in spite of the pain in her abdomen and twisted the dagger.

A gurgling sound escaped him as blood spilled past his lips.

She withdrew her dagger completely and shoved him away.

He fell backward, landing flat while blood pumped from his wound, from his mouth. His dark eyes reflected his shock.

She heard a shout behind her, but she had to bend forward against the pain of her cramps. Ryder would be fine.

She gasped at the new pain in her belly--not cramps, shallower, almost at the surface. Sharper. Near her hip, she thought, not her belly. It spread outward, intensifying. "Holy Gods!" she panted, bending farther forward. That didn't help, didn't alleviate the agony, but she couldn't straighten.

"Mena?"

Like a hot blade stuck beneath her skin to tear her apart from the inside out. *Oh, Gods.* "I'm fine. Really," she managed. "Do what you need to do."

She heard his growl, then another punch, a groan of

pain. If she could have, she'd have smiled, knowing he trusted her, just as she trusted he'd deal with the Harvester. But the pain strengthened, bringing her to her knees. Mena couldn't quite stifle her moan, but she clapped one hand over her mouth to contain any more--Ryder didn't need her distracting him. Sweat burned her closed eyes and soaked the back of her sweater.

And then the pain vanished. Like it had never existed.

Mena smiled, still panting as she rested her forehead on her knees.

It was over.

She didn't need to look to know that the goblet was no longer part of her tattoo. She was no longer the Medusa.

Something heavy hit the ground behind her, and she lifted her head to see Ryder running toward her.

"I'm fine," she said, pushing to her feet. "It's over." She knew her smile was even wider now.

He skidded to a stop in front of her, frowning. "What?"

"It's over." She stretched to touch just beneath a cut on his cheekbone. "I'm not the Medusa anymore," she whispered.

His eyes widened, and then a grin spread over his face. "*Yes!*" He grabbed her and hauled her against him. "*Yes!*"

Mena laughed until his mouth cut off the sound. He spun her around, and they both laughed between kisses.

Ryder finally stopped spinning. "Really?"

"Really. The cup is gone." She gingerly brushed her fingertips beneath the cut again. "You're bleeding. My protection spell didn't work well enough."

He shrugged. "I've had worse. You're sure?"

She smiled. "You're welcome to check, but I'd rather we had somewhere private for your inspection."

He growled, planting a hard kiss on her lips. "Let's go.

Before anybody else shows up, and they haven't gotten the newsflash yet."

Mena didn't argue. She didn't know how long it took for Ari to learn there was a new Medusa, but she didn't want to test him.

He caught her hand and turned toward the car. Stopped when he saw the Harvester on the ground. "Good." He squeezed her hand. Then he steered her out of the little wood.

Mena couldn't stop smiling as he drove them away. It was really over. She realized when the curse had lifted, when the goblet left her, her cramps had vanished as well. Gone.

Ryder found a motel about half an hour away, went into the office to check in, then dragged her into their room. She pulled away to go into the small bathroom and scrub her bloody hand and wrist clean. When she stepped out of the little room, he picked her up, carried her several steps, and dropped her onto the bed.

She laughed, in spite of the look in his eyes--that look that said he couldn't quite believe it was finished.

He jerked her blouse out of his way and tugged down the waistband of her skirt so he could look at the tattoo. His eyes widened, and he simply stared for a long moment. Then he grinned at her.

She held out her arms, and he came down into them, rolling to his side to hold her tight. She didn't mind the iron grip. They were both alive. Alive. And she was no longer the Medusa.

Happiness and relief welled up until she thought she might burst. "I want to go home, Ryder."

He leaned back enough to look into her face. "Have you decided where you'd like that to be?"

She shook her head. "It doesn't matter. As long as Mom is nearby and there's room for Jason to play and have a dog."

"He wants a horse," he said with a smile.

"Dog. He's been asking for a dog for three years."

"That was before Danny put him on a damned horse." Ryder's grin was mischievous. "We'll have to find a place outside the city that's big enough for a horse."

Philomena shut her eyes. "We'll talk about it." She had a feeling it was a battle she'd lose. And she didn't care.

Ryder's fingers slid up to her nape, and she let him tip her head back, opening her eyes. "You are going to marry me."

She resisted the urge to smile and raised her eyebrows. "I don't remember being asked."

He growled at her.

She waited.

He released her and rolled upright, then stood and set his hands on his hips. "You didn't think after all this that I'd let you go, did you?"

She rose, too, folding her arms over her chest. And waited. Her heart pounded harder, and she wondered if he could hear it.

Ryder dragged one hand over his head, rumpling his hair, and blew out an exasperated breath. Then he dropped to one knee in front of her, his expression somber.

Mena's jaw dropped as her eyes widened.

"Philomena Gregory, I hoped I'd have a ring to put on your finger when I did this, but will you please marry me?" He caught her hands in his.

Her knees wobbled. "Oh, my Gods," she whispered.

He smiled. "You didn't really think I meant it, did you?"

"I knew you did. It's why the amulet is gone." She let her weak legs have their way and fell onto her knees in front of him. "I knew you'd do what you promised, that you'd keep me safe. I trusted you to do it." She set her hands on his cheeks. "I love you."

His smile softened as she spoke. "I love you, too. Is that a yes?"

"Yes."

He grabbed her, crushing her to him, and she felt the burn of tears. Happy ones.

His heart beat fast against her chest, and his fingers flexed on her.

"Let's go get Jason and Aggie and fly to Vegas."

She laughed, tipping her head back. "How about we plan something after we find a place to live?"

He shook his head. "I've waited a long time for you, Mena mine. I'm not waiting any longer." He bent to kiss her, lightly.

She swallowed. The emotion in his dark eyes would be scary as hell if she wasn't feeling the same thing. "I knew you were trouble," she managed, sliding one hand into his silky hair.

He grinned, making her pulse quicken. "Only for you." He kissed her again, longer this time.

When they finally came up for air, their clothes were strewn around the room and their bodies slick with sweat. "I guess we can wait till tomorrow to fly to Vegas," Ryder said, nuzzling his way along her damp throat.

Philomena laughed, then gasped when his teeth grazed her skin.

She thought she might enjoy not being the Medusa. Very, very much.

EPILOGUE

Ari collapsed back in his chair. "Are you sure?" he gasped.

Alarm quickened Elek's pulse. "Are you all right, Great-uncle?"

"Are you sure she's no longer the Medusa?" he repeated.

"Yes, Mikolaus is certain." Elek didn't repeat his cousin's assertion that she and Ware were very clearly in love. His great-uncle already appeared on the verge of a stroke. The full, detailed report about his cousin's death could wait.

Ari squeezed his eyes shut. "Dear Goddess," he whispered.

A burst of light startled Elek, and his eyes widened before he realized the woman who had suddenly material-ized was Athena. He hastily dropped to his knees and bowed his head, his heart beating much too fast now, from fright or excitement, maybe both.

~

Aristotle flinched under the angry gaze of the Goddess who'd just appeared in his study, before he lowered his head. "My Lady." He braced one hand on the corner of his desk and fell to his knees, ignoring the pain in both legs when he missed the area rug and the hard wood pressed against his knees. "I am so sorry, my Lady."

"You have failed me again, Aristotle."

He shut his eyes. "I beg Your forgiveness."

"I grow weary of waiting for your family to fulfill its duty to me."

He dared a peek and found the Goddess's sandaled feet only a step away from him. "I apologize, my Lady," he began.

"I do not wish for more apologies, Harvester. I wish for results. I wish you to do your duty and kill the Medusa."

Aristotle closed his eyes, his heart rate quickening still more. "I will find her."

"You will have to start your search fresh."

His heart sank. Naturally She knew already.

"If you fail this time, Aristotle, I shall find someone who will not. Your family will lose my favor."

He felt light-headed. To lose the Goddess's favor... After all these centuries. His forefathers would be ashamed of his failures. He was already ashamed of himself, and more ashamed of his brother's failure. But to carry such enormous shame into eternity...

"I will not fail You, my Lady," he vowed, his voice shaking. "I will not fail."

"See that you do not."

When silence lingered, he knew She had gone, and he struggled to his feet, knees quaking. He sank into his comfortable leather chair, ignoring the way his lungs labored for air.

"I need some time," he said to Elek, who rose smoothly and left the room, looking grim.

Aristotle glared at his brother's picture where it sat on the corner of his desk. "This is all your fault, Iphis. Stupid, foolish boy, putting love ahead of family duty. Ahead of the Goddess." Aristotle swatted the photo off the desk. "You are gone and still, you will cost us everything," he snarled.

He knew the importance of succeeding, of killing the Medusa. His life and his family's honor depended on his success. He wouldn't let Iphis's lack of character ruin everything into eternity. No more monsters would get the opportunity to fall in love and evade his family.

He didn't mean to fail again.

ABOUT THE AUTHOR

Elizabeth Andrews has been a book lover since she was old enough to read. She read her copies of *Little Women* and the *Little House* series so many times, the books fell apart. As an adult, her book habit continues. She has a room overflowing with her literary collection right now, and still more spreading into other rooms. Almost as long as she's been reading great stories, she's been attempting to write her own. Thanks to a fifth grade teacher who started the class on creative writing, Elizabeth went from writing creative sentences to short stories and eventually full-length novels. Her father saved her poor, callused fingers from permanent damage when he brought home a used typewriter for her.

Elizabeth found her mother's stash of romance novels as a teenager, and—though she loves horror—romance became her very favorite genre, making writing romances a natural progression. There are more than just a few manuscripts, however, tucked away in a filing cabinet that will never see the light of day.

Along with her enormous book stash, Elizabeth lives with her husband of more than twenty-five years, with two young adult sons nearby, though no one else in the family reads nearly as much as she does. When she's not at work or buried in books or writing, there is a garden outside full of herbs, flowers and vegetables that requires occasional attention.

Website: www.elizabethandrewswrites.com

Light the Way Home

A Common Elements Romance Project novella

Single dad Nate Baxter has his hands full with his son and his haunted lighthouse. He doesn't have time to spend with a woman...especially one who won't stick around, like his ex-wife.

But Lucie Russo's not like other women Nate's met. She's sweet and sexy, and his mouth waters every time he's around her.

Will a family emergency cause him to break his relationship rules? And if he does, will his heart be broken too?

Hunting Medusa

The Medusa's Daughters Trilogy, Book 1

One murderous mission. One killer case of PMS. Who said "the curse" was a myth?

Ever since the original Medusa ticked off Athena by bragging about her beauty, her cursed daughters have been paying for that mistake. To this day, successive Medusas play cat and mouse with the descendants of Perseus, known as the Harvesters.

When Kallan Tassos tracks down the current Medusa, he expects to find a monster. Instead he finds a wary, beautiful woman, shielded by a complicated web of spells that foils his plans for a quick kill and retrieval of her protective amulet.

Andrea Rosakis expects the handsome Harvester to go for the kill.

Instead, his attempt to take the amulet imprinted on her skin without harming her takes her completely by surprise. And ends with the two of them in a magical bind—together.

Though their attraction is combustible, her impending PMS (Pre Magical-Curse Syndrome) puts a real damper on any chance of a relationship. But Kallan isn't the only Harvester tracking Andi, and they must cooperate to stay at least one step ahead of a ruthless killer before they can have any future, together or apart.

Warning: A hunter who's fallen for the woman he's bound to kill, a Medusa who must trust him with her life, and a magical curse only love can break.

www.ingramcontent.com/pod-product-compliance
Lightning Source LLC
Chambersburg PA
CBHW051213190726
48288CB00006B/1942